H. Marion Stephens

HAGAR THE MARTYR;

OR,

PASSION AND REALITY.

A TALE OF THE NORTH AND SOUTH.

BY

MRS. H. MARION STEPHENS.

WILL IS DESTINY.

Alas! O, alas! for the trusting heart,
When its fairy dream is o'er;
When it learns that to trust is to be deceived —
Finds the things most false which it most believed!
Alas! for it dreams no more!

BOSTON:
PUBLISHED BY W. P. FETRIDGE & CO.
1855.

STEREOTYPED AT THE
BOSTON STEREOTYPE FOUNDRY.

Damrell & Moore, Printers, Boston.

DEDICATION.

To the Women of America.

To the warm, true hearts, over whose impulses the frost of prejudice has not hardened; — who can feel for the tempted and the tried, though themselves may have escaped temptation; — who dare stretch out a hand to raise the fallen, even at the risk of being repulsed and scorned, — these pages are respectfully dedicated.

HAGAR is no ideal creation: and there are ten thousand Hagars the country through, who only need an encouraging word and a kindly look to wile them back to peace and virtue. Shall that word remain unspoken? Shall that look be withheld? And if so, who, think ye, will be the culprit in that great day, when all the passions, and trials, and emotions of the human heart appear unmasked before the face of our Father in heaven? While women trust, and men deceive, missionaries will be wanted, whose souls are armed with forbearance, pity, sympathy, and generosity. Let the spirit of the Mother Mary incite you to save rather than to destroy; so shall the stumbling block of despair be removed from the path of the erring; so shall we all be happier and better; and so shall be established upon the earth the creed of HIM who in *like* emergency found heart to say, "*Neither do I condemn thee.*"

H. MARION STEPHENS.

CONTENTS.

Hagar the Martyr.

PROLOGUE.

It was a stormy and tempestuous night! Torn and ragged clouds lay in great heavy masses, while here and there thin bits of haze drifted before the wind like scared and trembling birds!

It had been raining; but now the drops had ceased falling, and only a low, wild wail — the sobbing of the wind amid the trees — was left of what was come and gone at the bidding of the storm. Every where it was night. Not the soft, still night which whispers "peace" to the worn and weary ones of earth, but a night rayless and starless as the hope-wrecked heart of love, when its treasures have gone down into the ocean of despair.

The hum of busy life was gradually dying out of the city. The streets, with the exception of an occasional traveller, had been deserted hours before, and the lights had faded out of the different dwellings, until the night and the storm were about the only positive things to be counted upon. Even the Revere House, with its long rows of lights, was silent now, and only a glimmer from a distant window relieved its massive shade.

Almost within the shadow of this dwelling, in one of our most aristocratic streets, a mansion, whose external adornment had elicited many a sigh of envy, housed a storm of mental passion, outrivalling the atmospheric one that had but now lent terror to the night.

Up and down, up and down, all the long hours of that evening had the footfall of Hagar Martin dragged its slow length over the tufted carpet of her chamber.

What was it to her that the lightning swept in like a flood of flame through the heavy mass of drapery, which half shielded her open window? What was it to her that the rolling thunder pealed over her head, as if all the armies of heaven were in passionate warfare? The tempest without accorded well with the tempest within. The warring of the elements assimilated well with the warring in her own spirit of despair. It needed that to save her from positive insanity. She could bear wildness and desolation, for she was desolate and wild *in* that desolation.

Up and down, up and down, with her thin, white hands sometimes clasped above her head, sometimes folded over her bosom, but always with that quick, rapid step, as if trying to outwalk her thoughts. Sometimes she would pause for minutes, her eyes burning into the carpet at her feet, hearing nothing, seeing nothing — benumbed in every faculty. Once she paused before her glass, and leaning upon a marble slab, contemplated the rigid, gray-white face therein reflected. There were deep hollows upon either side of her forehead, and her eyes were rimmed round with that purple tint which tells of deep suffering.

"No wonder," she murmured. "No wonder; and the world so full of beauty from which to choose!" and again the quick foot took up its rapid tread across the floor. Another and another turn brought her once more before the glass. Her thoughts were going back to the time when she had been as wildly happy as she was now wildly miserable. What could have wrought the change? She was conscious of no wrong to *him* beyond exclusive worship and all-absorbing devotion; and yet conscience was whispering in her ear, "You should have told him — you should have told him." And yet she urged in extenuation, "What *could* I have told him? O, doubly, *doubly* martyr! O, fate, what had I done to deserve this punishment!" That happy time — she was remembering it all now; how she had suffered herself to dream upon the verge of a burning volcano; how she had awakened with that quick, sharp agony which comes but once in a lifetime; how she had struggled against it — against the knowledge that *he*, for whom she had sacrificed so much, was changing before her eyes; how she had tried to strangle the doubt of his untruth, before it had gained positive form; and how, in failing so to do, her heart had broken with its depth of agony, — it was all before her this night; all passing there, beside the plain white face in the glass. O for one moment's peace, though that moment saw her last on earth! O for one gleam of God's light, to show her the ending up of that fearful struggle, though that sight closed up her senses forever! In vain, in vain! *He had ceased to love her!* All of life's sorrows, all the great woes which had gone to make up her existence, were nothing to that one blow. To have lived and died a *slave*, with all the horrors of that life about her — ugh! The thought brings up the eloquent blood, till her whole face is flooded with crimson; and *then* a spectator might have seen that she had been handsome — a dark, rich style of beauty, such as is seldom seen in our clime of blue-eyed, soft-complexioned women. If the flesh had sunken from her cheeks, the ruby from her lips, her eyes still retained the old burning brilliancy which characterized the race from which she sprang. And she saw it all passing, like a kaleidoscope, in the glass before her. Struggle with it as she would, it was *there! He had ceased to love her!* The one idea of her soul hushed till it was almost silence. It was all before her. The bright, laughing face of earnest manhood which she should moan for, miss, and perchance never see again; the thrilling tones, so well remembered, which would be silent to her forever and forevermore; the eager, zealous interest in her weal or woe, which had passed away with affection, and which, more than all, she should need for incentive to future exertion,— it was all passing before her, till agony found voice, and she wept aloud.

"If he would only believe me — but *no! no!* — he listens to others who hate me for the love he has borne me. O, heartless, cruel that he is! Let him beware. He may call me *Martyr*, but more hearts than *mine* shall be wrung by the sacrifice; let him be sure of that. O, the blood of my race — the cruel, deadly, burning blood! Let him beware that it does not deluge him through the heart he has chosen to usurp my place." She was standing now, with face looking more thin and worn in the light of her gleaming eyes.

"Ay, let him *beware!* The worm may turn and sting the foot that tramples upon it; let him ——" At that moment her restless eyes fell upon an open miniature, lying with other trinkets upon the marble slab. With the sudden change which only madness knows, she caught it to her bosom, and smothered it with kisses. A step was heard in the great hall — a step so faint and low that only the senses quickened to intensity by much sorrow could have detected it. Crushing the miniature into her bosom, she crossed to a window, and flinging up the sash, leaned far out into the damp air to hide any trace of emotion. A light tap elicited a faint "Come in;" yet before the words were spoken the door opened, and a woman of some five and twenty years tripped merrily into the chamber.

"Up yet, Hagar?" she exclaimed. "Ugh! do close that window. It is horridly cold, and the wet is dripping all over your dress from the vines. We've had something of a shower. O, *do* come in!"

Hagar obeyed, mechanically, and her companion started, to see how haggard she looked.

"I needn't ask," she murmured compassionately, winding her arms around her; "I needn't ask. Walter hasn't been here this evening."

"No, Anna, he has left me — he has, indeed," she answered, shivering all over. A gleam of malignant joy overspread the features of her companion, passing away upon the instant.

"Nonsense," she replied. "This is just nothing at all. It will pass away again. Why, you have had a dozen just such pets; and yet he *is* a brute, any how, to treat you as he does."

"Not a word against him, Anna. It is all my fault. A truer, a nobler, or better spirit never dwelt in man's bosom than dwells in his. No; I abused my influence. I was impatient, exacting, and O, so horridly jealous, he couldn't understand it, because he couldn't know how fearful I was of losing him — and so we quarrelled. If he knew how I suffer — and how I miss him!"

"And what did you say to him after the quarrel?"

"I made every concession that a loving, suffering woman could make."

"And he ——?"

"Listened to it with his cold cynical smile till the words were frozen on my lips! To think that I — I, whom people think so haughty, so defiant, should beg for love as a criminal would beg for the life forfeited by some dark deed!

But let him beware! There is an end even to *my* idolatry."

Anna could scarcely choke down the triumph rising to her lips. After a short pause, she questioned, —

"And you sent for him to-night?"

"What could I do? Yes, I sent for him."

"And he did not come?"

The answer was broken by the opening of the front door; and immediately after a step, familiar to both, was soon heard ascending the stairs.

"'Tis *he!*" exclaimed Hagar; "and I was wronging him so in thought."

The dark face brightened into a sudden joy. The cheeks, which had been very pale, flushed into a vivid bloom, and she clasped her arms around her friend to save her from falling. Anna shook her off with such passionate fierceness, that at any other time, a mask would have fallen off which was screening the vilest and wickedest designs that ever entered a woman's heart.

"See him; *see him!*" she hissed, in a voice of concentrated rage. "See him, plead with him, and let him set his foot upon your neck again! I thought you had *some* pride, Hagar! I certainly did."

Hagar did not hear her. She would not have heeded the deepest thunder at that moment. To see *him* once more — to stand with him face to face, perhaps to feel his arms about her — that was all to her now. He had come at her bidding; that was something. What might she not hope for! She grew still and quiet. She saw the door open, and knew whose eyes were seeking her own. She heard words, or the sound of words, but the tension on her brain hid their meaning. She saw her friend pass to leave the room, but she did *not* see the distorted face of angry beauty which glared upon the new comer, or hear the words hissed out between lips white with rage into the ear of her lover, or some portion of the mysterious change she so deplored might have unveiled its reason before her. And that woman was her *friend!*

O that the almighty Father would sometimes strip the mask from selfishness, and show us what *is* false and hollow in this mocking old world of ours!

Hagar and her lover stood side by side silently on the hearth. He was very handsome — preëminently handsome, though the coldness of its expression now marred the beauty of his features. Finding Hagar likely to continue silent, he flung himself into a chair by the centre table, and began turning the leaves of an annual lying thereon. Quietly Hagar crept to his side, and raising his disengaged hand, pressed it passionately to her lips.

"You hurt me," he exclaimed, shaking her off, and lifting his hand from her clasp.

Hagar did not weep. It seemed as if there were no more tears in her nature, or, if so, that they were frozen. She did not even shrink, but sat silently gazing into the blue eyes that had for so many years been her heaven of happiness. He must have been aware of her gaze, for every now and then his full lips quivered with suppressed merriment, while his white hand went straying up into his hair. At last, as if some spark of pity had been blown into flame, he rested his arm upon her shoulder, and said, —

"Do you want any thing of me?"

Hagar could not answer. She wanted his love, and that he had taken from her. Again his question was repeated, and still unanswered.

"Well, if you don't want me, it is getting late, and I will go home."

"*Walter!*"

"Well?"

"Is this the end of all?"

"All *what?*"

"Our love, our intimacy, our happy association."

"I shall always be your friend, Hagar; nothing more."

Hagar's hands released their clasp, and dropped nervelessly by her side. This, then, was the end of all. How her head ached and throbbed! but that was nothing to the sorrow in her heart. Every where her eyes turned, they rested upon some memento of his affection. Her guitar lay on a table, untuned and unstrung. Elegant books, selected with a refinement of taste for which he was noted, were strewn in graceful profusion around the room; even sparkling *bijouterie*, from diamonds glittering like cold eyes in their diamond cases, to the tiny chain of gold which had been his first gift. How these things mocked her vision — these voiceless memories of his lavish affection! How should she live through the long years of the aimless future, with these silent messengers of lost joy forever before her! *The future!* In her present misery she had almost forgotten that; but now its dreariness rolled over her in a flood of bitterness, and, sinking upon her knees, she gave vent to the loneliest, dreariest sobs that ever agitated a human heart.

"Don't cry," said he, touched by the intensity of her sorrow. "Here, wrap something about you; you'll take cold."

This revival of old-time tenderness did not calm her, as he had evidently expected, and he was about gathering her in his arms, when the face of Anna McVernon gleamed for a moment in at the window full of taunting sarcasm.

"O, I beg pardon!" she exclaimed, in seeming surprise. "It is late, and I thought to find Hagar alone;" and closing the door, she retreated to her own room.

"Well, I *must* go; as Anna says, it *is* late, and time you were alone."

"O Walter, I don't deserve this; I *don't*, indeed. You will find it out some time, and be sorry for me."

Walter accorded her an unbelieving smile.

"O, you don't believe me, Walter. You *won't* believe me — but — there — there, go — *go* before I forget myself again, and say things which I shall regret when you are gone. Go, I say! You'll find Hagar a *woman* yet."

She pushed back the hair which lay in beautiful waves upon his forehead; she gazed mournfully into his blue eyes, as if searching for hope; she kissed his unreturning lips over and over again, murmuring, —

"You have wronged me, Walter; but you have been the world to me, and I forgive you. You will find it out some time, when it is too late, perhaps; but go now, and sometimes give a thought to your poor *Martyr Hagar*, who has loved you so."

He was gone! She heard the door closing behind him, and his step increasing the distance between them. A quick, sudden impulse seized her to see him once again — *only once!* to catch a farewell look at his face, which he would never know. She flung up the sash, and threw herself half out of the window. Yes, there he was. She could see him just turning the corner of the street. She would have known him far as vision could have extended; that graceful, manly form; there was no other like it to her. She seized a shawl, and wrapping it around her, flew, rather than ran, down the stairs, and out at the front door, leaving it open in her haste. One moment more and it would have been too late. Wildly she ran on from square to square, until she was nearly by his side. She could have laid a hand upon his arm, but did not, and followed quietly, gently, now that he was in her sight. There were no tears in her eyes now, but she regarded him with a fixed and dreamy gaze as she ran along, not near enough to excite his notice, yet near enough to see every feature of his face in the light of the street lamps as they passed. Presently he paused before a pleasant dwelling, and producing a key, placed the door of his own home between himself and his deserted devotee. She did not speak, but pressed closer and closer to the side light after he had passed through. She heard him exchange some light sentence with a person in waiting; she caught the last echo of his footfall in the distant chamber, and then nerveless, helpless, and motionless she sank down upon the stone step at his own happy home. Her wild prayer had been heard and answered. She had seen him once more; and by the white agony of her quivering lips, by the great drops of suffering which misery was forcing out upon her face, by the tight clinching of her thin hands, and by the heavy breathing which came in convulsive gasps from her over-charged bosom, that parting was destined *not to be the last.*

CHAPTER I.

THE SOUTHERN HOME. — THE FIRST LINK IN THE CHAIN OF CIRCUMSTANCE. — THE WAIF OF LOVE.

"In a beautiful home there is gloom to-day,
For a star in its beauty is passing away!
A spirit is leaving these chilly bowers,
And wending its way with the birds and flowers!"

IN a beautiful home — in a southern home, amid the flush of eternal flowers — 'mid the song of birds that never tire of warbling — 'mid the bright and beautiful things of nature — a noble woman, tired of the vanities and follies of this life, had lain down to take her last long sleep, whose wakening should be in heaven! Hagar — the saint — the improvisatrice — the martyr woman! Hagar, the superb, the haughty, the glorious queen of poesy and of love, lay languishing upon a bed of suffering — *dying!*

Hagar!

Did they who stamped upon her infant brow that bitter name know how surely she would work out its destiny in sorrow and in despair!

Hagar!

Name only for the crushed, the bewildered, the broken-hearted; and so they gave it to her whose pathway through life was to be on thorns! She had reached that pathway's end, and now lay dying! What was it to her now that the heart of manhood, that should have shielded, but only betrayed, now wept tears of blood to see her fading out — melting away into the shadow of death, as sunset clouds melt into the blue of heaven? Heavily throbbed the old clock in the hall, as if in agony to tell the minutes which were to be her last.

A strong man, paralyzed with remorse and grief, knelt among the curtains of the bed, pressing the thin white hand that had often sought his clasp but to find itself repulsed.

"Hagar — Hagar! has it come to this!" moaned the stricken man in the extremity of his grief. But Hagar did not hear him. Her eyes, supernatural in their burning brilliancy, were fixed upon the door; but there were no words upon her lips to express the desire so eloquent in its dumb appeal.

A slight movement of her arm brought to her side a gorgeous *slave woman,* who crouched in the corner of the room, sweeping through the curtains with her burning eyes, and catching every intimation of her dying mistress.

There were no tears in *her* eyes — nothing but a rim of deeper blackness circling the lids — to tell the depth of her anguish.

And how gorgeous she was! Only those who have noted the perfection of beauty to which the negro blood just merging into whiteness aspires can imagine for a moment the extraordinary beauty of this *white slave* of Carolina.

The opaque white of her complexion shone out in dazzling clearness, with just the tinge of bloom swaying backward and forward beneath her cheek. Her long hair swept in ringlets to her waist, with no more of a crisp or wave than served for the ornament of our modern style of beauty. Canova never dreamed of a more perfect form. The broad, sloping shoulders — the full, voluptuous bust, making more conspicuous the round, lithe waist, so perfect in its proportions — the round, taper arm — the hand long and slender — the feet beautiful in their extreme smallness! But the *eyes!* Let one but once glance into their burning depths, and there would be no thought for aught else. Let her once *speak*, and the melody of her voice drowned even the lustre of her eyes! Such was Minnie Claire, the slave woman, and personal attendant of Hagar Martin, who lay dying amid the luxury of her southern home.

Minnie raised the head of her mistress, and in so doing unclasped the strings of her cap. A flood of hair black as night swept over the bed, and mingled with curls only distinguishable by their purple tint.

The room was filled with weeping mourners; but there was one missing whose presence the dying woman most needed.

She had not long to wait, for the window opened from the lawn, and a strange, wild, beautiful creature flung herself half over the sill into the room.

"*Hagar!*" exclaimed a dozen voices, from as many persons, shocked at the sacrilegious act.

The girl, struck with the solemn-looking faces about her, paused, and dropped her apron full of flowers, which she had been all the morning gathering for the sick room of her mother. A shade of disappointment stole over her face, succeeded by one of perplexity. The dying woman turned her eyes imploringly upon the child, who sprang in, heedless of the crowd, and clambering upon the bed, threw her arms about her mother's neck.

"Hagar! my wild, beautiful Hagar!" the dying woman murmured, in tones which scarcely reached beyond the ear they were intended for.

"Loving, passion-hearted Hagar! O that here, in my dying hour, I could pour the experience of *my* spirit into yours — that I could save you from the broken reed upon which my soul has leaned! O for time — time — time!"

The brow of the speaker grew damp with death dew, but still she held the strange child clasped to her bosom.

"Speak, mamma," urged the timid voice, in a reverent tone; "don't fear I shall ever forget. Speak!"

The dark, round cheek, shaded with curls of raven hair, contrasted strangely with the faded one beside it.

"*Hagar!* — *my* Hagar! — read the world as you would a book, and fold away from its gaze thy strong, high heart before it yields to the voice of the charmer. Hagar! *Hagar!* For spirits such as thine there is the cross and the stake wherein to impale its yearnings! There are lessons to be learned in darkness and in sorrow. There are dreams from whose awakening death were a million fold to be preferred."

"I'm listening, mamma. I shall treasure all you have to say," murmured the child, whose burning eyes were reverently turned heavenward. For a long time the painful breathing of the mother was the only sound which disturbed the silence of the room. Minnie attempted to remove the child from the clasped arms, stiffening in death; but it was only the signal for a closer clasping, as if not even the King of Terrors could separate the loving and the loved. A tranced vision hovered about the woman, through which the future of her child seemed painfully distinct; for, after a moment of intense thought, with an energy only given to her in that last struggle, she raised herself from her pillow, and called wildly for her husband. In a moment he was by her side, with her head upon his arm.

"That girl, Alva — that girl, *Hagar!* I cannot die with a lie upon my lips! I have had such a vision I *dare* not. Hagar, Hagar! you are not *my* child — you are the daughter of ——"

It was her last sigh! Minnie had seized the child almost upon the threatened exposure, and held her convulsively to her heart. The group of mourners stood silent and apart. The conscience-stricken husband flung his arms frantically around his dead wife, while Minnie and Hagar alone stood tearless over the corpse.

"Not *her* child!" whispered one of the gossips. "This,

then, was her great grief. She was never happy like other women; yet who would have thought that Hagar was not her child! Whose *can* it be?"

Minnie's burning eyes flashed triumph upon the crowd, but no answer came to the question. One by one they dropped off, and left the mourners alone with their dead.

"Don't blame *me*, master — *my* master," murmured poor Minnie, laying her soft hand upon the husband's shoulder; "you know I would have died at any time to have saved her a moment's pain. I couldn't help it!"

Hagar's brilliant eyes were fixed wonderingly upon the pair.

"Hush!" said the man, between whom and the child the likeness was too great for a mistake in that quarter. Hagar blushed and turned proudly away. It was the turning of her first leaf in the book of deception. There were many more such pages in the book.

* * * * *

"Have you seen her? — have you seen her? — have you seen her?" were questions which circled like wildfire throughout Madame Delace's boarding school for young ladies on a morning after an event of peculiar excitement at that establishment.

"I dare say she isn't much," said Flora Bell, pouting her red lips to more than an ordinary size.

"Not *much!* We shall see whether she's *much* or not! Madame Delace says she is her father's heiress — worth half a million or so. We have no more chance of making conquests where she is than our Sally has of making *us* believe that beefsteak pudding is pigeon pie! It is too bad of Madame Delace."

"But did you mind her shoulder? It is a regular hump! Sally says her nurse let her fall when a baby, and she never got over it!"

"I suppose we shall have airs enough to make us sick! She's got a black waiting maid, and ——"

"Black! You don't call Minnie *black?* Why, she is as white as her mistress — whiter than Ella Rose is, enough sight," laughed a mad cap girl.

"Mind your own business! If I am black, I haven't got red hair! Lara King says he abominates red hair," flouted Ella Rose in return.

"Does he! Now, do you know he swore to me that it was his passion — compared it to sunset clouds, field lilies, and I don't know what else beside. O, depend upon it, Lara dotes upon red hair!" and the merry girl rang her voice out in a great laugh peculiar to her own happy self.

"But that is nothing to do with Hagar. What a funny name! They must have been hard up for a name when she was christened. *Hagar!* It makes one think of the outcast Hagar of the wilderness. Wonder if she is any relation? I dare say she will expect us to be very respectful to her; but I shan't, for one."

"Nor I, for another."

"No, nor I, for another. She's come to the wrong place for compliment of any sort."

"Girls, girls, girls! you don't know what you are saying. She is a stranger amongst us, at all events, and not big enough to be very formidable. We all remember how badly we felt in waking up the morning of our first day here, and finding only cold, strange faces around us. For the sake of that memory, let us treat her as *we* should have been grateful to have been treated in those days of our initiation."

"Thank you — thank you; you have made the place seem like home to me already."

It was an earnest, honest face that broke up the conversation so thoughtlessly indulged in, and a hand most perfect in its taper proportions which was extended to grasp the *other* hand of her generous defender. As the two palms clasped, Hagar Martin (for she it was) felt a thrill as of ice traversing her veins; and even while trying to thank her friend, a chilling, repulsive sensation took possession of her mind, and caused her narrowly to scrutinize the features of her new associate. There was nothing in the frank, honest glance which returned her own to predispose her in her regard. The eyes were dark and full — almost as dark as her own; while the face wore a calm, settled look, quite refreshing to dwell upon.

"Strange," thought Hagar; "I never felt this sensation before. She is too pretty not to be good." And with that questionable sentiment uppermost, she strove, by renewed exertion, to make amends for the wrong her first thought and first impulse had unintentionally committed. The sudden entrance of Hagar silenced the little troop of school girls — some from consternation, but most from merriment at their discovery; but in the slow glance which swept around the school room there was so much to disarm prejudice that those most inclined to defame were the first to defend her.

Hagar!

I never could describe children, much less could I do justice to the strong, wild, large-brained infancy of Hagar Martin; and so I pass it over, with its undeveloped fancies and precocious thoughts, — with untamable spirit, yet sensitive soul, — and bring her before the reader at a time when much that was good and all that was evil in her nature had acquired the strength of predeveloped womanhood. The death of her so called mother had left its lasting impress upon her. At first she refused all efforts at consolation. Only one of her entire circle of friends could control her in the slightest degree, and that one a young lad a year or two her senior, to whom she had been attached from her earliest years. Next to the parting with her mother was the pang she experienced in parting from her boy-lover, for such he had become to her in the fullest sense of the word. Keen, active, and uncommonly precocious, Walter Meadows was a fitting mate for the untamable Hagar. Others might storm, and rave, and entreat, but one look from him was a thousand times more effectual in result. Whole days, while the autumn sun lay warm upon the earth, they would wander away into the depths of the forest, or climb almost inaccessible hills in quest of amusement or adventure. Whatever he might do or say, it was her law and gospel. She was his defender on all occasions. Let any one but breathe harm coupled with the name of Walter Meadows, and her form would grow proudly erect, her eyes flash, and if she did not give them the lie direct, it would be because the eye of her father was on her. Dearly she loved every glossy curl that rose and fell with the passing breeze upon his noble brow; and dearly, after his boyish fashion, he loved the trusting child that, in her dependence, clung to him for sympathy. And so the years passed, till Hagar became frantic at the loss of her playmate, who had been sent to New York to study with a famous lawyer of that city. Then, and not till then, would she consent to become an inmate of Madame Delace's school in Charleston.

From the hour of her strange introduction, herself and Anna Welman had become sworn friends — such friends as we all remember to have had at some time or another of our childish years — such friends as many of us sorrow for with a grief known only to the waking dreams. Hagar was wild as the wind, free as the eagle, and impulsive as the mountain torrent, which sweeps over all barriers. Tempests which would thrill those about her with terror and dismay were to her the joys of her existence. She would sit at the window watching for hours the lightning as it played in fitful gleams around the rocks of her mountain home, as if she could scarcely resist the desire to be alone with the elements in their hour of darkest doom. Company was her aversion, now that Walter was gone. Her thoughts were company enough. Even her school chum, Anna Welman, had no power, when she chose to retreat, to draw her from herself. Then the solitude of the hills and the rocks, or the sea-girt shore, had charms alone for her. There, with rod in hand, or gun upon her shoulder, she would wander till the sun went down upon the mountains, and not unfrequently till the moon and stars were "lending torches" for her steps. You may be sure such habits tended to develop a nature at best untamable and erratic. Some persons voted it a harmless insanity, and as there was no malignancy in it, she was suffered to choose her own method of amusement. It was in vain the neighbors speculated from whence she got her fiery blood, from what source she inherited her rambling, restless disposition, or from whose milk she drank in that fierce, invincible, almost fiendish recognition of insult. They were there — elements that could not be controlled — that grew only the more wild, and fierce, and invincible under shadow of restraint; and when they questioned her father concerning it, and advised him to check its growth, he only sighed, and turned to matters of a foreign import.

And much in this way matters progressed till Hagar gained her fourteenth year.

CHAPTER II.

THE BELLE OF THE SCHOOL.—CROSS PURPOSES.—JEALOUSY.

THE summer was in its richest bloom about the hills and romantic dells bordering the academy grounds where Hagar was getting her wisdom. The trees were all a luscious, dreamy mass of quivering green, so broad, so dense that it was a mystery, known only to themselves, how the myriads of birds who flooded the air with song contrived to dive in and out without ruffling their glancing little plumes. But they managed it somehow. Lonely days there would have been without them, or without the ten thousand wild, free, living creatures who kept them company; or, for the matter of that, without the trees *themselves*, dancing and keeping up such a *rinktum* with their leaves all through the melting season. Madame Delace had taken good care of the pleasure of her scholars. Nothing could exceed the beauty of her house or grounds; and it was a perfect home thought to linger among the flowers and the heavy vines which invited a stroll on all sides. There was one little spot of all others that challenged especial admiration—a sort of natural arbor formed of great maple trees, from the tops of which, and all down the sides, drooped vines of gorgeous texture, so light, so graceful, and yet so thick, that the sun could only creep in through the interstices, and ripple in little pools of gold among the grapes. A heavy drapery of vines fell in a perfect sheet of embroidery, and formed a delicious curtain for the entrance to this sylvan spot. Hagar had taken the cultivation of this retreat into her own hands; and woe to the mischievous sprites that dared displace a single vine! On the side looking towards the turnpike she had arranged a window, at which she could sit and read or dream for hours and hours together. This was also the favorite resort of her friend Anna Welman. She had described it all to Walter in the many letters she had written him; had told him how rare and luscious the grapes were, which only waited the parting of lips to drop of their own accord into one's mouth; had told him of the flowers, and the birds, and the softly murmuring streams; had told him, with a minuteness which somewhat puzzled him, of the beautiful goddess of the arbor — pretty Anna Welman. Of late she had ceased to mention her young confidant. Perhaps Walter, in his replies, had taken rather too great an interest in her — had been too grateful for her kindness to his poor and lonely Hagar. One thing was certain; she did not quite relish Anna's curiosity regarding *him*. It seemed like an encroachment on her rights for any other girl to care for the color of his eyes, though they *were* the shade of the violet on the side towards the blue heaven; or to imagine the crispiness of his curls, though they *did* ripple like sunny waves over his broad forehead. She forgot that his many charms had been the incessant theme of her confidences with her friend, and finally came to drop the subject altogether. Not so her friend. Anna Welman was a born coquette; she could not help trying to win affection, though by so doing she was sure of breaking her own sister's heart. There are many such women in the world, unable to resist coquetry, yet meaning nothing in the end beyond a species of harmless pleasantry. If they would only reflect — But that is neither here nor there. Anna, as I have said, was a born coquette; and Hagar, with her quick instincts, felt her to be a dangerous rival. What Anna's thoughts were I should not like to say. It seems impossible to believe that, while sitting with her arm enclasped around her friend, she could be indulging in dreams of rivalry which were to wring that friend's heart. There are some inexplicable things in human nature, and this was one of them.

For days and days Hagar had wandered, restless and uneasy, around the house and over the grounds, yet never straying beyond sight of the domicile. The truth was, she had received a letter from Walter announcing a flying visit; and in her loving heart came doubts of the result thereof; she could not tell why — a presentiment, perhaps, but none the less painful to bear, that she was wronging her best friend by her ridiculous suspicion.

Never was sunset more glorious, never rang the good night song of the birds more cheerily, never whispered the leaves more dreamily than on the eve of his arrival; but the fates were against her even there. She had been sitting with Anna in their vine-wreathed arbor, watching the golden clouds melting away and brimming over into purple tints. Such troops of lovely fantasies! such floods of evanescent glory! She was wondering what it all meant, and where it all went to, and what made the night, with all its darksome shadows. Anna was leaning far out among the vines, framing as beautiful a picture in their fruity wealth as ever Rembrandt dreamed of or Angelo conceived.

"He will not come to-night," thought Hagar, as she stole away to view the setting sun from a more favorable point in the garden. Anna at first did not miss her, but continued leaning out, lazily plucking the grapes which dangled on all sides of the window. Presently she saw a shadow on the rich turf, and heard a step by the side of her. Thinking it was Hagar, she began in her accustomed method of addressing her when alone.

"*Bird-ee, dear,* ——"

"And bird-ee, dear," rang out a mocking, musical voice, while a pair of soft palms prisoned her head, and two warm, full lips took venturesome toll of her own plump, tempting ones.

"*Sir!*"

"I beg your pardon. How *could* I be mistaken?" murmured Walter Meadows, blushing and stammering like a school girl detected in her first love affair.

After a moment's embarrassment, Anna gracefully held out her hand to him, giving him warm welcome in the absence of their mutual friend, and explaining to him that *she* was the "bird-ee, dear" that was responsible for the amusing *dénouement.*

Hagar had caught a glimpse of him as he entered, and, flying along, she tore the drooping vines asunder, scattering the purple fruit in all directions, in her haste to greet him once more. As her eye took in the sight of her lover cozily seated by her friend, and conversing with the familiarity of old acquaintances, a flush of deeper red darted to her cheeks, and her eyes flamed out in gusty glances.

Walter sprang up, and would have taken her in his arms; but she evaded his clasp, and merely touched his hand in her chilliest manner. Walter gazed upon her in mute astonishment. Her letters had been so warm, so friendly; what could it mean? Conscious of no offence on his part, he wondered the more what could have given rise to her singular behavior. Anna could have told him; the very flashing of her eyes, the proud curving of her lips, had triumph in them. Not that she loved him; not that he loved her; not that she ever expected or wished him to love her — not *then,* whatever she might have done in the after years; but Hagar was jealous of her; Hagar — the proud, passionate, beautiful Hagar — was jealous of her. Never before had such a thrill of joy pervaded her being. Her sphere had heretofore been limited. Young men were novelties in that locality; and it needed no trumpet tongue to tell her that Walter Meadows was all the fond eyes of his loving Hagar had painted him. It was a detestable impulse, a fiendish determination. I shame to say that all her patterns are not extinct. Perhaps it would be as well not to say it; but then what would become of my story? Besides, I am disclosing hearts as they are, not as we would like to have them.

Anna did not long intrude her company upon the lovers, but left them with a graceful salutation, hoping to meet Mr. Meadows again during his visit. "Would it be a long one?" she paused in the doorway to inquire.

"No; two days at farthest."

Hagar caught his answer with trembling eagerness. She wished him to go, and she wished him to stay. If she was only at home! but *here* — no; it was better that his visit *was* to be a short one; for how could she *learn* while his eyes were between her and the book?

"Hagar, what have I done to be received in this way? *You* would have been met with no such freezing welcome as this if our positions had been reversed."

Hagar was subdued in an instant.

"I am *so* sorry, Walter — I am, indeed!" she cried, flinging her arms about him. She was only a child in years, reader, — just past fourteen, — and one who had always been allowed the rein of her impulses. Anna was three years her senior, and Walter six; so in reality her loving, infantile ways might well pass for those of childhood. In that light, however, none who knew her *well* ever ventured to class her. I do not think Walter judged of her as the womanly little thing she was. She was so large of her age, so fully developed, and so sensible on most points! In her love for Walter all other sentiments and sensations were blended. Of the passion of love she knew nothing, although the tinge of wild, warm blood swelling her veins predisposed her to enthusiastic demonstration in her own childlike way; but of its purity she was imbued — soul, sense, and nature. It did not surprise Anna, therefore, when, after her interview with Walter, she flung her arms around her neck, and, raining kisses upon her lips, her hands, and her hair, besought her forgiveness for her rudeness in the arbor scene. The next two days were days of happiness and joy to Hagar, as well as Walter. More attentive, more devoted she could not desire him to be; and if — as sometimes she did — she saw the beautiful eyes of her friend fixed mournfully upon his face, it elicited no sentiment but one of pity.

"Poor, dear Anna!" she would say; "I wish *she* had somebody to love as I love you, Walter. Do talk to her more; I never saw her so melancholy before."

And so he did talk to her; and, in talking to her, made the discovery that she was not only a very intelligent but a very attractive girl. There may have been a heart throb of pride in his bosom to think that one of her superior attainments should take such pains to amuse him; I presume there was. The *sex* are as susceptible to flattery as the softer stratum of society; or, at least, so it has seemed to *me*. I may be wrong; if I *am* it is no hanging matter, fortunately.

Well, the days passed, hurriedly enough to Hagar, and Walter had said farewell; but in parting with Anna there was an "*I love you, Walter!*" beaming from her eyes, which, all his journey home, haunted him, with a soft, sensuous, dreamy sensation, very far from being unpleasant. But Hagar was too busy watering the curls of her *friend* with her tears to perceive that *other* eyes than her own had received his last farewell — a merciful dispensation of Providence, which gave to her a few weeks more of unalloyed trust and affection.

CHAPTER III.

THE UNWELCOME SUMMONS.—THE FAIRY FRIEND.—THE LINK IN THE CHAIN OF CIRCUMSTANCES.

THE establishment wherein Hagar was domesticated, like all other establishments of the kind, gave sufficient material for the restless, excitable temper inherent in the nature of our heroine. I have always said, had I daughters I would never trust them within the pale of boarding school morality. There are too many elements of a clashing nature—too little purity of thought or purpose. A quantity of girls, many of them brimming over with the romance of a first plunge in the world's bath, congregate together, forming their own opinions of life, and oftentimes hazarding their teacher's displeasure, and their own expulsion, by acts of daring disobedience, which pass for independence and fearless breeding. I do not say that all schools combine these qualities to feed the restless mind; but those mothers whose lives, like mine, in their early times, were passed within the shadow of a boarding school, would hesitate long enough before sending a daughter to vegetate and form her views of the external life from experiences so erroneously founded.

As I have already premised, there was a wild, dark tinge of blood in the nature of Hagar that sent her heedlessly into every excitement calculated to stir and quicken the blood. Equestrian exercise was her delight and pride. She could sit the most fiery horse with the grace and ease of a thorough-bred jockey. Fences, ditches, walls, all were the same to her. It was a word and a leap; the beautiful Arabian understanding her lightest word, and paying the most implicit obedience. On one of her excursions, having traversed the country until she had lost herself, she came across a brook too shallow to wade, and too deep to cross in safety by herself.

"Trot along, Xerxes," she whispered in the ear of her Arabian, as she slid from his back to the ground. Xerxes, so commanded, stepped gracefully into the water, turning his head over now and then to see if his mistress intended following. Hagar laughed one of her wild, long laughs, and commenced picking her way across the water upon the smoothly-polished stones. When about half way across she paused, having come to a depth unexpected by her, and impossible to navigate. She was speculating upon the practicability of returning, when the bushes just at her hand by the water's edge gave a sharp crackle, and a young sportsman, gun in hand, pitched headlong through the mass, and landed in rather an ungraceful position upon the sand. Hagar turned sharply around, and would have suddenly retreated, but the ludicrousness of the position brought forth another of her musical laughs.

"I can't say, in our girlish idiom, Come here, and I'll pick you up, for you see I too am a prisoner," said she with a graceful bow.

The young man was on his feet in an instant, and in another moment at the side of Hagar.

" Excuse me if I pick *you* up then, as my position seems least onerous."

Without waiting her reply, he gathered his arm around her waist, and safely landed her upon the opposite side.

" As your knight-errant, it is only fair for you to inform me what nymph I have rescued from a watery grave."

" Nay, not so bad as that! Suppose now, instead of allowing you comfortably to bear me to the land, I had gathered *my* arms around you, and borne you to my cave beneath the water."

" Try it! try it! and see with what grace I will surrender."

" Look there!"

" Where?"

" As far as the eye can see!"

" I see nothing!"

" Give me your gun!"

A flash, an echo, and the noble bird lay bleeding at her feet.

" Ah, ha! glorious! Old Warland himself couldn't have made a better shot!"

" How cruel you are!"

" *Me!*"

" I should not think it— a soft, fragile girl, like you, to be so cruel. What's your name?"

" An impertinent question, Sir Squire."

"I am impertinent; it is a way I have."

"A very bad way, especially where ladies are concerned."

"What did you say 'glorious' for when you killed that poor bird?"

"It was too ambitious! It was soaring too near the sun, so I clipped its wings."

"How would you like *your* wings clipped, Miss Hagar?"

"*Hagar* — only Hagar; nobody calls me *miss*."

"Well, *Hagar*, then."

"There doesn't live the man or woman who could clip *my* wings. They were made for soaring."

"But you have no right to take life — even a bird's life. The poor thing is dead."

"And what is *death*?"

"Something I have no wish to define yet a while."

"Pshaw! You shrink from what comes to all. Now, to me, to die is to be free — *free*. Unfettered by mortal flesh — away from mortal ills! I never see death but I long to gather myself up and take a leap across the flood to that land of freedom, life eternal and unchangeable!"

Hagar drew herself up as she spoke, with a holy faith in her words which overshadowed the darkness of her face.

"I must study *you*."

"Two words to that bargain, Sir Knight! Who are you? Are you presentable, as Madame le School-*marm* says?"

"Rather. My name is Lee, at your service. An old name, and a good one! My grandfather fought, bled, and died in the service of his country, and I am prepared to do the same service by you!"

"O, thank you;" and Hagar made him a mocking bow.

"I have a thousand negroes at my service — own a farm — a score of horses — carriages too numerous to mention — and ——"

"Have a first-rate opinion of yourself, generally, eh?" broke in Hagar. "I shall be happy to make your acquaintance. You want a thorn to pierce that egotism of yours, and it will take me to leave you limp and reasonable."

"Take care. I may turn the tables."

"I'll risk it."

"May I try?"

"Certainly. There's my card."

"Why, you are at school with my Effie!"

"And who's your Effie, pray?'

"My Effie Rose! The dearest, sweetest, truest little Rose that ever bloomed! She can break a horse, ride a race, leap a hurdle, fire at a mark, and is the most dashing little dare-devil you ever — *Hello!*"

The last expression was caused by the leaping of a fence by a powerful white gelding, upon whose back sat, as if she had grown there, the same Effie Rose the young sportsman had just been describing. Down she came, thundering over the hill and waving her cap with an air of triumph which seemed to say, "Better that if you can."

"Aha, Charley! I haven't spoiled sport, I hope! How long since this agreeable rendezvous has been in vogue?"

"It is no rendezvous, Effie," began Hagar. "Charley — what's his *other* name? —O, Lee! Well, Mr. Lee happened here by accident just in time to rescue me from a watery grave;" and her merry eyes twinkled down into the still water lying at their feet.

"Never mind. I accept your apology. But take care of Charley. He's a desperate fellow — in his own opinion — a regular woman-killer! Why, I have been as good as dead these twelve months! O, by the by, I'm in search of you, Hagar. There's somebody at the hall who wants especial audience with you. A solemn-looking fellow, in deep black. I was lucky to find you. O, you rogue, Charley. Can't you let the girls alone one day out of seven? O, I've a rod in pickle for you yet. Come, Hagar."

As she wheeled her horse to go, Lee managed to seize a moment upon Hagar's hand.

"Let me visit you at the hall! I shall be miserable till I see you!"

"Don't believe him," chimed in Effie, who had caught the concluding words. "He said the same thing to me yesterday, and he will say the same thing to the next girl he meets. O, what a Charley!" And off they galloped to the hall, leaving Lee looking wistfully after them.

CHAPTER IV.

THE FATAL STEP. — THE DEMON MAN. — THE DESTINY SPELL.

> "There was a shadow on his face that spoke
> Of passion long since hardened into thought.
> He had a smile, — a cold and scornful smile, —
> Not gayety nor sweetness, but the sign
> Of feelings moulded at their master's will.
> A weary world was hidden in that heart;
> Sorrow and strife. It now could only feel
> Distrust in love — and mockery for those
> Who could believe in what he knew was vain."
>
> L. E. L.

I AM a fatalist — soul, sense, and spirit a fatalist! I believe that every turning point of our existence is so laid out that it is impossible to avoid its encounter; that every prominent incident of our lives has been set apart for us at the beginning. Things which in the world's vocabulary stand for luck and chance are fatalities — dire, dreadful, or agreeable fatalities, as the case may be. But sermonizing is not my forte; to those who would know the book from which I take my impressions of life, I can only say, from the leaves of my own experience. If that will not suffice, let them look down the track of their *own* years, and find there, dropped by the wayside, incidents which, adorn them as you may, still wear the features of fatality.

The setting sun was pouring its last tribute of gold upon

the little village of Eccleson (its romantic name) as the two equestrians galloped through an opening in the forest, and came dashing up the path leading to the academy. It was a beautiful scene, full of that still life which the night smile of the setting sun ever leaves upon the face of nature. There was scarcely a breath of air to ripple up the slumbering leaves, or trouble the emerald waters glistening in the rich light. The two girls for a moment seemed aware of the beauty of the sunset, for, giving their horses a loose rein, they subsided into a slow walk, almost monotonous in its measured echo.

With a quick impulse Hagar, who was in advance, suddenly wheeled around, and came to a stand in front of her companion.

"Why, Hagar, how pale you are! What is the matter?"

"I am going to meet my *fate!* I feel it here," — placing her hand upon her heart, — "here, Effie, as I felt it once before, as I lay in my mother's dying arms. There is a shadow rising between me and the hall — a cold, dreary shadow — a sort of mist, from out of which glimmers *something* — I know not what! If I was superstitious, I should say my mother's eyes — so wild, so mournful!"

"*Hagar!* The strong, powerful, self-reliant Hagar — Hagar that we all envy and half fear — is it *you* that are indulging in superstitious fancies? Come, you'll lose your crown if the girls get hold of it. I'll risk any thing worse than a *man* at the hall. Ogres and gnomes are bygones, more's the pity; and as for the shadow, why, it is the veriest fancy of a tired brain. Why, Hagar; poor little insignificant me, that haven't even a kink of genius in my brain to recommend me, am *your* superior *now!* I'll soon dispel your gloom; so follow to the rescue."

"Don't, Effie, don't be irreverent."

"I'm not irreverent; but when I hear one like you talking of fate, it seems too ridiculous to listen to. But see, there is the stranger standing at the window; do you know him?"

A tremor swept through the veins of Hagar, as her eyes were raised to meet those burning at her through the panes of glass.

"I tell you, Effie, the shadow is certainly falling. There is something more than fancy in all this; believe me, I should never feel so acutely the presence of a mere common stranger."

Hagar tossed her reins to the groom in waiting, and walked straight to the room where the visitor awaited her presence.

"You sit a horse as if you was born in the saddle, lady," was the remark which first greeted her ear.

"I love the exercise — the wild, free, glorious exercise. I always ride when I am out of spirits; it is an excellent opiate for thought. Did you ever try it?"

The stranger raised his eyes for the first time, and Hagar as readily dropped hers.

"You laugh, sir."

"How do you know? You are not looking."

This was a challenge, indirect to be sure, but too positive to allow her to pass it over.

"I'm looking *now!*" She laughed much after his own strain of bantering; and, truly, it must have been a stout heart that could have borne the eagle glance of her great eyes.

She did look, and such a face it was that met her scrutiny! Gentleness and ferocity, humility and self-reliance, tenderness and indifference, the antipodes of all good and bad passions, seemed gathered in warfare, and each fighting for supremacy. A forehead, low, broad, and massive, glittered out from kinks of yellowish-brown hair; cheek bones high and rugged; a firm, square-set mouth closed habitually with an expression of determination; lips full and prominent. Such was the appearance of his features when reposing in their awful stillness. But his smile — I have been trying to think of something to which to liken it. To sunshine? No; that is too pure a comparison. The glittering scales of the serpent were nearer its fascinating brilliancy. The gazer dwelt upon it with the same pleasing terror that a bird might feel when fluttering nearer and nearer to the open-mouthed charmer, charming to devour. You would not meet with another such smile within a circle of centuries. So dark, and glittering, and solemn; so profound, and silent, and convincing. There was no emotion it did not combine within its range of expression. That wondrous smile! — still, gentle, smooth, and seductive, it crept from feature to feature, lighting up that otherwise repulsive face with a radiance at once fascinating and fearful.

"You are taking your time over my face; I hope you like it," he said, after submitting to her scrutiny for some minutes in silence.

"Not at all. I have seldom seen a face I like less."

"Candid, at all events. Now, do you know, I like candor above all things. I don't believe there is another girl in the world that would have answered me so abruptly. Come, sit beside me, and let me talk to you. What do you see in my face to dislike?"

"I see sincerity overshadowed by cruelty. I see a devil's frown under an angel's smile. I see a will, a purpose, and a determination in the corners of your mouth, and I pray God that I may never be so unfortunate as to attract you."

"You *do* already attract me. I repel you, that is evident; you recoil from me! *Take care!* There is an instinct — a natural enough instinct — implanted in every heart to hunt that which flies from us. The excitement of the chase you know. Now, I possess more than my share of this instinct. Hagar, if I choose to wind my will around your repugnance, you could no more elude my grasp than you can free yourself from this arm till I choose to release you."

Before she was aware of his object, his arm had encircled her waist like a bar of iron.

"*Sir!*" The proud, the lofty, the magnificent Hagar in the embrace of a strange man!

"I beg your pardon, Miss Martin," he said, releasing her with all the gallantry of the southern race. "Your manner was so piquant — excuse me if I say abrupt — that I was tempted into a little harmless pleasantry. We are strangers again."

Hagar bowed, but the blush of shame still dyed her cheek, and her lip quivered with indignation.

"You have a message for me, I believe," she went on.

"Yes. Your father desires me to instruct you somewhat in relation to home affairs, and afterwards to conduct you to the Leclerk plantation. He is on the eve of marriage."

"*My father?*"

"Yes; is there any thing strange in that? How many years has your mother been dead?"

"Ten."

"That makes *you* fourteen; well, ten years of loneliness have induced him to enter once more into the bonds of wedlock."

"And who is the bride? Strange he has never written me."

"A Miss Montague, daughter of Montague the sheriff. Not a very lofty match; but he is old enough to brave the ridicule of neighbors; besides, Miss Montague is the handsomest woman I ever saw, not excepting present company, as one is in duty bound."

An impatient exclamation was Hagar's only answer to his ungallant remark.

"You are angry. Your pride is hurt, that your father should have stooped to a plebeian."

"No; I am too thorough a republican to care for that! *He was* the conservator of rank. I am wondering what overmastered his prejudice."

"Her beauty, perhaps; may be her *virtue*."

Hagar raised her eyes just in time to catch one of those strange, baneful glances for which his face was renowned. It lasted but a moment, and passed away again like the swooping of some dark shadow; but the sensation remained, telling her that there was some mystery, perhaps some vile plot, which her presence might counteract.

"You know her, then?" questioned Hagar, bending upon his face her own searching glance.

"*Know her! By* ——"

"*Sir!*"

"Pardon me. I am accustomed to strange spasms of pain. At that moment one assailed me, and — I trust you will pardon me. I have been rather unfortunate, I fear, in the impression my visit is likely to create. If you will excuse me, I will return now to my hotel, and give you the next few hours for the purpose of making the necessary preparations for departure."

He bowed himself out; but not before Hagar had taken in all the convulsions of that singular face.

"I never saw any thing so wild, so ferocious, in my life.

He looked like a hungry tiger, waiting to spring upon his prey. There's a mystery here. I must forget *self* for a while, and see into what sort of a net my poor father is placing his head. Poor father! he has never been himself since my mother died."

CHAPTER V.

PREPARATIONS FOR A WEDDING.—THE BEAUTIFUL BRIDE.—THE BROKEN FAITH.

"O, mine was but a perjured faith,
And mine a broken vow,
Else he I loved, and who loved me,
Were here beside me now."

THINGS turn out strangely in this rare old world of ours. Events tangle themselves up with events, incidents clash with rival incidents, so rapidly and imperceptibly, that one cannot help wondering

"If this be all of earth—
And nought beyond—O Death!"

For many years after the death of his wife, Alva Martin had eschewed woman's society for the cultivation of an expansive and noble intellect, which in all his early years had lain dormant. It was a season of great political excitement, and his eloquent appeals, somewhat stormy and passionate, stirred up the waves of public feeling, as the winds stir up the ocean's billows. He was practical as well as eloquent. He sent the scalping knife of his indignation to the heart of political antagonisms, and laid bare their discordant elements. He denounced to their teeth partisan traitors, who thought to climb into notoriety upon the downfall and disseverment of the Union. He dissected the elements and individualities of slave life — the flint and steel with which wrong-headed and wrong-hearted men have vainly endeavored to strike a fire which should devastate and lay waste our beautiful union of states. He was the people's idol; the pride, the boast, and the toast of his party. Bursts of genuine applause and enthusiasm greeted his appearance, while young men and old hung around him, anxious and happy to get a glance from the eagle eye, whose sturdy strength bespoke a heart immaculate in its untiring integrity. Candidates for office wooed his influence, and sought to propitiate his judgment in their favor. It was easy to tell when Alva Martin had left the trail of his fiery eloquence upon any of the boroughs of his native state. For days and days after, excited groups, with earnest eyes and flushed cheeks, would congregate for discussion or controversy. His eloquence was of the convincing kind, which not only carried conviction with it, but an ambition to emulate his lofty impulses. His honest zeal in behalf of his country, his self-absorbing, all-engrossing love of justice, in all its phases, was not allowed to go unrewarded.

In the fall of 183–, his name was up as candidate for a responsible station at Washington, and with an almost unanimous vote he was elected. It was during a fiery and passionate debate upon the floor of the Senate chamber that his eye was arrested, and his very heart almost stilled, by the sight of a young girl of gorgeous beauty, who sat gazing at him from the gallery, and whose parted lips and flushed cheeks told how much of soul and sense there was inwrapped in the eloquence of the stringent orator. It was in the centre of a graceful pause, while his hand brushed away the damp and tangled locks that lay heavy upon his forehead, that the vision first became prominent to his gaze. It was a truly Madonna face, shrined thence in its golden curls — a Madonna face, marred by an expression of repressed eagerness, but none the less lovely for that expression. The thrilling words — the arguments of massive strength which had swayed that multitude into demonstrative delight — had awed that fair, fresh beauty into a solemn stillness of admiration, a thousand times more flattering to the speaker than all the waving of handkerchiefs, or the more vociferous bravos which gave eclat to the occasion so long to be remembered.

Great sensation is always *wordless;* and the boundless enthusiasm, which burst forth in noisy tumult, annoyed, rather than gratified, the "star" of the day. How grateful, then, was the silent homage of that queen of beauty, radiating the chamber from her crowded seat in the gallery! All that remained of the speech (luckily it was nearly at its termination) was wild and erratic. He had fascinated his assemblage, however, and any incoherence or inconsistence of speech would now have passed without comment. He hurried on, impatient of release — impatient to see more, learn more of the fair being who had enslaved him. Never before, since the death of his wife, had woman's beauty stirred the slumberous depths of his sensuous heart. He had mourned for his young wife as they mourn who feel that half the love, duty, and honor belonging to their dead had been forgotten or neglected till the grave cast its long shadow between them and atonement. But *now*, the warm passionate beauty of that *lily* girl brought into being a delicious, craving, unconquerable love, which was half passion, and *all* madness. In vain he strove to shut his eyes to the picture before him. There she sat, more fascinating in her tender, languid beauty than had ever been to him the dark-eyed, passion-hearted children of the sunny south, in their most sparkling guises. Who was she? That was the one question of his tumultuous heart. To whom she belonged was another consideration. He would snatch her from them, if the next moment saw him an outcast and a felon. His she must be at all hazards! The wild tinge of Spanish blood which his mother had bequeathed him was boiling with impatience and desire. His vivacity forsook him; his eloquence paled before his extravagant passion, and excusing himself on the plea of sudden indisposition, he very abruptly brought his speech to a termination.

From the first encounter of eyes, Lola Montague (for she it was) had kept hers veiled beneath their long, shadowy lashes; nor was it till the voice of the speaker, grown singularly husky and uneven, announced the conclusion of the speech, that there was the least demonstration of life or vitality in that undulating figure. Then slowly and languidly she lifted them once more to where the speaker stood. A deeper flush melted into her cheek — a triumphant flush, for she knew, by intuition, what had occasioned the sudden indisposition of their orator. The fiery heat which filled his veins found no response in hers; she could not "love because that she did love;" but ambition was stronger in her breast than any other passion; she had made a conquest worthy the name — wealth, rank, social distinction; desires which had been as Utopian dreams to her young imagination, were here, ready for her clasp to close upon them. No longer the despised governess; no longer slighted for her position; no longer the *convenience* of those whose native possessions were not half of hers. It was of all this she thought, while sitting dreamily under the spell of eloquence. To disdain those who had scornfully passed her by; to read the deprecating glance of those who now disdained to recognize her existence; to plant her foot upon the necks of those who had humbled her, — O, *this* was a revenge too sweet to lose; and she determined to follow up the advantage she had gained. She knew that her taste was refined and critical; she knew that her education was thorough and practical; her glass told her that her face needed only the surroundings of wealth to make it as beautiful as a dream. With her husband, and such a husband, what more could her wildest ambition, her most luxurious taste, aspire to? She was still under the influence of such musings, when a hand rested gently upon her shoulder.

"Dreaming again, Lola!" said a manly voice in her ear.

The deep blush, the sudden start, the wild bound of her heart seemed striving to say, "Smother your ambition, or peace is gone forever!"

Coldly and silently she allowed her companion to adjust the shawl upon her graceful shoulders; then, taking his arm, she threaded her way out among the crowd. The statesman's eye had been the last to take in her own as she rose to depart; and, with a feeling amounting almost to exultation, she noted the jealous glance bestowed upon her companion; consequently, she was as much surprised as pleased to meet again at the door that same lustrous pair of eyes.

"Who is she?" murmured Martin, as she disappeared in the crowd.

"Why, man alive! you are not fascinated with Laird's governess, are you?"

"*She* a governess! *Impossible!*"

"*Why* impossible?"

"So haughty, so imperious, so self-possessed."

"And you may add, so self-reliant. All of these qualities she has in the fullest abundance. Nevertheless, she is the governess of as thorny a little piece of womanhood as ever you encountered, I'll be sworn. I've business at Laird's this evening; if you like, walk up the avenue with me, and see your dove in its nest."

"Is she accessible?"

"O, yes. Laird is a widower, with one child. Lola Montague's parents are poor, and cannot bear the burden of their own infirmities, much less those of a grown-up daughter. By the by, now I think of it, this Lola must possess rather more than the usual share of fascination. There was some trouble — I scarcely know what — between Laird and herself, that caused her to return home in a hurry. That was settled, however; but from what I know of *him*, I should not like his enmity. People think he tried to get her on his own terms, and, failing in that, intends to offer her *hers*. She has a cousin, or a lover, or *something*, which thorns Laird considerably."

"Does Laird belong here?"

"No; he passes the winter here with Lola and his girl. This is Miss Montague's third winter in Washington; and had she been half as rich as she is handsome, some one would have borne the bird to a golden cage before this time, I'm certain."

For some time they walked along in silence, when Martin again took up the thread of the discourse.

"You say if she had been as rich as she is handsome. Ought lack of wealth to stand between a virtuous, beautiful girl and her social elevation?"

"*No* — probably *not*, in the eye of *right;* but *might* has so ordained it, and there is no escaping its ordeal. These are things which we can't contend with. Society has elevated wealth over worth, and we must even bide its requirements."

"Not I, for one," stoutly asserted Mr. Martin.

"Eh?"

"If my fancy should chance to hit upon a poor girl, whose character would admit of sanction, her poverty would be the last obstacle I should allow to interfere with my happiness."

"But, my dear fellow, there are grades which never commingle. It would be impossible to take a wife from the medium classes and graft her upon the tree of fashion — impossible. We are, of course, only talking for talk's sake; but, believe me, no more imprudent union could be made than between a plebeian and an aristocrat."

"But a plebeian may be an aristocrat in desire, in taste, in refinement, and in intellect."

"Very true; but can you convince the world of that fact? Could you, loving your wife as your hot nature would be likely to love, bear to see her slighted, snubbed, or at best received with a questionable recognition? Why, you would be in hot water from one year's end to another, with the satisfaction of achieving nothing in the end but ridicule."

"Nevertheless, I am determined to try the experiment; that is, should I chance to meet a person worthy of the trial. But here we are at the hotel. To-night you say ——"

"At eight I'll come for you."

The companions separated; the one to speculate upon the possibility of a person in the lower ranks of life being recognized within the circle of aristocracy, the other to decorate himself in his most becoming garb, and to paint pictures upon the canvas of imagination, wherein a lily face with crimson lips and golden curls mostly predominated.

Lola Montague and her companion reached her home in silence. Being accustomed to a familiar reception, he went in with her and sat alone in the receiving room till Lola disrobed herself of her walking paraphernalia. For once the society of her cousin was irksome to her. She felt guilty of infidelity, at least in thought, and desired to be alone with her vascillating nature long enough to decide upon her future course. It was nothing that the noble and distinguished man had not even the pleasure of a speaking acquaintance. She knew he would find some means to effect it, and that its result would be an open and decided proposal. He was the soul of. honor, so his constituents said, and Lola knew his integrity too well by report to fear any thing but an honorable proposal.

"I was not pleased with Mr. Martin's admiration of you to-day, Lola," said her lover, on her return.

"For my part, I thought it exceedingly flattering," she replied, tapping her shoe upon the carpet by way of amusement.

"Flattering! The bold, undisguised stare of a libertine!"

"No, no, Charles; *not a libertine!* A young girl like me ought not to define the difference between an honest look of admiration and the disgusting fire of a libertine's glance. But you know I'm not like other girls, and I have *felt* the difference in the burning of my cheek and the indignant tumult of my heart often enough to be a judge. No; there was nothing that the most exacting nature could find to carp at in *his* earnest gaze."

"And you are pleased with it? Lola Georgiana, your ambition will ring the death knell of happiness!"

"You are right. I do not recoil from sharing your poverty, Charles, but I *do* your obscurity. I can't help it, and it is better I tell you so *now*, than when it is too late! To be rich is nothing; but to be great and powerful would be worth the sacrifice of even ——"

"*Even of my love!*"

"Even so, Charles. It is the first time I have had courage to say it; but I feel more to-day than ever before that my affection would die out in view of position and rank to which I never might aspire. It would be a lifelong misery to us both. I dare not — O Charles, pity me! — I *will* not risk the *after* torment of regretting unavailing evils!"

Lola's face grew pale and sad, but beyond that there was no visible agitation.

"It ought never to have been," she went on; "and something tells me now that I shall yet feel the misery I am inflicting upon you. My dreams have always been of ambition, and I cannot renounce them. I have tried, for I know I shall never again meet with a heart so true as yours; but they come again with redoubled force, and would madden me had my own act placed a barrier between them and fulfilment."

"Lola! Georgia! But no! Unworthy that you are, I will not plead with you. I leave you to your own reflection. If you still persist in this reckless ambition, farewell to love, happiness, every thing that makes life an object worth contending for!"

He was gone! and in one week from that time Lola Georgiana Montague was the affianced of Alva Martin. And what of him — the brilliant statesman? Passion outstripped all other sentiments. He lived in a maze of infatuation — to be with her, to listen to her voice, to gaze upon her glorious beauty. Life was at a standstill till he could possess her, till he could call her *his* by all the rights of wedlock! It was nothing to him that, with her small hands clasped over his arm, she had confessed her association with a younger lover; had confessed even her affection for him! That was nothing. He would make her love him. Such passionate and vehement idolatry could not help winning back a return. And Laird saw it all with evil eyes, thinking the while how he could be revenged.

Unexpected as the wedding was to Hagar, it was equally so to the neighboring families. Few were even conversant with the name or station of the bride. One thing, however, was conceded upon all sides, — that the aristocratic colonel — the severe and rigid stickler for rank and conventional position — would never degrade himself by taking a low-born bride to his bosom. Minnie, the gorgeous creole, having been summoned from her attendance upon Hagar, retained a cold, silent, almost sullen quietude amid the bustle about her. Questions were useless. What she knew — if, indeed, she knew any thing but that her master was upon the eve of marriage — she resolutely kept to herself; consequently, the most inveterate gossips were obliged to restrain their curiosity till a fitting moment for its indulgence.

While the hum of busy labor went on in the lower department, there were other rooms of the mansion concealing passions and emotions not often guests at a wedding banquet.

Mr. Laird, Hagar's visitor, had said truly that the bride of Colonel Martin was the most beautiful woman in the world.

Dare we intrude upon her presence, as she sits gazing from the window, with eyes fixed "too intently for seeing," upon the vast domain so soon to call her mistress? The tufted bloom of gorgeous carpeting will give back no echo to our tread; for all that taste could devise or wealth procure has been gathered to that home into whose precincts had come an unwilling bride.

I have heard it said that "beauty unadorned is adorned the most;" but I am no convert to the theory, although that regal-looking girl sitting in the depth of the window, with her crimson dressing robe hanging loosely from her shoulders — with her long, golden curls drooping over her neck and bosom like so many sunbeams — with her soft, white feet peeping naked from beneath an embroidered cloud — with her transparent bust heaving up into the light like drifts of snow, — I say, with this lovely, unadorned vision before me, I cannot help but yield my vote to the poetic and popular fallacy, clapping the hands of my admiration in token of approval.

O, beautiful! most beautiful! That sorrow should ever shade aught so exquisite, or despair dwell within the shadow of its charms! And yet she, so listless *now*, but one month ago rejoiced in that exceeding beauty which never failed to win her admiration; gloried in that *woman's* wealth — her own preëminent charms — which to the charms of those about her were as diamonds in a cluster of paste. *Now* so listless, so enervated. What could have wrought the change?

The more you gaze upon her the more visibly you mark the gloom which shades those classic features — a gloom ever and anon varied by a passing contraction of the brow, and a sigh which seems to be more the effect of habit than of present pain.

"It is your wedding day!" murmured a soft voice in her ear, the tones of which startled her from her dream. She did not look up after the first quick start, seeming conscious of the import of the words quite as mechanically. Minnie parted the soft, bright hair, winding each curl lazily over her finger, and drooping it down in radiant waves over her marble shoulders.

"It is your wedding day, lady," again murmured the tearful voice.

There was something in the tremulous tones that caused the bride to lift her eyes from their vacant resting-place.

"What should a wife bring her husband on her wedding day, Minnie?"

"For a husband like *yours*, honor, love, submission, idolatry!" And the slave's tall form towered in her enthusiasm.

"And if in the bride's heart there was no place for honor, no recognition of love, no belief in submission? What if idolatry was a name — perhaps a shame? — what if the altar of affection had crumbled under its weight, and borne down the heart's best garlands? — what if she gave him ashes for fire — withered leaves for love? — what if all that the world calls true, and pure, and holy had been charred out, blackened, smouldered, and only ruin lay where she had been?"

"O lady, better his marriage bed should be a shroud, — better the *grave* clasp than the clasp of arms wherein no thrill of love could linger! Your eyes are wild — your bosom throbs — there is a hungry ferocity in your face that I tremble to look at."

"No more, no more! There *is* desolation in my wedding day! I must speak to some one, or my heart will break. Minnie, do you know what it is to love — not gently, and timidly, and submissively, as women love, but as the storm loves the forest it levels — as the lightning loves the tree it blasts — as the ocean loves the bark it ingulfs? Can you imagine such a love? If so, what think you of an estrangement — of death without an unrelenting word — of the weary days and years that must follow? —

to have done injustice to one you worship, and not tell him so — to have parted with him coldly and angrily, while your heartstrings were cracking with misery? There are *some* sorrows lying too deep for words, Minnie! There — there; never mind! I talk at random sometimes, Minnie. Why, how incredulous you look! Come, child, come; it is my wedding day, and, as I live, time I was ready for my bridegroom. Why do you look at me so reproachfully?"

Minnie *was* gazing at her reproachfully — gazing down into that gorgeous face, where the bloom was deepening and coqueting with the lily of her complexion, as a thousand pretty waves — gazing down upon the rippling curls that quivered upon the neck and shoulders, and rose and fell as evenly as the warm bosom beneath them — gazing into those sunny eyes now shorn of their wildness, and wondering what the mystery was that had elicited that flood of morbid feeling, hoping that it was only a freak of the young bride to startle her, yet fearing there might be an under current of treachery that would yet endanger her master's peace of mind.

"Come, come, come! I'm getting impatient. I don't like to be studied so closely. You are a favorite with your master, Minnie — so *he* tells me."

The eloquent blood flushed up to the black curls of the slave, and then left her pale and calm as ever.

"I nursed his child," she said, clasping a string of jewels around the head of the bride.

"Not *them!*" she said, tearing the jewels from her hair;

"I could not wear them — my head would burst. There — hand me those flowers lying in the vase — I will select one."

"They are withering."

"No matter — let me have them! So — you nursed his child?"

"Yes, lady."

"How old is she?"

"Fourteen."

"Three years younger than her mother! It is laughable, isn't it?"

"*What?*"

"That your master, Alva Martin, — the dignified, learned, sober gentleman of the old school, — should have chosen such a harum-scarum, half girl, half woman little thing as myself. He had a good idea of courage, too, to defy the conventional rules of society, by marrying so far beneath him in worldly matters. I suppose I am ambitious — like display, handsome carriages, handsome horses, fine clothes, rich jewels, soft odors, refined associations! I shall have them all when I become Mrs. Martin!"

The young bride sat twining and untwining a long, loose curl over her taper finger, while Minnie went to the wardrobe to select portions of the bridal paraphernalia.

"He knows," she went on, still talking to herself, "he knows I do not bring him half a heart. He knows that it has been a struggle — a fierce, bitter warfare. I cannot love him, — he knows it, — at least, as I have loved — so blindly — with such mad infatuation. What if the idol *is* broken! — what if its crumbled ruin lies buried amid the desolation! — O, he should beware of the resurrection! Beware! — but no — no — no! What right have I, almost a wedded wife, to rake up the ashes of this poor, wounded heart, and fan the stifled embers into flame? No; he takes me to his bosom heart-wounded and cheerless! I should be a wretch — unjust, unkind, despicable — could I suffer one pang to reach the noble nature that has endured all, dared all, for my sake. It is over now. The last thought — the last wish! I have uncovered his image for the last time; and now that it is past, I shall be happy — very, very happy — ten thousand times happier than I could — have — been — with — O, my heart *will* break!"

And with a low, passionate wail she sank upon her knees at the window in utter abandonment of woe. Minnie, who had been a surprised witness of the scene, sprang quickly to her side, and would have raised her.

"Not yet, Minnie, not now. I shall be better by and by. Let me weep."

"This must not go on. Excuse me, lady; but there must be some way to avoid this marriage."

"O Minnie, there are times when the heart *must* claim sympathy! I must speak, or go mad! Your master knows it all, — how I grew from childhood with one to whom my whole heart was given, — how we were betrothed, and the wedding day appointed, — how there came a misunderstanding between us. He left me with the cloud still uppermost; and the following week, in a rambling excursion among the mountains, he fell in with a party of Indians, and lost his life in the struggle. You know how malicious the Indians on our borders are said to be. Of late there has a new feud arisen, and this has been the result. O Minnie, it was all my fault! I accused him of an infidelity which I was led to believe. I said things which no pure-minded maiden ought to have imagined, much less have given expression to. He was sensitive in the extreme — denied the implication, and left me. But there — I'm calm *now!* See who that is just entering the gate."

"O Hagar! — *my* Hagar! — my *foster* child-lady!" And before she could be detained for further questioning, she was down over the steps and out by Hagar's side.

"Your woman is very devoted to you, Miss Martin," said Laird.

"O, yes; she nursed me, and, in fact, has had the entire charge of me."

"Ah!"

Hagar, engaged in questioning Minnie, did not see the strange, glittering eye that rested upon her, nor hear that singular exclamation.

"It is a sad affair," whispered Minnie; "but I fear there is no help for it. Already the few persons invited to the wedding are assembled."

Hagar, without further ceremony, went straight to the room of the bride, and gave her own introduction. It was scarce completed, when a knock was heard at the door, and Mr. Martin, clad in bridal costume, entered the room.

"Welcome, Hagar, welcome. Your new mother, Hagar, — about your own age; you will get along swimmingly together. Courage, Georgiana," he said, lifting the small hand to his mouth. Then giving his hand to Hagar, he led her from the room.

"No confessions," he murmured, as he parted with his daughter at her chamber door.

It was evening — clear, still, and beautiful! The flowers had folded up their soft blooms; the streams lay glittering in their pebbled bed; birds, with folded wings, were twittering their last good-night; and the whole wide earth seemed lapped in repose.

Stately and beautiful as a marble statue, Alva Martin and his child-bride stood hand in hand before the holy minister. Except in years, a more fitting couple it would be hard to find. Out upon the lawn dozens of negroes hover together in groups, with a sad solemnity on their faces, as if there was some ceremony in progress that would materially interfere with their comfort. The old mansion has a still, slumberous air about it, as its gables rise in the moonlight; and the soft, green lawn, sloping down to the river's edge, lies white and silent in the rich light. Already the monotonous sound of the clergyman's voice reaches the wondering groups upon the lawn. A pale, sad face presses heavily against the open window, and although there are no sobs, tear after tear quivers upon the brown hands, showing that the eyes have been busy during the ceremory. Poor Minnie! Doubly a slave!

The last word lingers upon the lips of the clergyman, the irrevocable words have been spoken, when the sound of heavy hoofs of horses tramping in the distance breaks in upon the listening groups. Nearer and nearer they come; and now the bridle is flung to an astonished negro, and a tall, supple form strides into the mansion.

"It is not over, Georgia, it is not over! Say it is not too late!"

A quick, sudden start — a wild, shrill scream, and the young wife lies like one dead upon the bosom of her husband.

Quicker than thought the lights are extinguished, and the bride seized from her husband's arms. Strangers mingle in the *mêlée;* and amid shrieks, and oaths, and general consternation is heard the clattering of retreating horses.

Down by the river's side is a mortal combat! "Aha! It was *your* triumph! It is mine *now!* Aha! ha! ha! So perish all the enemies of Michael Laird, the outlaw!" And with superhuman strength the form of the new comer was raised from the ground and hurled into the river.

CHAPTER VI.

THE OLD MAN'S DARLING. — WOMAN'S WILL. — THE BAFFLED LOVER.

WILLOWDALE! with its antiquity, its quietude, and its gorgeousness; with its great hills, its drooping willows, its solemn dales. *Willowdale!* The very name ripples lovingly from the pen; and I love the stern stillness of its surroundings, for the rich haze of memory lingering amid its shadows. *Willowdale!* Never a wanderer overtaken by misfortune upon the road but some friendly instinct guided him to the moss-covered mansion of old Colonel Rose; never a tourist guided by his love for the beautiful that somehow or other did not, in the course of his peregrinations, stumble upon the massive homestead of Willowdale. It was noted, the country round, for the generosity, the urbanity, and the good breeding of the popular owner. Statesmen met there to discuss the doctrines and needs of their beloved country; rampant politicians made its great hall head quarters for fiery speeches, inflammable sentiments, and over-earnest declamation. Sportsmen met there to talk *horse*, book bets for perspective races, and exercise the colonel's splendid stud of imported animals, with which his stables were liberally supplied. The colonel was by no means a man of refinement. Liberal, generous, open-spirited, and even-tempered, he could not choose but be a favorite; but there was a lack of polish visible, which sometimes gave a loophole for the scalping knife of criticism among the sarcastic of his political antagonists, when the tide of electioneering ran high enough to lift him out of his racing element into the field of discussion. Daniel Webster the statesman and Daniel Webster his blood horse were, in his estimation, the two noblest creatures that ever existed; nor could any reasoning or argument convince him that mentioning the two in the same breath, and with the same spirit of eulogium, was in the least insulting to the massive mind which at that period was at its culminating point of splendor. The statesman, when the guest of Colonel Rose, as he often was, never failed to try the mettle of his namesake, or to add his mite to the praise which his master considered his due. In fact, Willowdale, at the time of which I write, crowded into its scope all the facilities for pleasure or amusement that had ever been discovered by the liberal-hearted colonel.

Having but one child — the Effie Rose of whom mention has before been made — it is not to be wondered at that in her all the wildness, the recklessness, the inconsiderateness, and the eccentricity of the colonel, her father, had been reproduced. She sat a horse as if she had been part and parcel of the same flesh. She was a complete calendar of the racing events of the entire century; could enumerate the names of the different antagonists, when and where they had trotted, what time they had made, who foaled them, and from what stock they sprang. Her father delighted in her knowledge no less than her independence. She was his pet, his joy, his one thing needful in her absence, and his perfect delight when at home. He had a neighbor, residing some four miles away, (that was the sort of neighborhood of those days,) whose lands joined with his, and whose only son seemed in his eyes made expressly to mate his only daughter. Had Effie been left to her free will, she would inevitably have fallen in love with Charley Lee. He was just her style of a man; nothing effeminate or *namby-pambyish*, but bold as a hawk, bright as a new button, and spirited as the pretty little Arabian which he rode with such matchless grace. From her earliest years he had been the companion of her rides and drives. They had crossed rivulets and clambered mountains together, until old Mother Dreslen, the Wild Woman of the Alleghanies, as she was called, used to say to herself, "It is easy to see what will come of *this* association."

Unfortunately, her father, in one of his communicative moods, led her into the secret that she was *destined* for Charley Lee.

"There will be no such property in the two kingdoms as the combined farms," he urged; "besides, the old man and myself have settled it."

That was enough for Effie. She was to be made a barter of, sold, traded away! and to Charley Lee, of all persons in the world! What would Charley think of it? or of her to allow it? No; she would *not* allow it! She would never consent to it! She didn't care two pins for Charley, any how; and if she did, she wouldn't be sold to him on those terms — not she! The spice of romance which made more piquant the rich flame of her disposition was likely to mar all the preconceived notions and plans of her father for future aggrandizement and elevation.

From the moment she became aware of her father's intention, her conduct towards Charley Lee changed from gentle dependence to uncurbed freedom. It was no longer "If Charley likes," or "Just as Charley says," or "Ask Charley;" but an independence of manner amounting nearly to indifference supplied her former submission. Nay, more; if demonstrative tenderness passed for any thing, she was as good as engaged to a young Virginian merchant who had found excuse for delay among the wild old hills of Carolina. The school at which Effie had been educated was but a couple of hours' ride from Willowdale; and of course her Saturday evenings found her at home, listening to the croonings of some bedridden servant, praising the industry of the young colored population, and dispensing her good words and her kind smiles liberally within the precincts of her romantic plantation.

Among the slaves she was an angel of light. All the honest, faithful feelings of their nature were called out by the invariable kindness of their "young missis." They were always sure of her ear and her sympathy; and woe to the taskmaster who had abused his authority! From him her smiles were averted, and her cheering words withheld. That was the great threat and the great punishment on Willowdale plantation, and one which kept its working people in greater subjection than any terror of corporeal punishment could have done. That last, be it said with pride, never disgraced the beautiful vicinity of Willowdale. Luckily for *me*, my experiences of slave life have been among the humane and the benevolent. I have passed many years of my life investigating, as far as practicable, the peculiar institutions of a slave country. I went south with all my northern prejudices warm within my heart. The first sight of a *slave* was to me a sensation of itself alone — a something no more to be *re*produced in description than to be the second time experienced. I made my home for years on a plantation where slaves were part of the family; not in point of actual association, perhaps, but as far as needs, desires, and humane treatment were concerned. No wonder, then, that I look with dislike upon those who, by a vigorous pen, strive to waken all the bad impulses both of master and slave, and wedge in the life already in bonds of servitude by stricter vigilance and a greater severity of discipline. However, it is not here that I choose to discuss the right and wrong of slavery; not here, where the point of my story hangs upon one of the *evils* of slave life — where its *dénouement* will expose a flagrant outrage perpetrated through the medium of the laws by which the slave becomes human property. No; I will leave the subject to those whose impulses urge them to oppose the human traffic, which to me is the *only* horror of slavery. It will take a fresh chapter to start fairly again with our pretty Effie Rose.

CHAPTER VII.

THE ROMANCE OF REALITY.

THERE were to be grand times at Willowdale! It was *race week!* We lose much by not entering into the spirit of the races as they do at the south. To them *race week* is a point in the calendar of their happiness. They anticipate for days and months in advance. It is the theme of conversation among the old turfsmen, and a matter of intense interest in circles just becoming aware of its importance. The course is one grand, gorgeous masquerade; — the lithe and beautiful horses — the hurry and excitement around the betting stand — the glittering of carriages bearing in their freight of loveliness — the jockeys, in their pretty sporting dress of crimson and white — and, more than all, the grand stand, where the chivalry, the wealth, and the fashion of the whole southern country congregate to witness the trials of speed between the well-trained competitors.

It was the evening before the races that the balconies, the platforms, the lawn, and, in fact, every observance point of Willowdale was crowded with gay and lively people awaiting the arrival of Effie and her train from the school.

Old Colonel Rose glided here and there and every where among his guests, looking the full-faced, merry-eyed, rosy gentleman of the old school that he was, and making a liberal tender of hearty courtesies, cordial words, and welcome phrases.

"It is getting late," he said, in reply to some question. "It is well that I ordered dinner an hour later than usual." The words were scarcely uttered when a cavalcade wound round the corner of the wood, and came galloping up the lawn and through the gate to the mansion.

It is well it was a mansion in the fullest sense of the word; for what with the crowd already in waiting and the crowd in company with Effie, accommodations else had been any thing but on a par with *Carolinian* hospitality.

The host forgot his dignity in a father's affection. He ran as fast as gout would let him, and, heedless of the remaining parties at the door, he held Effie encircled in his arms.

"My pride! my joy!" he exclaimed, kissing her eyes, her lips, not forgetting her nose! "My blessing! There! away with you! Run up stairs, while I welcome your friends. You'll find a host awaiting you."

But Effie did not profit by his release.

"I have a *particular* friend to whom I must introduce you, and for whom I must ask your hospitality."

"Of course, Effie; any of *your* friends, you know— But, I say! where's Charley? I don't see Charley any where. You haven't left Charley to come by himself?"

"Am I Charley's keeper?" she laughed, blushing and placing her arm within her father's. "Charley puts on airs of late. I was obliged to unseat him, take him down a peg, you know. Hush! Mr. Wells, father awaits to welcome you. Mr. Wells, father; father, Mr. Wells. There, make yourselves acquainted. I hate these formal introductions."

Colonel Rose extended his hand, without releasing Effie, however, and the moment courtesy would allow him, he drew her away to the end of the balcony, for the purpose of a serious talk, as he said.

"I've heard something of this before, Effie. But I say now, you can't think of giving up Charley Lee for *him*."

"Charley Lee, indeed! Mr. Wells loves me ten times where Charley Lee don't love me at all."

"Nonsense! fiddle-de-dee! *love!* What do you call love? You never saw this fellow till within a month. Of course, he fell in love with you. Every man between twenty and twenty-five falls in love with every new face that comes along; but how long will it last, Effie? that's what I want you to think of. Here's Charley, — handsome, rich, — all the girls are after him. There's Miss Angier; she would go on her bended knees to get him."

"She had better take him, then. Here he comes, looking as glum as a Grand Turk. Let me cut ——"

"No, you don't. Now, you just treat him decently. I command it! Well, there, don't draw up in that manner; I mean, desire it."

Charley Lee did, indeed, look glum as he came slowly towards the mansion. Effie stood with one hand prisoned in that of her father, and with the other decapitating certain rosebuds that clambered over the palisades, by aid of her riding whip. A comical, saucy smile was the only greeting she accorded her quondam lover.

"Effie likes you, Charley, for all her stubbornness; indeed, she does."

"Do I?" and off went another bud from the clinging vine.

"I'm obliged to her," was his frozen reply

"Come, now, don't *you* be huffed. She don't care two pins for this Mr. Wells, nor he for her, for the matter of that. It is impossible; it isn't the nature of things. Young men don't know their own minds ten minutes at a time ——"

"That's what I tell Charley ——"

"Shut up, will you? I say your *city* young men go crazy after every pretty girl they meet; to say nothing of platonic affection for pretty wives. They are as the vane of our weathercock up there, and not half so reliable; they would disappoint romancers if they wasn't. Come, make up now, before you go in; and don't let me hear another word of this childishness. Effie is always telling how much she thinks of you."

"Why, father! Don't you believe him; don't you *dare* believe him. I wouldn't have you; no, not if there wasn't another man, or *boy*, in the world."

So saying, Effie wrung her hand from her father, and rushed into the house.

"Something must be done, Charley. It is all because I let out about the property. She's romantic as a toad, and be hanged to her. I don't see who she took it from; not from me, that's certain. She can't bear the idea of being made a barter of. But never mind, now. Let's go in and devise some means to put a spoke in this Mr. Wells's wheel. He shan't have her, that's certain! Why, Effie would die in reality. She couldn't bear it. Come, come, cheer up. I've a plan in my head, and if that fails it will be time enough then to give her up. Come."

What a week it was for the gay, the brilliant, the gorgeous guests of Willowdale, — that race week of 183–. How many bets were lost and won, with a zest known only to such as enter fully into the excitements of sporting! "Going to the races!" There were bright-eyed girls, with their attendant cavaliers, intent upon surprising the dense crowd with their superior horsemanship. There were the sombre old gentlemen of a past age, trying to warm their stagnant blood by sight of the carnival, so inspiring in its details. There were gay parties of all ages; elderly matrons, chaperoning their rolicking charges; young maidens, bent upon conquest and triumph; girls, cantering along sedately and coyly by the side of watchful papas and mammas in barouche or travelling carriages, and girls dashing along with an impetuous grace which spurned all control, other than that of their own, over the mettled charger yielding to their guidance! Liberty and license were the order of the day. All hearts drank in the excitement of the scene, and, for once, gave rein to the most liberal enjoyment and hilarity. If the scene on the thronged thoroughfare was so exciting, what word would convey a sense of the gorgeousness of the course and its surroundings? The stand, filled with the perfection of southern beauty, looks like a fairy bower amid the coarser elements of the crowd. Beautiful dames, who would elsewhere shrink from such public gaze, here receive the ovation which beauty always wins from manliness and gallantry without a frown of resentment. In fact, admiration on these occasions is too freely tempered with respect, to cause other than pleasure at its bestowal. From the grand stand Effie Rose looks gracefully down upon the crowd, nodding to this one and smiling at that, seemingly unconscious of the presence beneath of melancholy Charley Lee. Ever and anon his eyes wander to the "observed of all observers," and then plunge into the crowd with a stiletto gleam quite *bravoish* in its expression. Effie Rose is chaperoned by the haughty Mrs. Thems, a lady in every sense of the word, even to that of having once had her day of beauty. Her heavy velvet dress gives a superb haughtiness to the oval face, and corresponds well with the marked dignity of her manner. She does not condescend even to enter into the general excitement which characterizes the last "home stretch," but sweeps her superb eyes over the flushed crowd, as if astonished that any thing on earth could create so great a *furore*. At her side are her two daughters, one a merry, saucy little damsel of sixteen, the other a second edition of her own haughty self. Effie blooms under her jaunty little riding hat, and Charley Lee thinks she looks handsomer than ever in her long skirt. Grace is in her every motion, even to the method in which she clasps the folds gathered in her slender little hand. She bends her laughing eyes upon the gloomy lover, and is upon the point of motioning him to her side, when a new acquaintance claims her attention.

"Are your bets all taken, Miss Rose?" he asks, in a bantering mood.

"Every dollar," was her retort. "Unless papa replenishes my purse, or I win the next heat, I have only my heart and hand to stake. I have been particularly unlucky to-day. My favorite has balked me dreadfully."

"I'll take that *last* bet, at all hazards."

"What, my hand and heart?"

"Yes."

"And what do you offer in return?"

"My Selim, here — pure Arabian — original stock — fleet as a bird, and kind as he is fleet."

"I'll book it."

"On the next heat, or the termination of the race?"

"O, the heat, by all means."

"Effie!" exclaimed Charley, angrily.

"Here they come," "Clear the track," "Hurrah for Gray Eagle," "A hundred on Blueskin," "You've lost," were exclamations of the excited crowd. "And *you've* lost, Miss Rose," was the exultant affirmation of the victors in their antagonism.

"O dear," she laughed, "here's my hand; how will you take — across your cheek or over your head," and she made a movement to strike. "Please leave me my heart."

"No, no. I shall call for it yet. That's not fair. I was prepared to dismount Selim on the instant."

Charley gave the whole party the benefit of a scornful scowl, and struck off into the betting stand. Here he encountered Colonel Rose, and taking him apart, laid his complaints at his feet.

"It is of no use, colonel; while Effie imagines she is sold to me for the benefit of the estates, she will never consent to be mine; and with all her tormenting, I do believe she likes me."

"I'll settle that; call at the house this evening. Don't be surprised at any thing which occurs; only play *your* part well, and if she loves you, I'll guaranty to see her Mrs. Lee in a week's time."

"Impossible!"

"Not at all. Women are strange animals. There is no telling what they'll do. Tell them they must, and they'll see you hanged first. Tell them they shan't, and they will break their necks or their hearts to do it. I've summered and wintered them, and that's the only way to get even with them."

The sun was flinging its last stream of golden light over

hill and valley, as the brilliant cavalcade took up its long line of march from the race course. If going to the races had been a theme of grandeur and excitement, returning from the races was still more picturesque. There were faces elate with success, and faces gloomy with defeat. Some urged their tried steeds to the top of their strength, while others slowly traversed the crowded streets. There was a little grumbling, considerable swearing, and a confusion of tongues worthy of Babel. However, the day ended up as it had begun, or rather with a contemplation of past happiness, instead of anticipation of happiness to come, in the minds of those who had been active participants of the pleasures thereof.

CHAPTER VIII.

The Fearful Secret. — The Great Wrong. — The Plot of the Demon Man. — Hagar's Doom.

Slowly, very slowly, the homestead of Alva Martin recovered from the shock attendant upon his nuptial evening. Hagar felt most profoundly the need of that dear maternal bosom, that, in her precocious childhood, was ever ready with words of gentle wisdom to counsel and to direct. How empty the house seemed, and lonely! The master, stricken down by the sudden bereavement, sat silent and alone, scarcely deigning to come forth from his desolate chamber. His love for his beautiful bride had been stormy, turbulent, and tempestuous. He did not ask if she returned his love — he did not even think of it. She was weak, vain, and frivolous. The name of Martin of Le Clerk was one of the oldest and most responsible on the Carolina records. She had played a bold, deep game to accomplish the aim and object of her life — so bold and deep that even the infatuated lover was fain to close his eyes upon what else must have been palpable and mortifying. To have a position among the haughty dames of southern aristocracy, — to wear a name the loftiest of all, — these had been the gems for which love, peace, and affection were bartered.

Nor was it possible that, upon the eve of consummating her ambitious projects, she could have forsworn them all to elope with her returned lover. That she had been forcibly borne away during the confused scenes of the evening no one could doubt; and as the lover had also disappeared, it was easy for suspicion to point the way of her escape. Martin, in his sane intervals, raved and threatened all manner of punishments upon him who had thus deprived him of his beautiful bride; while Hagar, with forethought beyond her years, soothed and caressed him, and by her own placid demeanor endeavored to withdraw his mind from the one subject which threatened his reason. With consternation she saw the influence that Laird — the dark, stern companion of her journey home — was acquiring over the shattered mind of her father. There was something so sinister, so designing in his meek, smooth assumption of manner, that the young girl shrank from his approach with the undefinable feeling of dread which characterized her first approach to him. More than once had she detected his dark, lowering brow growing darker beneath her father's threats against the abductor of his wife, while at such times his surveillance of herself was so intense, so searching, that the flush of anger *would* spread upon her face in spite of her efforts at self-control. To make matters worse, Charley Lee had become almost a constant visitor at the Le Clerk farm. From the first a spirit of antagonism, too plain to be mistaken, had arisen between the two men, which oftentimes threatened open warfare. It was a painful evening to all parties — the one on which Charley Lee first broke up the monotony of the dwelling. It occurred after a warm and impetuous tender of his heart and hand to Effie Rose, and of her decided and unconditional refusal.

"I want a *friend*," he said, taking both of Hagar's hands within his own; "I want a sister; I want soft, cooling hands, like yours, to keep the fever from my brain, that threatens to spring there because a madcap girl — a wild, silly, will-o'-the-wisp girl — refused to become my wife. Torment her! It is because she *won't* have me that I feel as if I couldn't live without her. What ought I to do?"

"Do!" And Hagar laughed a low, contemptuous laugh.

"There — don't treat the subject in that way! Of course you never were unhappy, because you never loved; but the time *will* come — it comes to all, sooner or later — when life's calm ocean rises into a storm — when all that is so quiet now will be surges, and foam, and tumult, and you will either be shocked to pieces against some rocky fate, as I am now, or be drifted away upon its surges into a calm and quiet existence."

"You talk like a boy, Charley. One would think that the most distressing of calamities had befallen you, instead of which it is only a whim of your lady love to try your affection. However, I will do the best I can for you — I'll see Effie myself. We are rather unsettled here at present. Father, as you must have heard, has never quite recovered the shock of a few weeks ago."

"And what does he keep that ferocious looking Laird about him for? There is something wrong there, Hagar. He was the constant companion of that girl whom your father narrowly escaped marrying——"

"He *didn't* escape, Charley. If ever she should return, she is as firmly his wife as the laws of the state can make her. I sometimes half suspect——"

"What, Hagar?"

"Nothing — nothing. I was thinking aloud——"

"A very bad habit, Miss Martin, if you'll allow me to say so," broke in the voice of Laird.

Hagar and Charley both sprang to their feet; but there was such an imperturbable gravity upon the intruder's face — such an unconsciousness of having given offence, or committed an impropriety — that neither of them could rebuke the intrusion.

After a few moments' commonplace talk, Lee called for his horse, and bowed himself out.

"A pleasant fellow enough, Miss Martin," said Laird; "a trifle impressible and fickle; but the rough angles of the world will polish that in time."

Hagar deigned no reply, but began reading a book which she had dropped upon the entrance of Charley.

"Why do you prefer this room to the parlor, *Hagar?* — it is very cheerless."

"*To be alone!*" she replied, not raising her eyes.

Laird stood gazing at the girl from the position he had taken, while over his face ran, by turns, all the good and evil passions of his nature.

"What a singular, provocative little vixen you are, Hagar! and what a time I shall have in taming you when — we — are married!"

"*Sir!*"

"How delicious it will be to strike out sparks of fire from that heart of oak! — how original and pleasant to watch the taming down — the quivering and the going down of the candle of defiance into the socket of subjection!"

"*Sir!*"

"What a spicy, piquant little tiger-bird it is!"

"Then mind its *claws!*" exclaimed Hagar, flinging the book violently from her hand. "Married to *you!* I have seen the time when there was a fascination in the dark, strange men that get into the world by chance — I have even dreamed of the sensation it would be to *tame* one — to subdue one by force of affection — to remove the monster's claws, and play with it, while all around trembled with the expectation of seeing me torn to pieces; but *you* — *you* — *you!*"

Hagar drew a contemptuous breath, as if nothing could express her utter detestation. Hagar was a girl of quick impulses and quick resolves. She had formed her estimate of the *man* too truly not to crush his aspirations as a suitor. No circumstances — no *set* of circumstances — could induce her ever to receive him in that light. All the while that she continued speaking he stood before her, his eyes lighting up, his smile — that fearful smile, of which I have before spoken — glittering over his face, giving it the semblance of a handsome *fiend!*

"Good! good!" he laughed; "I didn't believe you had so much spirit! Proud, beautiful vixen that you are — *you* — standing there the picture of incarnate scorn — you inspire me with impatience! I long to begin my task; and by the powers it promises to be no *easy* one! Come, when shall it be? Name our wedding day."

"Sir, you insult me!"

"Shall it be a month — a week hence? A week is a long time to wait. Say to-morrow."

"*Never!* Don't fear but my *father* shall know of this insult."

"O, *tell* him, by all means! Let him order me from his door — let him bid his servants spurn me from his threshold — let the lightning of his eye and the thunder of his tongue beat upon me as yours do now — still I tell you I am your destined husband! No other man can circle that quivering form in his arms; no other man can pillow that proud head upon his bosom; no other man can call you *wife!* Be arrogant, scornful, defiant if you will, — you will call me *husband* yet!"

"Leave this room, or by the God above us, you shall know whom you insult with such impunity!"

The fire which had been glowing and darkling in Hagar's eyes seemed growing into flames. Laird folded his arms, and gazed mockingly upon her white face and quivering lips.

"*Begone!*" she thundered again, all the concentrated passion of her nature bursting forth in an incarnate storm.

"You *shall* obey me!" she exclaimed, starting towards the bell rope with a lofty bearing. Laird caught her in his arms, and held her fast.

"Delicious! *delicious!*" he exclaimed. "What a mass of coquettish arrogance it is, to be sure! Don't struggle; you won't free yourself. I hold you fast; fast as — whew!"

Hagar, in the insane anger of the moment, had wrenched her hand, and dashed it with all her strength into his handsome, smiling face.

"*Now* will you let me go?"

"Yes; but you have rung *your* knell! I might have had pity — compassion, had you been any thing but the fierce, relentless thing you are."

"I detest your sympathy; I scorn your pity. Release me, I say, or I will alarm the house, and have you sent neck and heels out of the window."

"But first you must hear me. You think your father's bride fled with her lover."

"Yes, of course. But what has that to do with me?"

"You think they are now enjoying each other's society somewhere, do you not?"

"Yes; but ——"

"Wrong, altogether wrong. He came between me and *my* love; robbed me of what made up my life; he sleeps at the bottom of the river, while she pleads with me for mercy, as you will plead yet in a prison of my own designing!"

"Monster! O, it cannot be."

"Do you think I would tell you my secrets, were I not sure of your silence? As my wife it will ill become you to betray me."

"Your wife! Once for all, let this mockery cease. Once for all, I tell you that the grave should receive me, rather than *you*, even were you not the guilty thing you confess to be."

"And I tell you, proud girl, as you stand here the concentration of scorn, that one word of mine could divest you of these broad lands, this princely mansion, these symbols of great wealth. I tell *you* that one word of mine would make you abhorred, detested; a thing to shrink from, to point out and jeer; an object of pity and compassion to the meanest of your people."

Hagar had released herself from his grasp, and was now walking rapidly up and down the room. Laird was deadly pale with passion.

"By my soul," he exclaimed, wiping the cold perspiration from his brow, "had I not sworn to be revenged, I could find it in my heart to unmask the traitor and turn it out upon the world in its true colors!"

"Silence. I have heard too much. I insult my station by listening to such a tirade of nonsense. Let me pass."

"Not till you hear me. To-day you spurn my offer of marriage with the imperious glance of an empress; to-morrow, more humbly than ever criminal sued for forfeited life, will you beg for the restoration of my favor."

"If I thought so ——"

"*If!* There is no such word as *if!* You *will* ——"

"Don't interrupt me. I say, if I thought I could be so lost to sense, dignity, shame of womanhood, I would blacken my face, paler than my betraying heart, and set myself up for sale to the first bidder, as a slave and a craven."

Hagar swept her eyes up over her companion's face, where they were transfixed with horror at the sight of diabolical, malignant passion thereon displayed.

"You said *slave*. Ay, that is the word! Lift up the drooping fringes of those proud eyes, and see there the rim of opaque blackness, indigenous *alone* to the slave. Examine those long, taper fingers, whose heaviest task as yet has been to toy with a book or a fan; or press back the clasp of lovers' palms, and mark the indentation of mingled color which circles the nails; then raise that mass of curly jet, and trace there the short crisp wave of hair that separates the negro from the white; then, if that suffice not, go to your mirror, girl. Take feature after feature of that superb face. Examine them individually — the luscious lips, the high cheek bone, the broad, low forehead, the unshapely nose — all bright, gorgeous, and fascinating *together*, but apart and distinct, undeniably African."

Hagar had sunk into a chair, and was slowly, mechanically examining the hair, the hands, while the sparks died out of her eyes, leaving their surroundings more perceptible than ever. She might have been a statue, so still, so silent, so aghast did she appear.

"Have you never suspected this?" questioned Laird, somewhat touched by the stony nature of her grief.

She raised her eyes as if bewildered; she gathered up the drooping rings of her black hair.

"And I was so proud of it," she murmured. "Tell me all — all! Or why have you told me at all? Suspect! how *should* I have suspected? So proud, so honored, so respected. O, to be a child of shame — and *such* shame. *Now* I know what *she* meant in dying. A *slave!* O, ignominy! O, degradation! Where, where shall I hide my head?" And sinking down among the cushions of the sofa, she gave vent to indescribable moans of anguish.

"Your husband, that *will* be, is alone conversant with the secret. It is not to his interest to betray it."

"No, no, no! It cannot be. I'll not believe it. You say this to alarm me. You say this because I am dark, and deformed, and desolate. You think to get the Le Clerk estate with *me*. Only say so! Only tell me it is the estate you want. It shall be yours, but not encumbered with me. Only say you will be content with the estate;" and she bent an imploring glance upon him that ought to have moved a fiend.

"Hagar, we have gone too far to recede. You should not have defied me to tell you secrets, which might in other hands condemn me. No, Hagar, my wife, or *my slave!* It is for you to decide."

"I cannot endure it! O unsay those horrible words, or

see me fall at your feet a corpse. Tell me, was — was — *Who was my mother?*"

"*Minnie — the quadroon slave!*"

With a face whitened with anguish, she moaned the name of Walter; then rolled from the sofa, and lay still and motionless as if she was indeed dead.

This dead calm was not of long duration. Left to herself, she soon recovered enough to comprehend that some terrible calamity had befallen her.

"My father — he will tell me if it is indeed as that man says."

Summoning all her strength, she dragged herself to her father's door. The room was closed. Upon opening it, and creeping in to where her father sat in his study chair, the very blood in her veins seemed turning to ice. Erect upon his seat, with his head resting upon the table, her last hope, her beloved father, sat frigid in his eternal slumber.

The last plank to which she had clung was indeed shivered. The chain of circumstances was gathering about her.

Poor Hagar! Hagar the Martyr! how truly had your prediction been realized.

9

CHAPTER IX.

THE DEFIANCE. — THE RESOLVE. — THE ESCAPE OF THE WHITE SLAVE.

IT was after a stormy and a fearful scene, that Hagar sat gloomily by the window of her own private room. Laird had expressed his determination either to make her his wife, or to bring matters to their severest issue, and had given her till evening to make up her mind. The last glimpse of the sun was resting upon the hill tops, and the shadows were gathering thick and heavily under the hedgerows of the garden, and among the folds of drapery around the window. Was there no hope for her? Not one. Must she wed with him her soul abhorred, or become that doomed and degraded thing the disclosure of her birth would make her. The sins of the father were indeed descending upon the head of his child; and yet, after the first agony of thought, there was no sentiment of reproach in her heart toward the author of her being. Had she been poor, degraded, suffering, any thing but a *slave*, she would have arisen in the power of her own womanhood, and laid bare the vileness, the grossness, and the inhumanity of the monster. Her will was fettered as her hands *must* be, unless she consented to his desire. In the midst of her meditations, two men were seen to turn the corner by the lawn gate, and approach the house.

"*So soon*," she exclaimed, springing to her feet, while her face, hands, and lips were frigid as ice.

"They have come," whispered Minnie, whose swollen eyes showed that she shared the misery of her child-mistress.

"I will be with them presently," was the calm reply.

Hagar went to the glass, rolling the long rings of hair mechanically over her fingers. Bathing her eyes, she took a small vial from a secret drawer, and placed it in the folds of her dress.

"If worst comes to worst, this at least will save me," she muttered; and with another long, earnest gaze at herself, she turned and walked steadily to the parlor.

Laird was standing by the fireplace, leaning heavily upon the mantelpiece. He started forward at her entrance, and led her into the centre of the room.

"This is Mr. Templeton, clerk of the probate, Miss Martin," he said, by way of introduction. "He comes here with a license to make us *one*, Hagar, or (he hissed in her ear) *to arrest you as a slave*." Hagar recoiled, as if a serpent had stung her.

"By Heaven, *no!* By the merciful Father, *no*, *no*, I will *not!* Don't touch me," said she, clutching with savage eagerness a cane, which she knew concealed in its centre a short, thick sword. "I'll be no *slave* — no wife that's worse than slave! There's no drop of slave blood in my veins!

I am as white as you are, as free as you are, and I will not be enslaved. There's a land where all God's flesh is free; where groans, and tears, and bondage are unknown; where man is man, though the outward covering *is* a shade of blackness; where *worth* is the coin that passes current from grade to grade of society, and where the felon who persecutes a helpless woman is a felon still, though gold should be a carpet for his feet."

Like a fierce animal at bay stood Hagar; her dark and fiery beauty growing more dark and fiery with each word, that flung off like sparks from her outraged heart.

"Chain the mountain fawn, cage the free eagle," she continued, in her wrath, "but never hope to subdue Hagar Martin! If the laws do not protect me, God *will.* You dare not harm me. I am no property of *yours.* At the very worst, it would take time to *prove* all you have asserted; till then, I defy you, I scorn you, I detest you, as all good men and women will detest you when your unrevealed crimes shall have been plucked from your heart, and laid bare before the astonished eyes of a world that has hitherto held you in some show of respect. Now, do your worst; it is power *against* power, and God help the right!"

Proudly and firmly Hagar turned to leave the room. Neither party opposed her, knowing for the present, at least, she was beyond their malice.

"What is to be done *now?*" questioned Mr. Templeton of his crestfallen client.

"Set spies about the house, intercept all egress from the grounds, and proceed at once to investigate her birth."

In passing through the hall, Hagar's quick ear caught the words, and in a moment her resolution was formed.

"They call this freedom!" she murmured. "Only let me escape the horrible fate awaiting me — only let me set foot upon untrammelled ground, and to thy cause, O God, I devote my remaining life!"

All that evening, Hagar and Minnie were employed in gathering together all the valuables among the profusion of gifts, which, from time to time, had been lavished upon her by her father. There were some hundreds of dollars in her possession; and, among her jewels, collateral security enough to raise, in case of emergency, perhaps a thousand more. All these were carefully culled, and placed about her person in a way to secure their possession. Then dressing herself in her coarsest apparel, and ordering Minnie to do the same, she went carefully to the stable, and with her own hands saddled her favorite Selim. Leaving him there, she returned for Minnie, and in another hour they were on their journey from the parental home.

But under the moonlight and over the thick sward, dew-gemmed and fragrant, stole Hagar and her slave-mother, as noiselessly as their steeds could move. At an easy pace, long before daylight, they could reach a place of compara tive safety; and well Hagar knew every foot of ground for miles and miles away. Her love for reckless roving, for exploring almost impassable ravines in the mountain interstices, now stood her in good stead; while the faith, which had never failed her, in the *strong arm* above now gave a lighter impulse to her heart, and urged her to believe in her final escape from that horrible man.

For hours and hours they rode in silence; sometimes climbing steep, almost perpendicular hills, at other times picking their way down over immense cliffs that every moment threatened their destruction. At another time the terror of Minnie would have been too great to attempt so perilous a descent; but in the distance, *liberty* beckoned her on — *liberty*, that she knew only by hearing others descant upon its beauties; now, a little more strength, a little more endurance, and she would know of her own experience what it meant.

All at once Hagar roused herself from the deep thought that had held her silent during their journey. Her quick ear had caught a sound, distant, but distinct; a rumbling, trembling sound, as of horses' feet trampling swiftly the deep distance. Nearer and nearer it came, till there could be no doubt of its source.

"Rouse all your energies, Minnie, for flight! We are pursued!" she exclaimed, tightening the girth around the saddle for the better expedition of the race she saw in the perspective.

"My Lord, what *shall* we do?" moaned Minnie, ready to fall to the ground for fear. "You know how they punish runaways. O, I wish I had never started. We might have known they would have caught us."

"*Woman!* Coward! If the worst comes to the worst, we can but die!"

"O, but I don't want to die! Why couldn't you have left me in peace? You see now what will come of it. O, I wish I was safely at home."

"*Craven!*" hissed Hagar, clutching at the drooping rein of Minnie's horse. "Dismiss your fears, and try to save yourself by flight, or by the heaven above us, I will lay your coward carcass under the hill yonder, for the crows to peck at! Come!"

"Stop," thundered Laird, his voice leaping from hill to hill, until it pierced the ear of Hagar.

"Never!" shouted Hagar back again. "Liberty or death!" and dashing her spur into the side of Selim, she flew down over the precipice, with Minnie at her side. It was a contest of strength against strength. Hagar rode an Arabian, fleet as a deer. Minnie was mounted upon a blood horse, quite as fleet, but more powerful; while Laird, scarcely a mile behind them, rode as strong and enduring an animal, who could make up in bottom what she lost in speed.

The defiance, which drifted on in broken echoes, was met with a mocking laugh by Laird.

"Let them vaunt their security," he said to himself. "It is impossible for them to escape."

On and on they flew, the pursuer and the pursued; now striking the sparks out from the massive rocks, now fording some shining bit of water — anon beating down over the hills, and then leaping wildly through the crackling bushes.

Selim begins to pant and breathe heavily, while the perspiration falls from his sides in a shower of light. Hagar whispers a word in his ear, which he evidently understands. He sees the stalwart horse which Minnie rides, closing in with him, neck and neck, and pushes on more rapidly than ever. They cannot even hear the ground rumbling under the feet of their enemy, and so content themselves with having distanced him for the present.

"If Selim only holds out," murmurs Hagar.

If! What a word of meaning it was to her just *then!* Selim begins to tremble in every limb. The moisture still streams from him, and his eye glares with painful light.

"Poor Selim! Good Selim! One effort more!" murmurs his mistress, patting his head, as she leans over in her race.

In vain. The horse that Minnie rides thunders past like some white monster; his breast heaving, and his eye flashing fire.

One more effort, and the beautiful Arabian closes up the gap, and passes his companion at supernatural speed. But it doesn't last. Nature is exhausted. He falls behind again, and in a few moments more is far in the rear. It is now impossible to describe the horror of the scene. Far ahead, Minnie rides like some midnight fiend bent on diabolical intent. Far behind, the ringing oaths of Laird break up the silence that lies asleep among the wooded hills. The Arabian has strained every nerve to save his mistress — in vain. in vain! With a deep groan, almost *human* in its agony, he reels, trembles, and falls beneath his load!

"Ah, ha! ha, ha, ha!" shouts Laird, as he comes mockingly up, and stands over his prostrate *game*. Hagar does not heed or hear him. She is kneeling by the side of her beautiful Selim, holding his quivering head in her lap.

"To die for me — to die for me!" she murmurs. "Poor Selim. Poor beauty. I might have known it would be useless!" The poor animal tried to rub his nose against her shoulder, as she leaned over him. It had been his method of showing his regard, but even in that he failed from weakness. Turning his eyes to her face, he gave her a look of mute eloquence; lapped the hand that caressed him, and, without a struggle, lay dead at her feet.

Poor Selim!

Minnie, seeing the turn that matters had taken, put fresh speed to her horse, and, in her terror, paused not for impediment of mountain or of stream. But she was too little game for Laird to hunt, under existing circumstances. Hagar was all he desired, and her he had before him.

Casting a longing look at her dead Arabian, she silently allowed her persecutor to place her before him upon his horse. Back over the mountains, and through the valleys; back under the moonlight, and through the leafy shadows. That darkest hour just before day found them still trampling the clover blossoms and the fresh flowers that sprang in rich profusion all along their path. Not a word had been spoken. But for the heavy beating of her heart,

Laird might have held a statue in his arms. He was beginning himself to indulge in a superstitious tremor. He tried to shake it off, by thinking how fate had favored him in the present instance. He had a brilliant future before him. Hagar surely would consent to be his wife, rather than have her disgraceful origin exposed; and as for Minnie, he was rather glad than otherwise that she had escaped. He knew she *would* escape, for being a favorite servant, she was always provided with a pass, that would carry her safely to any part of the slave territory.

As Laird neared the homestead of Hagar, a feeling of superstitious awe took possession of his mind. Her own death-like stillness, the deepening of the night's last shadows, and the solemn quietude which pervaded nature in its rest, all told upon him with irresistible force. He even began to meditate upon the systematic tyranny with which he had followed up the strange wooing of Hagar, and to speculate upon the feasibility of yet setting her free, and burying in his own breast the knowledge of her birth; but when his good angel's influence was uppermost, the tall old cupola of the Le Clerk mansion came in view, with its ambitious aspirations, and all his good intentions vanished as a dream.

"Hagar."

No answer.

"Hagar, we are home again."

"*Home!*"

"It remains with you to make it a peaceful or a stormy

one. Escape is impossible, and your next attempt will not be so lightly passed over; believe me."

"Walter! Walter!" exclaimed Hagar, in her despair.

"*Walter!* O, yes; much Walter cares for you. I have heard of this before. But Walter has forgotten you long enough ago."

"False, false! I'll not believe it!"

"You will believe your eyes, I suppose. I have a paper containing the positive announcement of his marriage to the daughter of his employer."

"Impossible!"

"You shall see for yourself."

"O, impossible! He could not be so base."

"What do men think of their boyish vows? Why, just nothing at all. So make up your mind to become Mrs. Laird, and all the rest will come with time."

Hagar made him no answer; but, arriving at the door, she sprang from his arms, and fled up the long stairway.

"Let her go! She will not attempt to escape again at present," muttered Laird, as he led his horse away to the stable.

Hagar flung open her chamber door with a dash of her hand, and would have buried her head in the bed, but that an apparition, so pale, so pure, and yet so lifelike, rose up and supported her. It might have been a marble statue, so immovable did it seem. One hand was held close to her breast, while the other pushed back the clustering curls which showered over the face and neck, even down to the fragile waist, which seemed scarcely an arm's span.

"Who are you?" exclaimed Hagar, on whom the events of the night had left their superstitious impress.

"Don't you recognize me, Hagar? Am I, indeed, so changed?"

"Georgiana, *mother!* O, how glad I am to hear a human voice. But stay; you fled with a lover. You insulted my father's memory. You are no fit companion for a true woman."

"Hagar, it is false! all false as the man's heart who planned and executed to suit his own interest! Laird removed me while I lay insensible, or rather his minions did. He lured into, what he supposed to be, deadly combat the lover of whom you accuse me. Hark! I hear his step in the lawn. I have come to punish him. Listen. Years ago he committed an act which won for him the deadly feud of the old woman of the mountain. Pretending to forgive him, she has followed him up, slowly and surely, to her revenge, and this it is. She was present, at his request, on the fatal night of your father's wedding. She sent the men who captured me to her hut on the mountain, but watched him as he dragged his victim to the water's edge. He thinks that former lover of mine dead by his own hand. He thinks he sleeps his last sleep under the water of the river yonder. But this old woman, with a faithful servant, rescued him, and had him also carried to her hut. It is only now that he is able to confront this fiend, and bring him to judgment. Our preserver kept the run of his movements; knew of his absence this night, and had us both conveyed here, to await his return. He is below, waiting the proper moment to appear to him. Laird is coming; chance and the right protect us!

"I must say a word to you, Hagar, before ——"

"How came *you* here? And where is that old fiend, whom I had for your security?" exclaimed Laird, as he entered the room.

"*Here!*" The door of a closet suddenly opened, and a weird-looking, haggard old woman stood in its door. "Here is the old fiend you called for, ready to answer any questions you may ask, and to ask more, perhaps, than you can answer."

"Hag, devil! Do you think *your* word would be taken against mine? Go home, and learn wisdom."

"Ah, ha! ha, ha! I learned *my* wisdom years ago; when the last moans of my heart-broken child — broken by you, Michael Laird — rang in my ears! When her dying groans called on me for vengeance! vengeance against her destroyer! And *you* thought a *mother* could forgive the destruction of all on earth she prized, and live for his pleasure, as you thought I was living for *yours!* O, fool! fool! fool!" And the old woman swept out of her frame, and up and down the room, casting upon him the most withering glances.

"Go home — home, I say — to your den upon the

mountain, or I will have you dragged there, to see it destroyed before your eyes!" hissed Laird, between his white lips, while his whole frame trembled with excitement and terror.

"There is no home for me in this world. You took care of that, years ago. O, *man, man!* Where is your conscience, that you can look down the track of years, upon all the evil you have committed, and upon all the hearts you have broken — to say nothing of the murders of innocent victims, who came between you and your plans!"

"You'll drive me mad! For God's sake, leave me!"

"You drove *me* mad years ago! Why should I spare *you?* That you may do still more evil? That you may kill these helpless women, inch by inch, to secure their silence? That you may stifle my voice, that its tones may not ring in the halls of justice, denouncing you as a *murderer!*"

"'Tis false! I am no murderer!"

"Why, then, does your face turn to ashy paleness? That is not the look of innocence. Or, if my word be doubted, look there — there! ha, ha, ha! *there!*"

Laird did look, and with one loud wail, sank trembling to the floor.

"Take him away — take him away! or by all the fiends you shall answer for it! What does he here? He should be ——"

"In the river, under the waves! Dead men tell no

tales, but the waters sometimes give up their dead. Look at him; ha, you dare not!"

"He is convulsed," exclaimed Hagar, springing to the side of Laird. She attempted to raise his head, but over his white lips, staining his neckcloth and vest, a little pool of blood was flowing.

"He'll harm no more," muttered the old woman, stooping over, and placing her hand upon his heart.

"He'll harm *you!*" he screamed, making a violent effort to regain his feet. It was useless.

At that moment his eye fell upon Hagar.

"Walter," he muttered, between spasms of pain; "Walter, ha, ha! Here — here is the paper — papers don't lie — he's married — and if — ugh! this pain! Can't some of you help me? or are you devils, all? Who would have thought the water would have given up its dead! Outgeneralled, outgeneralled," he went on in broken ravings.

"Call in the servants, and have him placed in a bed," said Mrs. Martin, ringing a small hand bell.

"Thank you — ugh! — you are not the worst of women, Georgie, if you did — O, what pain I do suffer!"

Hagar held the paper in blank despair.

"Read it — read it. You'll find what I say is truth — Walter — your — Walter — is married — to — the — O save me, Heaven."

Laird had fainted with pain, and was borne insensible to

a chamber, where the best of attendance could be rendered. Hagar had no thought, no care for him, now. He might live and denounce her, or die and bury her secret with him in the grave. It mattered not to her; her sun had gone down into a night of hopeless gloom.

CHAPTER X.

The Fatal Step.

"Alas! O, alas for the trusting heart,
When its fairy dream is o'er!
Then it learns that to trust is to be deceived;
Finds the things most false that it most believed.
Alas! for it dreams no more!"

All the next day, and for days afterwards, Hagar sat in her own chamber as one in a maze. The privilege of thought, much less that of deliberation, seemed wrested from her forever. Her youthful mother-in-law lost no means of awakening her to the present, but to no avail. The town was in a tumult in consequence of the recent disclosures, as far as Laird was individually concerned. Lawyers were deep in the property (debts and credits) of the deceased Alva Martin. A competence and something more remained to his wife and child; but to that the latter was quite indifferent. No one could fathom her thoughts or imagine her intentions. She gave no answer to the various questions addressed to her; and when Walter's name was mentioned as being in a manner connected with her father's will, she only drooped her head the lower, as if that name was the last feather to the load of her misery.

So things progressed, till one morning the family found her room vacant. No letter was left — no line by which they could learn her destiny. Scouts were sent out, here, there, and every where; but no trace of even the most remote nature could be obtained. A girl answering her description was seen in the streets of Charleston, and it was thought she took passage from thence in a vessel bound to Boston. Only the commonest material of clothing was missing from her wardrobe; but all her valuable *bijouterie* had disappeared, proving that flight, and not suicide, was the means of her escape. The subject in time became a nine days' wonder, and then dropped, till the name of Hagar Martin was almost forgotten.

But of the martyr girl! What of her? Far away in a land of strangers she had wandered, companionless and alone, determined to know the truth regarding her boy lover. Far away and alone! What was it to her that the world looked coldly on while her heart was breaking? She would know, she would see with her own eyes, she *would* be convinced; and if, as Laird had said, Walter had forgotten her, why then farewell hope, happiness, every thing in this world! It was an easy matter to ascertain the locality of Walter. The address of his employer was as familiar to her as her own name. Enough that after weeks of anxiety amounting almost to frenzy, she ascertained beyond a doubt that he who had won her young heart had won it only to forget her. His marriage is announced with the daughter of his rich patron! All after that is pain, sorrow, bewilderment. What is the world to her? What has she to live for? Who cares whether she lives or dies in the agony of her despair? *One.* Yes; *unfortunately* for her, there is one who feels her anguish as if it was his own.

One! Hagar! girl! rouse yourself from the apathy of your despair! Your foot is on the precipice! One step more, and you are lost to all eternity! Father of mercy, gather your arms about her! Angels, protect her, for she knows not what she does! Too late! too late! Alas! *One,* and that a figure of dazzling brightness, who bends above her, clasping her thin hands, and pleading, in a soft, sweet murmur, "The only thing that loves you on the earth." *Such love!* the love of the serpent for the dove! She does not quite realize the purport of his words.

"Let *him* see that you can live without him." *Him!* He has triumphed by his sophistry — that brilliant man of the world! He might have talked "love" to all eternity, and only the murmur of his voice would reach her ear; but her *pride!* that was the vulnerable part of her nature; that the unprotected fort to which he brought all the force of his bewildering battery.

He triumphed! Hagar has become the martyr of love, the wreck of womanhood, the outcast, the worse than slave! She does not comprehend it yet; she neither hopes nor fears. There is *one* to meet her with kindness, and him she tries to love. Impossible! O, *how* impossible! Thoughts will come of her infant home, of her boy lover, of her days of innocence; but nothing positive, nothing to make her grieve, or to convince her of the false step she has so recklessly taken.

And now the months have crept almost into a year; *how*, Hagar scarcely knows. She has been insane — a quiet, harmless insanity, but still insane. Ever beside her is the handsome, dazzling figure which tempted her to desperation. Ever around her rustling silks, and flushed cheeks, and eyes trained to captivate and to insnare. She is too simple, too innocent to know the meaning of this display, but something tells her all is not right. From its little crib a tiny face looks out from endless folds of lace, and puts up its pouting lip for a *mother's kiss!*

A mother's kiss!

"Tell me what it is, and why I am here," she questioned the woman who seemed to be at the head of the house.

"I *will* tell you, poor, young, innocent mother. This is no place for the like of you. Go — go — no matter where; any where from here."

"But why do *you* stay here?" was the shy, childish question.

"O, I — I am used to it. It is nothing to me." The dark, penetrating eyes of the woman flashed wildly for a moment, and she leaned her head on her hand in silent thought.

"Is *your* mother dead, too? and did the one *you* loved desert you?" pleaded Hagar.

"Child! child! you torture me to madness!" exclaimed

the woman, springing up, and pacing the floor rapidly. "I tell you you *must* go! I'll not have the curse of *your* ruin on my head. This house is a hell, where the weakest of our sex and the worst of the other congregate to break every law of God or man. And he who brought you here — he is a villain. Come with me."

Silently she led the way through a long hall to a chamber in the distance. Softly opening a closet which communicated with a glass door leading to another room, she drew Hagar within, and pointed to the occupants of the chamber. One look was enough. Seated by the side of a girl as young, as beautiful, and as brilliant as himself was the man who had allured her to this scene of crime!

"Now," said the woman, as they once more stood in her own chamber, "go! Here is money, plenty of it; take it, and sometimes give a kindly thought to one 'more sinned against than sinning.' Flight may make for you a better fate than mine, and it can't make a worse one."

O, thank God, there is *good* in all! That one deed of this lost woman will shine in the day of God's reckoning with a lustre that shall overshadow a thousand failings. Think of it, you mothers and daughters, who, secure in your own strength, forget the boundless intensity of passion which has wrecked the heart and hope of thousands as pure as yourselves. Perhaps that single pearl dropped in the cup of bitter degradation may plead for her in that day as for one that had bartered her happiness for the worthless flower that had withered in her hand.

CHAPTER XI.

Flight of the Martyr.

The next phase in Hagar's life was that of a young girl, with an infant scarcely less helpless in her arms, wandering away in quest of an uncle whom she had heard of in Charlestown. Street after street was labored through in vain, till nature gave way, and the helpless mother sank with her charge upon the step of a pleasant dwelling. Now came a scene of bustle and excitement. Fortune had favored her at last. The house was the one she had so long searched for; and, what was better, Minnie had found it a refuge in her escape from slavery. Her uncle was a rough man, but not unfeeling. After an explanation and a sufficiency of oaths he sat himself down to *think*. The world mustn't know it; his friends mustn't know it; Walter — for whom he entertained an especial regard — he, of all others, mustn't know it. And so they planned and schemed, and finally concluded — as Hagar resolutely refused to part with her child — to have it left at their door in a basket. The poor thing, however, saved them the trouble; for, after a few days of suffering, they laid it to sleep with the birds and flowers in the Charlestown graveyard.

After the burial of her child Hagar seemed to awake to a new life. She was then scarce sixteen, though the ravages of sorrow had made her look much older. It was months before she fully comprehended the nature of the sacrifice that she had made of all that renders holy and beautiful the cestus of womanhood; but when she *did*, it was with that species of horror which was worse than unconsciousness. "I can never hold up my head again," she would murmur to her uncle. He was a substantial man — was old David Warren — and, what was more, a good man. He believed it best for all parties to conceal the history of Hagar, and to encourage her in a life of virtue and propriety. He had convinced himself that her heart was sound, and that was enough for him. She had sinned, but it was with an unconsciousness of evil that all the truly good would forgive; and so he strengthened her resolution, and helped her into the broad and open field of thought which heretofore had seemed shut against her. Her uncle's wealth brought around her a large circle of friends, amongst whom were Walter Meadows (who had come to Boston to practise) and Anna Welman, who, having finished her schooling, had returned to triumph in the field of Boston aristocracy. She had taken care to resume her acquaintance with Walter, for she had watched him growing up in the splendor of his intellect — handsome, talented, and popular. Thus far her siege upon his heart had proved unsuccessful; but hers was not a spirit to grow discouraged at slight rebuffs. Walter had never married.

The announcement in the paper that Laird had given Hagar had been premature. There had been a talk to that effect, and he had even engaged himself to the consumptive daughter of his beloved benefactor; but she had died before the consummation of the ceremony. Her death left Walter free in person, as he had ever remained in heart. It was not long before he proposed to Hagar in something more earnest than the boyish declaration of their former years; but she, in her quiet way, assured him that their intimacy could only be one of friendship. In vain he pleaded with her to think it over; she had done so; and, though she went a shade paler at the thought, she quietly advised him to turn his eyes and his heart elsewhere. He did not see the convulsive weeping which always followed these rejections, or he would have *felt* the secret which stood between him and wedded happiness.

But Anna Welman saw it all — saw it with eyes full of jealous rage — and inwardly vowed that, sooner than lose *him*, she would destroy the rival who, with all her assumption of calmness, it was easy to see gave back worship for worship, as far as the sentiment bestowed by Walter might resemble it. For this purpose, as in the days of their schooling, with the most treacherous intent she ingratiated herself so firmly in the good will of Hagar that the two were seldom separated. All her thoughts, wishes, and aspirations were shared with her friend; nor could any one have convinced her that what seemed so real were but the jealous impulses of a rival heart striving to undermine her with her lover. With Hagar's impetuous and stormy nature it was impossible that Walter in time should not have come to be so acknowledged. At first she strove against it, heart and soul; but her own wishes were so in keeping with his own that she could not resist yielding to his love, although strenuously refusing to become his wife.

"It never can be, Walter — indeed, it *never* can be!" she would say, when over urged. And so it went on, year in and year out, till Hagar had reached her twentieth year. Long before that there had been a "new star" in the literary firmament, whose brilliancy for the time created speculation enough for the good gossips of Boston. At first the name of the "new light" was kept a profound secret. It was not long, however, in leaking out; for Hagar's garrulous uncle was too proud of the *honor* to allow it to remain in doubt; so Hagar was obliged to wear the laurel she had so honorably won. Hagar was much courted; what woman in her position is not? and there were plenty in their own hearts who could find subject matter in her free and independent life for scandal and contumely. She could *not* help it; she could not school her impulses to be one among the million; she must do what her nature approved, in despite of the cold, critical world, who watched her with a jealous eye. At that time, unfortunately, she lost her uncle. His property being all left to her disposal, she removed from Charlestown to Boston, and took a resi dence in the vicinity of the Revere. Anna Welman still kept up the greatest intimacy, while her heart was boiling over with spleen. There were plenty of persons to join her in the disparagement of Hagar. Even men — no; I will not degrade manhood by classing with it this nondescript breed, this clique of pantaloon scandal mongers — but things calling themselves *men* would league together to annoy and defame her. Now, scandal in a woman is simply contemptible; in a *man it is disgusting.* We naturally expect better things of them; are inclined to look up to them as the inheritors of the right and might, which unquestionably descended to them from the earliest ages; but when they forget their dignity, and assimilate to themselves the meanest foibles of *our* sex, they cannot wonder if woman, acting upon the same principle, should arrogate a portion of their exclusive right. Your *men* tattlers are invariably cowards. They will meet you with a treacherous smile and a close clasping of hands before the words are cold or the ink dry with which they have tried to stab and blacken your reputation. They will fawn and flatter like a whipped cur, while their soul and strength were directed to the one purpose of dragging you down to their level. I never meet with one of this "stab-in-the-dark" class of men without wondering for what good end God Almighty formed them. For my part, I am inclined to think they are the *hell* of this world — a sort of breathing retribution for the sins of omission or commission with which human frailty is burdened. Perhaps some one of my readers may ask, "But why devote a chapter to their benefit?" I will tell you. I *know* a clique of this kind who will say, "The author is writing from her own heart." And if I am, what then? I have seen so much of the heartlessness of society, of its assumption of virtues which it does not possess, of its attempts to *seem* rather than to *be*, that I have grown reckless and fearless of the critical bravo's stiletto; that I have determined to paint out real scenes and real characters; at the same time premising that my associations have been with a class of people no more given to error than are those of the "bread and butter" writers whose works abound with angels. My war is not with the unfortunate, but with the *masked pretender;* not with those whose circumstances in life have thrown them into false positions, but against hypocrites and dissemblers. If

> "I have not loved the world, nor the world me,"

at least I do not *fear* it; and while necessity bids me write, common honesty and common humanity shall dictate the material, despite the venom of would-be critical and whipper-snapper censors.

Hagar (as I had begun to write when my pen took a freak and darted off in another direction) was the centre of a circle celebrated for its wit, its independence, and its intellect. Her home was the resort of the gifted and the noble; and many a brilliant inspiration, which in matured form won highest honor, blossomed into life in the genial atmosphere which genius always creates. If in reality her impulses were too masculine for the recognition of the world, those who knew her *well* forgave her. Her charity was proverbial. No needy person ever turned empty-handed from her door, and no unfortunate ones were forced to take the last step in guilt for lack of her friendly clasp to hold them back. And yet — and yet — simple words, meaning so much! Underneath this quiet calm of her external life there was a stratum of fire — a leaf of her heart folded down from the gaze of the world — a tempestuous sea, which was perpetually casting up darkness and destruction, — the memory of that period in her life when the earth was covered with darkness like a pall; when hope, strength, fortitude, all were sunk in the whirlpool of despair. Her friends called her capricious; they could not understand that sudden recoil of the spirit which would sometimes, in the midst of a brilliant conversation, roll over her in a flood of bitterness. "If they knew all!" she would sometimes moan, in the sickness of her heart; "if they knew all!" But what that *all* was, no human eye had ever seen, no human ear had ever heard.

And yet Anna Welman is conversant with it all! Anna Welman watches, with her great dazzling eyes, the mental tortures which ever and anon wring the bosom of *her friend.* She sits with her in the clear, still starlight, till Hagar's heart goes out in sorrowful dreams, and she forgets that she is not alone. And she ponders upon the time when Walter shall have learned it all, when Hagar shall have been discarded, and when *she* shall be installed in her much-envied place.

And so the time passes, till incidents tangle themselves up with incidents, and wind themselves in mockery around the struggling girl.

CHAPTER XII.

PRETTY ELLEN'S PHILOSOPHY.

TO leave the suffering and the sorrowful, — thus far the staple of my story, — and come a little nearer home, if there is one thing more than another for which I have an especial eye, it is for rich and tasteful adornments. One can't have too much of a good thing, so long as elegance and judgment rule the parade. If nature had cast a vote to make me wear pantaloons, I think my talent for spending money to good effect would have been enormous; as to *making* it, that would admit of argument.

If you are good at clairvoyance, I am going to take you with me into just such a "love of a room" as I should like to live in, if wishes were horses — quite a charming little room, with great blooms of flowers on the carpet; and splendid pier glasses, reaching from the floor to the ceiling; and crimson curtains, so folded in with costly lace that you might eye it from one week to another before guessing where one began or the other left off; with statuettes, and vases, and costly pictures; with books, and music, and engravings; in short, with every thing which a bright little lady, with more money than prudence, would be likely to pack into her private *boudoir*, I suppose I ought to say, as I'm writing a novel — but between us, it was only a parlor on a very expensive and altogether Aladdin-like style. The room, at the time of our entrance, had three occupants; one an elderly lady, — elderly for our times, when one is positively old at forty, — the other a beautiful girl of sixteen or thereabouts, and the third party a chubby little boy, in disgrace, for having, after the twentieth remonstrance, dragged his pet kitten into the room with its head downwards, causing on the part of said kitten a series of vigorous struggles, out of which it had come victorious, and escaped under the dress of the elder lady of the party. If her words were to be believed she could show the marks of its claws.

Chubby Cheeks looked as if he doubted the assertion, and wouldn't object to an ocular demonstration. "I can say my lesson," said he, sliding down from his perch just far enough to set his foot upon the kitten's tail. The unexpected action caused the kit to turn a somerset over the lady's foot, who, be it known, if she had a weakness, it was in her fear of cats.

"Go, you naughty boy," said she, putting him away; but the whole affair had been so ludicrous that the younger companion caught him struggling in her arms, and laying him upon the hearth rug, gave him such a succession of rolls and hugs, that he was as glad to escape from her as the kitten had been from himself. The incident which favored his escape was the entrance to the room of a stately, grim-looking gentleman, on whose face a smile would have been out of place.

"What is this, Ellen?" said he, haughtily surveying the now blushing girl, who still knelt upon the rug.

Thinking to put the best look upon the matter, she turned her face laughingly to him, and extending her hand, said, "Please pick me up."

And such a face it was; so bright, so wicked, so saucy. No one could tell exactly how she looked, so changeful was her expression. She might not have been handsome, in the common acceptation of the word, but she certainly was very lovable — very.

Mr. Veazie — for he it was, and by and by in very *un*-novel fashion I'll tell *who* he was — walked with great dignity and precision, and took his seat by the window. "Now don't be angry," said she, following him up, and flinging a handful of rose leaves at his head; at which audacious liberty the elderly lady looked perfectly horror stricken. "Don't be angry; I've a favor to ask; and if you must be angry and can't help it, wait till it is granted, and say no more about it."

"You want more money, I suppose," said he, gravely.

"That's just it, uncle Ben; there, I'll call you uncle Ben for a week, if you won't refuse me;" and as the title was one which she well knew revolted his dignity, she half repented her sauciness the moment she had spoken. "Well, *uncle Veazie*, then —— *Now!*" said she, drawing an ottoman along by his side, and crouching down like a kitten.

"How long since I supplied you fully?" he questioned.

"Un —— why, two or three days ago."

"And what's become of that last hundred?"

"Gone," said she, looking as penitent as she could, upon such short notice.

"Gone? where?" he continued.

"Spent," she replied.

"And you want more?"

"Um-ps," said she, with a comical face.

"I can't spare it," said he, moving away and taking a book.

"What!" said she, in surprise.

"I can't spare it."

"*You* can't spare it! Who asked *you* to spare it? I only want my *own;* and what's the odds whether I have it now or next week, or next year? Had I been asking charity, Benjamin Veazie, uncle though he is, is the last person I should have ventured to apply to;" and a haughty flush of indignation lit up her pretty face.

"I will consult the leger, and see when you can have another instalment," said he, rising to go.

"You'll do nothing of the kind," said the spirited girl, placing herself between him and the door.

"What right have you to limit me in my expenses? They who gave you guardianship over me never set *their* bound to my extravagance, and certainly you shall not."

"It would have been better for you if they *had* exerted a little parental authority," he exclaimed.

"It would have accorded better with *your* spirit of meanness, I dare say, if they had," she replied, her eyes crawling over him with contemptuous defiance.

"And what they neglected to do, I shall perform for them," said he, stamping his foot with a rage which he could not conceal.

"O, do, do, *do!*" said she, pacing backward and forward. "*Do!* If I want a bonnet, or a shawl, or a dress, I shall say to myself, 'You are limited, my fine lady! Your own is *not* your own; you are not fit to be trusted!' Or, if a beggar wants a mouthful of bread, I shall say to him, 'I can't give it you *now;* I'm limited! I shall have some money again one of these days, next month, perhaps, or next year, and *then* — if you can do without food till *then* — come to me! I'm limited, *limited!*'" said she, growing warmer and warmer with each word. "As if tastes, and feelings, and impulses, and desires, could be *limited!* As if will, and inclination, and want, and contempt could be limited!" she went on, fiercely aggravating each word. For the first time she raised her eyes and looked scornfully at her uncle.

"Have you done?" said he, with contemptuous gravity.

"As if I could help hating a man who tries all in his power to make me wretched — whose greatest misery is to see me happy. As if I could help scorning the man who takes every opportunity to annoy and vex me. No! thank fortune, you are no blood of mine, though you call yourself my uncle. Nothing so mean, so hateful and contemptible, ever belonged to our family, and I'm sure, had my father known how you would abuse the trust, he never would have placed it in your power to worry and torment me as you do." She hastily wiped her eyes as if she was ashamed of such a waste of feeling, and tried to summon a stoicism quite unusual to her. "Once for all — am I to have the money I want?"

"No!" was the determined reply. "If you choose to run into extravagances and follies beyond your means, I choose to restrain you. You'll thank me for it yet."

"O, I dare say; thoughtful man! considerate man! Of course, money is worth something handsome, now, in these hard times; but *that's* nothing! Of course, a double interest *tells* with *some* people — not meaning *you!* I beg your pardon; I thought it was *my* fortune you was speculating upon; I find it was *yours!*"

The beautiful, wayward girl was gone. For some minutes Mr. Veazie stood leaning his head upon the mantelpiece. From the first symptoms of a storm, Mrs. Willard, the mother of the offending Ellen, had taken her boy and left the room. He was evidently brooding over the insulting expressions his ward had used; was striving, by nursing his anger, to break up the influence which, notwithstanding his perverseness, he could not help knowing she exercised over him. He was neither selfish nor greedy, and yet such was the implication of her recent taunts. She had been placed under his control a wild, intractable girl, with expensive habits which had never been restricted, and a fortune greatly impaired by these habits. He had been her father's earliest friend, and often mourned in secret this same waywardness of spirit and disregard of advice, which now he was endeavoring to counteract in the child.

Perhaps she had found out — for women are quick at such work — that this seemingly cold and insensible man, with half as many years to his age as she could count months — this cynical, repulsive, severe man, had become by degrees entangled in the web of fascination which had been woven for more susceptible game. Be that as it may, if he *was* a captive, never lion bore his fetters with more impatient chafing than did this severe guardian of a teasing, tormenting, beautiful girl. If he had all his lifetime treated the subject of love with most unmitigated contempt — if he had not scoffed at it, abused it, and scorned such as fell victims to its power — the galling chain of servitude would have been less hard to bear. The more he felt convinced of the sweet influence Ellen was exerting over him, the harsher, harder, and more repellent he became to her. What right had she, a thoughtless, heedless, careless girl, to awaken in his seared heart emotions which had a whole lifetime been strangers to it? What right had she to intrude her sweet face between him and his dreams; between him and his waking thoughts; between him and the world which had been his love; and create a longing, yearning, unsatisfied desire for something unattainable and beyond his reach. Never a *party* man, or a *society* man, until she needed his guardianship, now his evenings were occupied in fulfilling such or such an engagement, to which his ward gave brilliancy. In vain he strove to blind himself to his infatuation — to believe it a duty to save her from the dazzling brilliancy of false appearances. The fierce (more fierce for the necessity of concealment) anger with which he saw her gay, chatty, and communicative — the life and soul of her "set" — would have convinced him, if nothing else had done so, that he was most safely bound in the fetters of that arch-rogue Cupid. Never had this same Cupid such revenge of scoffing humanity, and never did he exact so hardly the tax due his dignity, as in the instance of Mr. Veazie.

And this it was that rendered him so severe and tyrannical. To feel himself thus snared by a child, with the best feelings of his nature at her mercy, was quite enough. He would do any oppressive act to keep that knowledge from her own tantalizing self. He could imagine the mocking laugh with which she would receive an acknowledgment of his affection; and that he did not hate, and annoy, and purposely vex her was because invention was at fault wherewith to find material. And Ellen — what of her? Sometimes, when glowing and heated with conquest after conquest, — for she was a belle and a beauty, — when life, despite the clouds of her home, seemed a season of brilliant, gorgeous, never-ending excitement, — when the gifted, the proud, and the beautiful swam like visions before her bewildered senses, — a hard, harsh figure would intervene — a severe and repellent face would glimmer before her mental vision, in the study of which she was prone to find relief from the unsubstantial flummery — the ten thousand and one nothings which go to make up the bulk of society. Did she love that stern and uncompromising man, who, of all the world, openly defied and thwarted her in every way? The idea was too ridiculous to win a second thought. And yet it was certain that, when weariness or satiety, or that dreariness of spirit which at times comes to the gayest of us, overtook her, he of all other men claimed her thoughts and regrets, and won from her heart a secret promise to deal more considerately with him, and not so often cloud his brow with the mischievous pranks which, after all, were only mischief. I have often thought it a pity that people so wilfully misunderstand each other. One half of the misery of human life arises from it — at least, such has been my experience. Ellen had scarcely gained her room before she repented the warm words and warmer temper she had bestowed upon her guardian. It is as much as my word of veracity is worth to describe Ellen Willard just as she was, with all her virtues, faults, eccentricities, and blandishments upon her head; and yet there is scarcely a social circle in our midst that has not in it an Ellen Willard under some other name. Full of thoughtless and untamable spirits, she was perpetually running her curly head into mischief, and laughing herself safely out of it. Singing, dancing, riding, or talking, she was equally at home, and equally fascinating. To say the truth, the generality of her sex were more worried for her character than they would have been had she been twenty years older and defective in person, and more lenient to her whims than they could have been but for that thirty thousand in the perspective. I'm sorry to own it, but my sex are not quite angelic in their temper to one who has the reputation of knocking down tenpins and gentlemen's hearts with equal facility. I don't think women are quite aware of their *habit* of dissecting character on every occasion. It seems an epidemic with the generality of the sex. The warmest friends — the truest and most intimate — find some mote in each other's eye when talking to a third party. I remember once being taken to task for my avoidance of *women* gatherings. The same evening chance called my interlocutor and myself to a party in which women predominated. From the time we sat down to the time we rose to depart, a constant flood of small scandal overwhelmed all efforts at intellectual conversation. "There," I said, when once in the street; "you blame me that I do not cultivate my own sex. You have had a specimen of their employment. By this time I am over the coals, and before they have done with me I shall be in tatters; and yet they wouldn't say a word to injure me for the world. I tell you, when women are alone they are inveterate scandal-mongers!"

I wish the progressive people would take the subject in hand — they couldn't do better than to fine every woman who speaks ill of a neighbor unnecessarily. But, bless me, how I have wandered! If, however, I have held a glass wherein cliques can see their folly, it won't be wandering in vain. Scandal-mongers don't get half lashing enough, any how. But of Ellen. If women fought shy of her presence, the men made it up in over-devotion. Never was girlhood more petted and idolized than hers; and never did maiden dispense her smiles and repartees with greater prodigality, yet fairness of division, than did pretty Ellen Willard. And her guardian saw it all, and inwardly chafed and fretted at what he could not control. Had she lived in the days of dungeons, her chance for liberty of speech or person, I fear, would have been exceedingly small. As I was saying, the quick impulse of her sweet, childish disposition turned her anger to penitence, and without waiting to change her mind, she tripped down stairs again in great humility. She never thought of herself or of her own dignity when wrong, however inadvertently, had been done.

"Please forgive me," she murmured, half laughing. "I won't do so any more."

"O Ellen, you should be the last to taunt me with meanness! You know, as far as reason is concerned, I never deny your wishes."

Ellen had a torrent of self-accusation to pour out, which quite subdued the stern guardian, and wrung from him the very check for money which he had denied her a moment before. Ellen flung her arms about his neck, and protested that she could do without it, if he needed it; and there is no knowing what he might have urged in her moment of self-abasement, had not the announcement been made that the horses were at the door. Ellen's maid, also, appeared at the same time, bearing the riding hat and whip of her mistress. If there was one thing that Ellen could do better than another, it was to manage a horse. She had a perfect passion for horses, to indulge her in which her guardian had made her a present of a superb animal, which, she justly affirmed, could do any thing but talk. The lithe, supple limbs — the close, glossy coat, so smooth and shining — the neck arched and graceful as a swan's — the head sitting upon it in superb haughtiness — all were admiration points in her eyes, upon which she was never tired of descanting. There was, too, evidently, an understanding between Noble and his lovely mistress. His eyes would brighten at her approach with restless, eager joy; and though every nerve would quiver with joyous expectancy, no backing, or curvetting, or shying would endanger the beautiful burden, whose exquisite form matched so well with his own faultless exterior. Ellen was turning to leave the room, when the door suddenly opened, and a servant made his appearance.

"Are you at home, Miss Ellen?" he asked.

"I don't know. Who is it?" And she held her hand for the cards.

"Mrs. Welman, the Misses Welman, and Mr. Florid."

"Mr. Florid?" asked Mr. Veazie, flushing to the temples. "No! she is *not* at home."

"O, ain't I, though! Here, Mary, take my hat and whip; and, John, ask the party in, and then exercise Noble. I shan't ride to-day — unless, indeed, Mr. Florid chooses to be my escort."

Mr. Veazie bit his lip, and turned to the window in silence. Ellen sent a smile of triumph after him, and yawned a bewitching little yawn, sacred to the party whose entrance broke it in half.

Mrs. Welman was one of the new-fashioned, energetic, *manly* sort of women whom every body disliked, yet every body feared to offend — rather limited in her ideas of right and wrong, wealthy enough to defy any opinion that stood in her way to pleasure, and liberal enough to buy that charity which is supposed to cover a multitude of sins. The world treated her with prudent respect, because she was one of the tremendous kind who insisted upon a why and a wherefore to every thing. Few persons were daring enough to come under the sledge hammer of her sarcasm, for it was generally understood that when once the lion in her nature was aroused, the lily itself would have left her hand stained and spotted. She was one of those pests of society who dissect and gather up every record of those with whom they mingle. There was no hiding the skeleton from her eyes. The world might not see it, but it was clear as daylight to her searching eyes. There was no shutting the dark corner of the heart from her inspection — she knew every secret of it as well as did the owner thereof himself. Her daughter Anna is already familiar to my readers as the companion at school of Hagar Martin. The dark points in her mother's character were fully inherited by her; and with such an instructor, she was not far behind her in selfishness and dissembling. Allie, the youngest, was a quiet, shy little girl, to whom Ellen was really attached. There *was* a Mr. Welman, — so report said. No one ever saw him at home, or mingling in the society that his wife frequented; but at the close of day, a pale, worn, heart-broken individual was usually seen entering the area door of the dwelling; and this, they said, was Mr. Welman, *the millionnaire!* Allie, quiet as she was, was too beautiful not to be a thorn in the side of her ambitious sister; so no objection was made to her earnest wish to pass the evening in the basement with her father. Her sister said it was because young Altimus, the new clerk of the Welman firm, spent a portion of his leisure hours therein; but her father knew it was to make some amends to him for the ingratitude and coldness of her mother and sister. It was a beautiful sight, however, to see her young, innocent head bent lovingly over her father, or seated by his side, reading to him from some book which would amuse him. The Welmans had long been obnoxious to Mr. Veazie. The lash of Mrs. Welman's tongue was no bugbear to him, whatever it might have been to others; but he disliked her most thoroughly, and had often expressed the keenest dissatisfaction at Ellen's recognition of them. This day, in particular, he was opposed to their being admitted; for (what, in his eyes, seemed an insult to the pure girl under his guidance) they were accompanied by a most notorious libertine, who was even then the talk of the city, from an *exposé* reflecting little honor and less manhood upon him.

"What is the news?" was, as usual, Mrs. Welman's

salutation. "Of course you have heard of Harriet Lee's elopement — and with Tom Harris, of all persons in the world! It seems to me, if I was going to run off, it would be with somebody worth suffering the censure for. I suppose they think old Lee will be glad to hush it up, and come to terms; but he won't. I know him like a book; and they may bet their life he won't."

Ellen laughed, and presumed it didn't matter, so long as he had got Harriet.

"O, don't it, though!" she exclaimed. "Trust Tom Harris not to know the value of money. Besides, they do say he isn't over and above fond of her, any how!"

"Not fond of her! What did he take the trouble of running off with her for?"

"Why, for what *will* be hers when the old man steps out. But that's nothing to the scrape George Worrell is in."

"What's he done?" queried Ellen, glancing over to Veazie, to see how he was bearing the flood of small talk.

"I suppose you know he has lost his clerkship at Honeywell's?"

"Indeed! No — we are out of the way of news. It is quite a godsend when *you* call — we make up for lost time. It is about as much as poor *we* can do to take care of our own affairs!"

Mrs. Welman looked suddenly up at Ellen; but there was such a demure, innocent expression of her face, that she could not think there was meaning in her remark.

"Tell Ellen, ma'am, about George and the Honeywells."

"It is about the funniest thing out. But I never did think much of Mrs. Honeywell. She is rather fast for a married woman — eh, Florid!"

The gentleman addressed vouchsafed a sickly smile, and complaisantly smoothed his mustache with the ivory leg on his polished ratan.

"How was it?" he asked, in an affected drawl.

"Why, Mrs. Honeywell was always sweet upon George before she was married, some folks say. Any how, she got him the situation with her husband, and seemed to take an especial pleasure in his company. One day, old Honeywell, who, it appears, began to think there was something in the wind not quite the cheese, sent him home of an errand, and followed shortly after. What occurred I don't know, I'm sure, nor don't want to. I would have taken her part, for, after all, I don't know as she was so much to blame; but, would you believe it? when I called the next day to sympathize with her, she told me, blunt as could be, that if people would mind their own business it would be just as well for them. An upstartish thing."

"And George is turned away?"

"Turned away? I guess so; you don't think Honeywell would have him there, after catching him in an intrigue with his wife?"

"Nonsense, Mrs. Welman; I saw him in the store this morning," answered Mr. Veazie.

"O, ho! there's Cynic! I didn't see you before. Well, I had it from Mrs. Somerby. I don't know where she got her news; but I had mine straight enough! Any how, there's some truth in the report of Mrs. Western's following her husband to a place where he had no business as a married man. They say she pitched into him right and left, knocked his hat off, and tore his shirt."

"No, ma'am, you haven't got it right. She heard he was going out to ride with some woman, and watched the stable when he came home. It was a funny scene — better than any of the dramas at the National."

"Why, I never knew Mrs. Western added jealousy to her other charms," said Ellen, laughingly. She was taking a mischievous pleasure just then in the writhings of her guardian.

"Jealous! O dear, yes; she thinks every woman that looks at her husband wants to get up a flirtation with him. She makes herself, and him, a perfect laughing stock. Every body knows what a flirt he is; and the idea of her keeping him tied to her apron string is funny."

"Why, Anna," chimed in Florid, "I saw *you* out riding with him the other day. Better not let her know it, or insure your curls. She hits from the shoulder."

"Yes; I was crossing the bridge when he came along with that splendid team of his. He was alone, and I was alone. Besides, there was no harm in riding with him if people were not so malicious as to make harm of it. The next day I was honored with a call from her. She would have been quite ferocious, but I drew this bit of a dagger, and laid it on the table beside me. I don't know what she said then — some hifalluten about riding with other people's husbands. For my part, I have no pity for a jealous woman."

"I believe you," muttered Mr. Veazie, rising and walking to the window. Even Ellen was getting uneasy. Here were persons tolerated in good society, making boasts of indiscretions, to use their lightest name, which ought to start the blush from purity's fair cheek.

"But have *you*, Mr. Veazie. It strikes me, that when you have a wife, jealousy will be on the other foot."

"And it strikes me when I have a wife, it will be one whose sense of self-respect and womanly modesty will preclude all possibility of jealousy."

"Ay; but there is such a thing as a person being jealous without a cause."

"No sensible person, Miss Welman. Where I love, I must respect. If I was unfortunate enough to be the husband of a woman who, for the gratification of her own foolish vanity, could stoop to make me appear contemptible in the eyes of the world, or of those about me, I would ——"

"Well — *what* would Mr. Philosopher do?" interrupted Ellen.

"Hate her — detest her — *kill her!*" he retorted, flashing his eyes full upon the questioner.

"O dear, bless me. A pretty prospect for *somebody*," sneered Anna.

"Don't be alarmed, Miss Welman. It won't be you!"

"Heaven forbid! The woman who marries you will

want the patience of Job, backed up by the seven cardinal virtues, to bear with your old, capricious behind-the-age views," retorted Anna, crimson with rage. "Come, Florid — ma'am, let's go!"

"But you haven't told Miss Willard what you came for. You let such trifles excite you," whispered Florid, bending over Anna. "What do you care for an old grampus like that, as long as I don't find fault with you?" Anna shook him off, by no means appeased.

"O — ay! a costume party, Ellen," broke in Mrs. Welman. "We are getting up one for Wednesday; that's Anna's birthday, you know; and we want a 'Dudu' for the occasion. There are plenty of girls in the city that would jump at the chance, but we intend being rather exclusive; besides, your eyes and your hair would be just the thing for 'Dudu;' Byron's 'Dudu,' you know! Of course, you have read Byron's Don Juan."

"No; I have not advanced in my fashionable education that far, Mrs. Welman," answered Ellen, with a slight shade of seriousness. "Uncle tells me there are other poems of Byron preferable to that one for my perusal, and in this instance I judge his taste is better than mine."

"O, how can he say so? Don Juan is delicious. I could repeat it by heart," was the enthusiastic rejoinder of Anna.

"Not here, if you please, Miss Welman. Ellen's taste meets my approval, and I should be sorry to have it perverted. There are some poems I should be sorry to see in the hands of my ward, and the one you specified is among the number."

"Well, this is interesting, at all events," broke in Mr. Florid, who had all along been a quiet spectator. "I propose adjournment, although Miss Willard looks beautiful enough to tempt a longer visit, if she could be prevailed upon to say any thing agreeable."

"I *couldn't* say any thing agreeable to *you!*"

"Why?"

"Because I don't like you well enough."

"Sincere, at all events," muttered the crestfallen man.

"Sincerity is oftentimes impertinence," rebuked Mrs. Welman.

"In what manner is Mr. Florid offensive to you? Most women admire him. Don't you think him handsome?"

"I haven't thought any thing about him. It is speaking pretty plainly to one's face; but since Mrs. Welman sets the example, it must be right. I always feel, when Mr. Florid is by, as I used when beautiful Fido was in the room. You remember Fido — the handsomest wretch of a dog that ever lived, but so mischievous! And when I see a man externally so attractive, and know that he perverts those gifts, and makes them the lure to insnare susceptible hearts, I always shun him and his influence as I would a distemper. Mr. Florid will pardon me; but I have some odd notions about me, which even the example of Mrs. Welman can't quite uproot."

"Ellen is ridiculously fastidious," said Mrs. Welman, as

the party were on their way home; but the little sprite had pleased her stern guardian, and in an hour after, she was out with him on the shell road, driving a pair of beautiful horses which it required all her strength to hold in and manage.

CHAPTER XIII.

LAWRENCE, THE MESMERIST. — THE ADVENTURE AND ITS CONSEQUENCE.

"AN adventure! an adventure!" laughed blithe Ellen Willard, bursting into Hagar's parlor one evening, just as the sun was flooding the room with gold. With both hands she held up the skirts of a riding dress, while the little janty hat, cocked upon a bunch of crisp curls, made her look saucy enough to fascinate any body fond of the picturesque.

"Well, what is it?" said Hagar, kissing the warm, full lips, while she disengaged the hat, and sent her servant off with it to her chamber.

"*Well, what is it?* Yes, I guess so; a regular romance, in three volumes. You see, uncle having gone to New York, and mother to sleep, there was nothing left for me to do but to saddle Noble, and take a turn or two upon the shell road. Well, just as I was passing the Common, something startled Noble, and away he went like a flash of lightning. The fact of it was, I had lost *his* head, though I didn't lose my own. The women screamed, and the children shouted, and the men — well, I don't know what they did, for just then ——"

"An angel descended from the clouds, I suppose," laughed Hagar.

"No; but an angel of a man descended from his trotting sulky, flung himself upon Noble, caught me in his arms, and landed us both in the softest kind of mud. Here's a specimen of it," said the merry girl, holding up her draggled riding skirt.

"Were you hurt at all?"

"Not a bit. When Noble saw how ingloriously he had acted, he turned short of his own accord, and came back to me. My preserver — don't that sound romantic, eh? — my preserver gave me a lift, raised his splendid great eyes to mine, told me his name, and asked permission to call upon me here this evening."

"And you ——"

"O, what could I do? He had saved my neck, for I suppose that would have been the end of me; and I couldn't be uncivil, especially when he told me he was a stranger in the city — a Mr. Lawrence, I believe, of New York."

"Lawrence, did you say? — what Lawrence?"

"That's more than I know. I couldn't ask many questions with all Charles Street gaping at me as if I was a show got up for the occasion. I only know he was handsome as a picture — something like you; that is to say, a handsome likeness of you, with the tiniest bit of a mustache, and a pair of eyes that — Lord bless me! ——"

That last exclamation was the result of a sudden encounter of that pair of eyes looking at her with a very quizzical expression, while their owner was evidently waiting an opportunity for explanation.

"In your — what shall I call it? — not an accident — which gave me the privilege of being of service to one so beautiful," — and the intruder raised his hat in eloquent admiration, — "you dropped this bracelet, which it was my fortune to find; and I have made it an excuse for this untimely visit. Am I forgiven?"

What could she do? Stifling her incipient embarrassment, she gave him her hand, — which, by the by, he held quite as long as the exigencies of the case demanded, — led him up to Hagar, and gave her an introduction.

"Who did you say that was?" questioned Mr. Lawrence, as Hagar left them chattering like old friends, instead of the strangers they were in reality.

"Hagar Martin. You must have heard of her. Every body knows her, by reputation at least, — so smart, so keen, so witty, — quite the *lionne*, I can tell you, in Boston. But you mustn't fall in love with her!"

Mr. Lawrence blazed his eyes upon the bright face before him, as if it would be rather hard to fall in love with any thing but that. A blush and a slight hesitancy in expression showed Ellen to be not altogether unconscious of the tribute to her charms; but after a moment she rattled on again.

"Whoever marries Hagar must be quite a superior person. I don't think she would care any thing about beauty, so that there were goodness and manliness enough to make up the loss. You see she has always been alone, as it were, and most persons think her haughty and proud; but she isn't, only to those she dislikes."

"I hope I shall never come under the range of her displeasure."

"O dear, no! She will like you, I know."

"Why do you think so?"

"I saw her reading your face while we were talking; and I know she was pleased with it."

"Why so?"

"There is strength in it. Hagar likes strength — strong thoughts, strong acts, strong speeches. These are what Hagar likes, and these she read in your face."

"And *you?*"

"*I?* O, I am a wilful, wayward little thing. I like to be cared for, to be petted, and to be loved; at least I suppose I *should.* But if I loved unworthily, or one that couldn't love me in return, why, there would be an end of it. But *Hagar!* let *her* love once, and it will be terribly in earnest. She would go through an ocean wild with the foam of a thousand thunder clouds to serve one she loved."

"*You* like strong terms, too, I see."

"Yes; I've caught them of Hagar."

"I shall like Hagar, and, I'm afraid, love *you.*"

"O, there is no danger of that while she is round; and so I constantly tell uncle Veazie, when he objects to the persons I meet here."

"And who is 'uncle Veazie'?"

Ellen's face darkened for a moment. In the pleasure of her new friend's society she had forgotten that he would be likely to object. Lawrence saw the cloud, but gave her time to answer.

"O, uncle Veazie is — I hardly know what he is. A guardian, I believe they call it; a tyrant, I think, sometimes. I have always had my own head till lately. He draws a tight rein. That reminds me I was charged with abundance of orders to Hagar about my morals, manners, &c. However, having forgotten some, I may as well make up my mind not to remember any of them."

Lawrence had risen to go, and stood leaning against the mantelpiece.

"Can't you adopt me for an uncle, or cousin, or something?" he questioned, drawing Ellen towards him with a premature familiarity.

"I'm afraid that would be dangerous," she laughed.

"Something nearer, then."

"We have known each other scarce an hour."

"And yet it seems as if I had known you all my life."

"Hagar is returning; she mustn't hear such language."

"One kiss, then."

"*Cousinly?*"

"Any thing you please."

He drew her unresistingly to his heart. His deep eyes rained down their light into her own, with a weird, wild influence that bore off all self-control. She allowed him to draw her closely to his heart, to press her lips over and over again; nor until the door closed upon his retreating form did she awaken from the trance wrought by the wonderful influence of Michael Lawrence, the mesmerizer.

CHAPTER XIV.

THE UNWELCOME VISITANT. — STARLIGHT'S GRAVE.

A CHANGE had come over Hagar, and she grew paler and thinner than ever. She wrote more powerfully of human passion and of human despair, and the world wondered that an intellect like hers should coin its music into passionate wailing. Another year had passed — a year that had made strange havoc with her health. As she grew into notoriety, her success won for her the envy and petty jealousy of a clique of scribblers, who determined, in their own grovelling spirits, to undermine her fame.

"It is too bad!" said she, "too bad," as she clutched, in nervous haste, a paper in which some wounding allusion was made to the mystery of her young life. "So long ago — so much as I have suffered, and in all these years to have the single error still staring me in the face — still striving to drag me back into deeper perdition. *O God, have these men hearts?*"

The cry with which this question was given was so wild, so despairing, that it seemed as if it *must* force some answer out of heaven. O, how she wished the past, with its maddening memories, could be swept away where she might never hear of them more — where she might never be reminded that in this bright, sunny world, over which the blue heaven bends so smilingly, there were hearts so cruel, so unforgiving, so relentless, that common charity fled from their approach! To struggle as she had struggled for redemption, to atone in bitterness of spirit as she had tried to atone, and then to have the hands of *men* busy in seeking her downfall, O, it was too terrible! She threw up the window, that the cool air might fall upon her heated forehead; but the calm, and the quiet, and the holy softness of evening brought no comfort to her. What was life, if man was less forgiving than his Maker? O, *you* who follow up the repentant Magdalen with insinuations and reproaches, you who bar her to virtue's path by every conceivable means that malice can suggest, remember that it is *you*, and not she, that will be called upon to answer her guilt before the throne of Him who hath said, "Neither do I condemn thee."

Hagar still clasped the fatal paper in her hands. In a moment of womanly tenderness, when her yearning heart longed most for some answering voice, she had yielded to the passionate entreaties of Walter, and they were again affianced. In the fulness of her joy, she had closed her eyes, and resolutely refused to look upon the consequences which might accrue from such a deceptive step. And now, Walter must know it — must hear it from her lips. She had not long to wait. A ringing step was bounding through the hall; a joyous voice was breaking up the silence, while Hagar's heart was shuddering from the self-imposed task.

"Never more, Walter," said she; "never more!" and she shrank out from the enclosure of his protecting arms.

"Why, Hagar, what's the matter?"

"Walter, we must part. You'll hear a story of — something which may be true or false; but whatever it is, or however you may shudder away from me, never think there has been love in my heart for any human being but you! Never think there has been a wish that you did not share!"

Dizzy and exhausted, she was near falling, and only that his arms were again closing around her, she would have sunk to the floor.

"Hagar, for God's sake ——"

"Don't speak to me, Walter; don't touch me! Walter, many years ago, when I was young — *too* young to comprehend the enormity of it — I sinned, in a way that God sometimes mercifully forgives, but man never ——"

"Hagar, stop! I'll not hear it from *you!*"

"I have tried to outlive this blot," she went on, growing paler and paler, while her eager, earnest eyes grew yet more lustrous in their expression; "I have tried, God knows how hard, and I had hoped — but that is past now; I had hoped to pass my life — it will not be a long one at best — but I had hoped to pass it with you. It is impossible, Walter — you understand the word *impossible.* O my God, this cup is too, *too* bitter; I cannot bear it!" and, rushing past him, Hagar flitted like a spirit up the stairs, and locked herself into her room. O, how cold and dreary this world had become to her! What a mockery of goodness and charity were all the semblances of truth!

"What is the matter with Hagar?" questioned Walter of Anna McVernon, as she stepped out from her concealment among the curtains. I need not premise that it was her hand that had prepared the last drop of poison which had imbittered Hagar's cup. Month after month she had laid watchful and incessant siege to the heart and hand of Walter Meadows. In vain her mother ridiculed and painted, in strong terms, the life of comparative poverty she would necessarily lead with him; in vain contrasted the splendor of McVernon's establishment — the beauty of his equipage, the costliness of his furniture — with the possible "parlor and bed room" which Walter would have to offer She loved him with all the force of her perverted nature, To secure him, there was no crime too deep, no villany too wily, for her enacting. But Walter was a true-hearted, honorable man. The very forwardness of her overtures, and her open and undisguised admiration of him, only caused him to avoid, as much as possible, without offending her. At length, wearied out by incessant rebuff, she threw herself away upon the wealthy old man who bought her, as he would buy any article of adornment, because she would add grace and dignity to his establishment. But even that did not prevent her secret designs upon the heart, at least, of Walter Meadows.

"What *is* the matter with Hagar?" again questioned the bewildered man.

"I — I don't know! Perhaps this note can explain the mystery," said she, picking up a crumpled note which she had dropped for the occasion, unperceived by him. To see that manly brow contract as with a sudden pain — to see those sunny eyes cloud over with indignation and dismay — to see that handsome face grow flushed and pale by turns, and the healthful form droop as under some fearful shock — O, any heart, but the one seared and scarred by constant dissembling like hers who contemplated this scene, would have relented, and endeavored to retrieve the wrong so surely done. Not so *her's!* There was a malicious pleasure, a fiend-like cruelty, in the wild-beast eyes with which she took in the amount of pain inflicted.

"My darling Hagar," so the letter ran, "how can I thank you enough for the meeting you so kindly granted? In all the years that have passed, you have been my heart's dream — my worshipped idol. By the angel-spirit of our early-lost 'starlight,' I conjure you to see me once more before I leave the city. Only once! It may be the last time of asking, and surely you owe me that gratification."

"Infamous!" said Walter, crushing the letter in his hand. "I *knew* ——." He hesitated, while a deeper flush stole up over his fine forehead. No, he would not breathe a word against her, lost and depraved as she was. He checked himself, and ran his eyes once more over the cruel lines. It was no dream; there they were, cold, cruel, horrible. And this, then, was the cause of her agitation; the return of an old lover, and — the — only one she had loved.

"You had best be present at the meeting," suggested the woman-fiend. *The meeting!* He had not noted that. He would be there. He would confront her — accuse her of falsehood and duplicity, and then — farewell ambition, love, hope, every thing which goes to make up the life of a man.

The meeting was to be at the house of Justice A———, a singular place, he thought, for an assignation. He wondered that the justice, whom he had ever considered an honorable and high-minded man, should countenance such a thing! But if Hagar was thus guileful and treacherous, where could he look for sincerity? Taking the address, he left the house, and wandered away miles and miles into the country.

O woman! *Fiend!* Smile in the consciousness of your successful scheme; but remember there is an eye above you who counts every groan you have forced from a desolate heart. It is now *your* turn to triumph, *but to-day is not always.*

CHAPTER XV.

THE UNWELCOME VISITANT.

HAGAR locked her chamber door, and threw herself in utter prostration upon the floor. She could not weep — she could only feel.

"Too bad, too bad! and I so young to sin!" was her perpetual moan. The sun had gone down, and the stars were out in summer brightness, as if no crime, no sorrow, no despair was in the world over which they smiled. The air seemed suffocating. Hagar rose, and gathering a light shawl about her, ran down the stairs and out into the street, on and on, through crowds of laughing, chattering people — on and on, across streets and past houses where happiness had not forgotten to dwell; on, over the long, cool bridge, past the navy yard, past the prison — O, even its inmates were less wretched than she! — past the vine-wreathed cottages! The graveyard, with its still, white marbles gleaming in the moonlight, lay before her. O for strength to reach that little group of mounds, shut in with thin, whitewashed palings! O for God's power to lie down to sleep as those she loved were sleeping! The gate is cleared at last, and with a sad, pitiful cry — a cry which seemed to say, "My God! my God! why hast *thou* forsaken me?" — she flings herself by the senseless stone, her long, white arms stretched around it, with her face pressed to the ground. How long she had lain there it is impossible to tell. The moon was high in the heavens, and the night wind rose and fell through the branches of the tree over her head.

"O that I had died with thee, my child! O that I had died with thee!" she moaned. "No hope! no light! O, how good *they* ought to be who can afford to hunt *me* to my ruin! My child! my child!"

A shadow fell over her, and crossed the grave upon which she had flung herself. She did not perceive it, but kept on murmuring, —

"My child! my child!"

"*And mine!*" said a deep, full voice.

He spoke — that new comer — almost in a whisper, but it seemed in the awful stillness to be a peal of doom, rather than a voice. She unwound her arms from the cold stone, and looked up through the moonlight into the handsome face bending over her. It must be a dream — the very nightmare of a troubled brain. God knew if she had sinned she had also suffered. Surely the Almighty, in his mercy, would not inflict so horrible a punishment upon her; or, if so, why, then come death.

"*And mine!*"

Again that sound penetrated to her ear like the rushing of many waters. She could not be mistaken. He was there, bending over her, breathing into her ear; he, that had counselled her to break God's holy ordinance; he, that had taken advantage of her great grief to make her the thing she abhorred. He was there, and forever and forever all was most surely lost!

"You do not speak to me, Hagar!"

"What can I say to you?" she began, while her face, which had flushed at the sound of his voice, went very pale again. "What can I say to you? I never loved you, that you knew; yet, so knowing, you led me into temptation. You loaded my young life with shame; you made me abhor and shrink from myself as from some polluted thing; you made me bear with me, through all these long years, a hidden stain; a stain that has eaten into my soul; that has cankered my best impulses; that has risen up before me at all times, in all places, under all circumstances, till I loathe myself for the crime you won me to perpetrate."

She raised her wet, mournful eyes to his face, as if she would read there some retreat from the horror that was pursuing her.

"Hagar, do you think I have not suffered too?"

"*You!* and what should make *you* suffer? Do you not know it was a laurel in your crown of glory? Do you not know that it was a gem in the setting of your fame? Harmless pleasantries, innocent amusements, trifling inconsistencies, when a man tramples upon all that is sacred and holy in human nature! But the victim! what for her? The averted eye, the curling lip, the crushing, damning sneer! O, wonderful world! O, discriminating society! Stamp *libertine* upon the brow of man, and it is the magnet to draw all womankind fluttering around him, like moths around a flame; and if their wings *do* get scorched by the contact, why, woe, woe to *them*, and glory to *him!*"

Hagar leaned her head in her palms, as if conversing rather to herself than to him who listened.

"Hagar, Hagar, go with me; be my wife. The future shall repay you all the wrongs of the past. I have watched you at a distance; I have seen you brave, defiant, scornful, and felt how superior you were to those who would cast you off like a poisoned weed, did they but know the circumstances of your life. I have seen you goaded on, almost to madness, by the arts of a bold, bad woman, and I have waited the right moment to come forward and save you. Will you be my wife?"

"No, no! it cannot be; it is impossible. If I sinned *then*, when I did not know, as I know *now*, how wicked it was, think how much greater would be the sin of giving myself to you, while my heart is full of its wild worship for another! Think what it would be to have that other face always coming between me and my honor; between me and my duty; between me and every thought and impulse. Think what it has been to have that other face beaming on me, and I not able to look up to it in innocence; and what it would be to feel that I had forever divorced myself from its sight; and leave me."

There was such an imploring, wistful look in the speaker's eyes, that the man of the world was subdued — awed into obedience; and taking her passive hand, which she neither gave or withheld, he imprinted a kiss upon it, and hurriedly walked away. Hagar watched the last trace of the shadow, even till only the crackling echo of a distant footfall came back upon her; then nerveless, hopeless, aimless, she closed her eyes, and drooped in utter unconsciousness upon the grave by which he had left her.

CHAPTER XVI.

The Christian Menial.

When she awoke, the morning sun was shining full and bright upon her pillow. She had no consciousness of returning; no consciousness of any thing but a dull, heavy sensation about her heart, such as might have been the remnant of a bad dream. She rose to dress herself, but was too weak to make the requisite exertion. She rang the bell, and Meggy, pale and worn with watching, came out from among the curtains.

"What has happened?" questioned Hagar.

"Where did you wander to last night, lass? A gentleman — he *was* a gentleman, too — brought you home in his arms, and took you up stairs, O, *so* gently. O, darling, such sighs and such sobs! It isn't much when other women cry, but when *you* sob, it is enough to break one's heart — it is!"

"Hush, Meg, hush! Was any one here when I came?"

"Yes; Walter was just going out. He looked at you, and he looked at the man, and he scudded away as if he'd seen a ghost, instead of a handsome, beautisome gentleman!"

"That will do, Meg. You needn't wait."

"I didn't think it was very pretty of Walter not to stop long enough to see if you was alive or dead."

"Walter was right, Meg. Fate has done its worst. O, it was so wrong to deceive him. It was so wrong to suffer him to love me. He will cast me off; they will all cast me off; Meg, all — all;" and Hagar burst into a passionate flood of tears.

"I won't cast you off, darling. I didn't cast you off when I knew all about it; the sin, and the suffering, and all. O, my love mayn't be like the love of them as has book larnin' to teach 'em, but it began in your cradle, and will only end when they bury my heart in your grave." And the old faithful creature clung kneeling to the feet of her mistress.

In that moment all difference in position was forgotten. Hagar stooped over and drew the old gray head up to her heart, kissed the worn, wrinkled face over and over again, crying all the while as if her very nature was dissolved.

"Don't, Hagar, don'tee," whimpered the faithful nurse. "I don't know much ways to comfort any body, but I have heard an old minister say, 'When the world forsakes us, then the Lord will take us up.' And you, poor innocent lamb that you were, how could you know what dreadful deed you was doing?"

"That is no excuse, Meg; no excuse for me at all. I ought to have buried myself in the depths of the ocean, before ever joining in with the untainted and the pure. I ought to have died before I had ever shown my face in the world again. I ought — I ought. O, I wish I *had!*"

"I'm astonished!" said Meg, changing her tactics, and giving her charge a little petulant shake. "I'm astonished to see you take on so. Why, when you first came home with a puny little baby on your arm, you didn't take on after this fashion. Where's the one of them that's so good, or so kind, or so charitable as you are? Where's the one of them as *hasn't fell*, that's fit to hold a candle to you in point of goodness? Let them cast you off, say I, if they dare to, and see what our heavenly Father will say to them, when their turn comes! Wonderful pretty, indeed, if people are to lie and cheat, and scandalize their neighbors, and pass through the world with heads as high as Hamer's, as the Bible tells of, while you, who have injured nobody but yourself, and who have repented and repented until there is nothing more to repent of, must shrink into nothingness and be cast off! I only wish I was a prophetess, for their sakes. I'd tell them that God never made one *human* a judge of another; that he never intended one human should trample another into the hopeless dust of misery; and that there are thousands of sore, bleeding, penitent hearts, here on earth, that will rise up in the day of judgment against them who barred up their road to repentance, and say, 'But for *you*, and for *you*, and for *you*, I might have been saved.' God help me! but I wouldn't be the one to put between a fallen woman and her way to atonement; no, not for all the diamonds in *Golgander's* mines."

She probably meant Golconda's mines, but as her matter of speech was better than her manner of speaking, Hagar did not think it worth while to correct her.

"Come, cheer up, honey," she went on, smoothing out the tangled curls, that defied any thing like proper training. "Cheer up; the worst can but come to the worst. You can write all around them, and when you are dead they will print your book, and get a monument for you, and be sorry that they hunted the life out of you; so they will; that will be a treat, won't it, pet?"

Whether it was Meg's rude, homely speech that cheered the mourning girl, or whether it was that her tears were all spent, I do not know; but certainly an expression of her old defiant nature stole over her face, and she rose calm, collected, and almost as determined in her strength as she had been before the accursed paper which sounded her doom had fallen into her hands. All that day she spent in writing; not for publication, but, I think, though the papers were afterwards destroyed, they were in part confessions, and acknowledgments, and words of love, to be opened only after she had ceased to be.

From that time there seemed to be a presentiment of coming death. Not that she contemplated self-destruction; her naturally pure and good impulses would have shrunk away from such an idea. If she had sinned, she could bear to suffer till God saw fit in his mercy to prepare her bed and take her home. That day, fortunately for her, several letters came to her from unknown sources, each one containing some sentiment of the affection her writings had inspired. That was no unusual thing, and these tokens had done much towards convincing her that she was not altogether unworthy of Walter; but to-day they were especially acceptable. She wrote to Walter, entreating him to come; and it was in answer to this solicitation that the scene described in my prologue occurred. Her nature, as I have said, was strangely wild and tempestuous. She thought if she could only see him she could school her heart to take a final leave. He came, as I wrote before, and, not knowing the treachery of Anna McVernon, his strange coldness overwhelmed her. She pleaded with him, and was repulsed. Had he asked for an explanation, all would have been well. He did not, but took for granted what her evil genius had insinuated. When she arose from his door, after following him home, it was with a will and a resolution, which, defiant of consequences, she had determined to effect. Could Anna have read her heart at that moment, she would have fled from the coming storm. "At Mrs. Welman's party; at Mrs. Welman's party." That was the object to be gained; that was the point to be arrived at. Till then she would be patient; she would bear to suffer, and then her life's duty would have been done.

CHAPTER XVII.

RETRIBUTION.

WALTER sat and read:—

One who has loved you immeasurably, one who has echoed your sighs and suffered with your suffering, implores an interview. I shall be at home to no one but you this evening. Will you come, and forgive the desperate impulse which counsels this step? ANNA.

Walter crushed the letter in his hand and—*thought*. Time had been when such an unwomanly invitation would have been met by open scorn; but now he was suffering. He wanted some *woman's* consolation, some *woman's* affection. He wanted to lay his throbbing head upon some *woman's* breast, and there learn the secret of the great calm and peace which he read in the eyes and on the lips of all around him. He wanted the thrill of some woman's soft hand to mesmerize away the throbbing of his brain. And *he went!*

Leaving him time to travel the distance of three squares, I have a word to say of Walter in general and his never-do-wrong set in particular.

Walter was a thorough man of the world; a man whose natural instincts had been moulded in that fastest of all fast schools of nature — New York. "*Love is possession*," had been his war cry on Love's battle ground, while his experience told him possession is death to love; and yet, with all his heart and soul, with every impulse of his somewhat vacillating nature, he loved Hagar. The idea of her delinquency froze his blood to ice. It was nothing that, like his sex's prototype, the butterfly, he had drifted from lip to lip, from flower to flower, till passion had lost its freshness, and possession its power; but her he loved must bring to his treasury the purest dew upon the flower of affection. *Deception!* that was what he shrank from. To be sold by a *woman!* O, *that* was *too* much of a good thing! And now for the characteristic of the sex. Men, in their vain-glorious pride, arrogate to themselves the title of "lords of creation;" there is not so easy and confiding a dupe in all that creation they lord it over as what is termed a *blaze* man of the world. I don't mean the class of silly simpletons that Nature sent on to the earth especially to become footballs for coquettes, but of that *wise* set of creatures who sleep with one eye open on society; who will rattle you off a string of maxims as long as the moral law about the inconstancy and untruth of women; "fast livers," who crowd ten years of common existence into one, and who would be greatly amused at the idea of any woman trapping them. Why, at the very moment that they curl their lips in haughty disdain, and dare a woman to deceive them, they are putting their feet into snares which a blind man might see. And so it was with Walter. If he had taken as much thought, or reposed as much confidence in Hagar's integrity as he did in that of Anna McVernon, much sorrow to both would have been spared. Ah, well! some lessons are worth learning, though they are learned in sorrow.

Standing before a superb mirror, a woman gloriously beautiful was drinking in the admiration of her own voluptuous charms. A robe of India muslin, thrown open from the throat and gathered at the waist, covered, but did not conceal, the swelling proportions of a luxurious bust. If coquettish women only knew how much repose there is in those soft, thin muslins, no other material would intrude upon an in-door costume. I have known more men to lose their — heart, I had nearly written, but as there is a question in my mind whether it was not the *heart* instead of the *rib* that was beguiled from Adam, I revoke, and write *head;* I have known more men to lose their head at sight of these hazy, cool, delicious toilets than from the effect of the rarest magnificence of costume. Their presence is as soothing as a narcotic, as bewildering as a dream, and as fascinating as a — a — I don't know any simile to fill up the sentence. Anna McVernon knew what she was about; let her alone for that. She had played her card too well to lose the game now. Had Walter's heart yielded at her first onset it would have lost half its value. Anna was none of your common *intrigants.* There was an intense excitement, a bewildering joy, in following up a flirtation till her own heart was caught in the rebound.

"Take care of her," whispered Florid. "She plays a bold hand. Gorden broke his heart for her, and he will cut his throat if he sees you with her."

Walter smiled with an air of provoking coolness.

"And as for him," said Florid, "he is as good as married. He hasn't a thought for any thing but Miss Martin."

That was enough said. Another woman loved him; from that moment she determined that he should wear her chains. More men than Walter Meadows have owed a most inexplicable success to the knowledge of being beloved by another woman. It is a singular anomaly of human nature that no heart is so valuable as when belonging to a third party. I have heard women say there was no pleasure in conquest unless they were ousting some one else. If I thought any such blood as that ran in my composition, I would let it out and fill my veins with milk and water as a more worthy substitute. But there is little honesty of purpose in this rare old world of ours. One man's mistress is every man's target, and one woman's lover is the property of every woman who chooses to try the strength of her fascination. But this is an unnecessary interpolation. The world can "gang its gait," for all I care. No one should meddle with love that wants peace; and so — had I been in their confidence sooner — would I have told the whole party who were playing at such cross purposes.

A ring at the door startled Anna from her pretty contemplation, and flung her down in a most studied and graceful attitude upon the luxuriant lounge. One hand was thrown carelessly above her head, while the other listlessly toyed with the long silken ears of a rare King Charles spaniel that crouched by her side.

As the door opened she started in pretty perturbation, and, rising, gave her hand timidly and with an excess of confusion to the young and handsome visitor whose presence she had solicited.

"Mr. Meadows — Walter — do you despise me — do you? O, speak to me! say something! break this horrible spell! I thought I could explain why I had sent for you without compromising myself as a woman — myself as a wife; but, by Heaven, I cannot!"

Anna trembled from head to foot, and would have fallen but that the arm of Walter enclosed her voluptuous form. She had counted too much upon her own strength, upon her own morality; or rather upon that policy of purpose which throughout her life had passed for morality. "Thus far shalt thou go, and no farther," had been the text laid down for her passionate impulses; but now the boundary was passed, and upward and onward, sweeping over every other thought, came the flood of impetuous excitement. It was a moment alike dangerous to the peace of both. With her form still cradled upon his bosom, he had sunk down upon the lounge from which she had risen on his entrance. Her beautiful arms had crept up over his shoulders, and were folded lovingly around his neck. Her sweet breath, coming in quick, heavy gasps, stirred the soft curls that shaded his noble brow. Her warm, full lips, parted just enough to reveal a set of pure and pearly teeth, seemed wooing him to their clasp; her white, womanly bosom, just rising into view over the folds of muslin, rose and fell with the tumultuous heavings of the heart beneath it.

"I do love you so! I do love you so!" were the sounds which from time to time fell upon Walter's listening ear, as closer, nearer, and with greater *abandon*, she yielded to the intoxication of his embrace. The statue had warmed into life; the marble heart had grown wild with its passionate fire. O, man! man! when will you appreciate that entire sacrifice of self which the woman who loves you ever yearns to make? There might come moments of great agony yet, following in the wake of that one triumph hour; but to make *him* happy, if only for a moment — to make *him* forget the outer world of disappointment and sorrow, if the next moment gave her eternal remorse, — that was the passion cry of her tumultuous heart — that was the only thought which reached her dizzy brain. To be *his*, if the next moment saw her a corpse at his feet — to be his, if it stained her after years with hideous deformity — to be his, if she could know — could be sure of it — that that moment would stamp "*unpardonable sin*" against her upon the scroll of doom! There was nothing left of the cold, wily woman of the world but a mass of dangerous passion, of delirious idolatry. Her only idea was that *his* arms were clasping her; her only prayer that he might owe to her instrumentality one moment of entire happiness — a prayer which, cruel and heartless as she had been to others, the Almighty was too merciful to grant.

Walter still held her in his embrace, though conscience told him of an irreparable wrong; still listened to her passionate words, although his own heart could not reciprocate; still suffered himself to be beloved, though he knew the flame was feeding upon the very lifestrings of the infatuated woman.

"*I do love you so!*" she murmured, pressing her moist and dewy lips passionately upon Walter's. "I thought the icy barrier of pride which *has* shielded would still save me; but *you* are here, and I have forgotten every thing that I ought most to remember! It is no *new* dream," she went on, sadly, "no new dream, but a lifelong love; and when I have seen you wasting your wealth of heart where it was unreturned — and when I have looked into your noble face as I do now ——" Here the great, glorious eyes met his with such an audacious, maddening glance, that what *had* been of conscientious scruple melted beneath the fierce flame of lawless passion.

"I WILL love you, Anna!" he exclaimed; "I *will* forget every thing but you — my glorious eagle, my beautiful — " *ruin* he ought to have added; but just then, when her utter *abandon* had sent the blood coursing like fire through his veins, when his eyes were filling up with lustrous brightness, at that turning point in human nature where the sublimity of manhood is overshadowed by animal grossness, a step was heard in the hall, and a servant made his appearance at the door.

"Mr. McVernon desires your presence in your dressing room."

Had a thunderbolt fallen at her feet she could not have been more thoroughly startled.

"How long has he been at home?" she questioned.

"An hour or so, I believe; he sat on the balcony for some time, knowing that you had company."

"Treacherous balcony! cruel chance!"

The lounge upon which they were sitting was against the window, and he must have heard all—*all!* Ah, woman—*fiend!* it is a long lane that has no turning; *your* turn is coming. Perhaps you will have occasion to remember wrongs done to one whose only harm to you was in daring to love where you had cast your eyes.

Every vestige of passion, every remnant of tenderness, every trace of emotion, vanished from the heart of Anna, while her old selfishness and fear of detection usurped their place.

"An *eclaircissement* is *sure;* you must protect me," said she, looking wildly up into Walter's face.

"Prove to me that Hagar is false, and I am yours eternally."

"*I will*, at the party to-morrow night." I can gain that much reprieve, she thought, if matters are really as bad as I apprehend.

Anna summoned up all the impudence and confidence it

was possible to command, and proceeded to meet her husband.

McVernon was a gross, sensual-looking man, of about forty-five years of age, upon whose face the ravages of a dissipated life were deeply ingrained. Having been a dissipated debauchee himself, he was prepared to put the worst construction upon, and treat with the least delicacy, any thing approaching to infidelity in others. He was the leader of that class of pests who can never see a man and woman in conversation without shrugging his shoulders with a knowing leer, as much as to say, "Oho! sets the wind in that quarter?" He had mingled with the lowest class of women until his respect for the sex was limited and distorted. Anna Welman had been admired for her "good points" in a physical sense, as he would have admired a fine horse or a noble dog. He first saw her at the Cambridge races, looking down with flashing eyes and flushed cheeks upon the close contest between two favorite trotters. He saw her from the judges' stand, leaning like a statue upon the railing, her eyes following the horses; and from that moment he saw nothing else. In vain Goodwin trotted his beautiful Charmer backward and forward past the stand; even his skilful driving, which had heretofore been an admiration point with McVernon, passed for nothing. He chattered incoherently, betted at random, took all the odds any one chose to offer, and cared just three straws whether he lost or won. Just then a shrill cry of horror and dismay startled the echoes with its force. The sulky containing one of the drivers, by mismanagement or design, had been run into, and horse, wheels, vehicle, and driver were all mingled in a tangled mass. Pale as marble, Anna flew out of the balcony, down the stairs, and out into the thickest of the excitement. While the men were talking, she, by some process unknown to herself even, disentangled the horse, gathered the broken pieces of wheels from about the wounded driver, clasped him convulsively to her heart, and fainted in his arms. Whether the handsome, manly little fellow who thus became openly the recipient of her sympathies was known to her it was impossible to say. His *eyes* said yes; *his lips said no.* If his lips told the truth, he had hard luck, for no one believed him. In the distance, Mrs. Welman looked on in utter astonishment. McVernon raised the fainting girl in his arms, too glad of the chance to find fault with the means, and bore her into the house. Mrs. Welman, knowing his antecedents, as indeed she did those of every person of note, warmly thanked him, and accepted his escort home. It was a long time before people knew why Mrs. Welman ceased to countenance the track, or why Anna blushed so deeply whenever her mother would allude to "Mr. — Mr. — I never *can* remember that fellow's name — he that you got up such an amusing scene about, Anna."

That same "*Mr. — Mr. —*," whose name her mother never could think of, would have been a pretty severe thorn in the pride of the Welmans, but for the ridicule which was the sharpest weapon her mother could use against her.

Passion once sated, and McVernon tired of his beautiful wife. Another, younger and fairer, had taken his senses by storm, and he was determined to rid himself of Anna. Here was the chance he had been longing for, and he was too coarse to care for the scandal, too indelicate to heed the wagging of that world's tongue which such an *exposé* would set going.

"Well," said he, as his wife stood calmly before him, "what excuse have you for such conduct, madam?"

"Such as what?" questioned Anna, quietly.

"Such as lying in your lover's arms," retorted he, trying to look as grave as possible, considering his joy at the discovery. "Don't attempt to deny it; don't try to exonerate yourself. I saw it with my own eyes — my own eyes — and you will allow me to believe *them*, I hope."

"And who else saw me?" she questioned.

"Nobody. Wasn't it enough that I should see it? If I had cared any thing about it, I would have murdered the pair of you; but I don't. All I want is a divorce. With such a husband as I am, I don't see how you could take up with that Meadows."

Anna laughed a long, low laugh.

"That's right; that's right; add insult to injury. I was going to portion you off with enough to keep you from starving, for the sake of what the world might say; but now you may whistle for your bread and butter, for all I care."

"You horrible old villain! you detestable old nightmare!" exclaimed Anna, furious with passion.

"Don't stop; go on. Any thing more that's pleasant? You won't have long to rave; and when I'm rid of you I'll marry again; do you hear that? Your detested old nightmare can get your betters, my beauty. Understand that?"

"Yes; and when you tire of *her*, you'll *will her to Charlestown bridge!* and if she happens to fall over — *accidentally*, you know — why ——"

McVernon turned pale, then livid, and then, with a loud scream, fell down at his length on the floor. Anna rang the bell, her eyes glistening with ferocious joy, and ordered the servants to convey their master to his room. The usual restoratives were resorted to, and, when consciousness returned, as Anna bent over him with apparently tender solicitude, she murmured in his ear, "Another word about Walter, or the *divorce*, and take the chances of another fainting fit!"

"Mother knew that woman was telling the truth," she muttered to herself, as she went out slowly to receive some visitors.

CHAPTER XVIII.

The Death Struggle. — What the Waves said.

McVernon was a gross man — a selfish man, but not altogether heartless. There were germs in his nature which, had they been cultivated by the hand of kindness, would have made him a true, honest, and solid citizen. Wealth, which has made more bad men than ever poverty accomplished, had done its work of perversion by him. Things which would have stamped another man with scorn were passed over, as far as he was concerned, in view of his enormous wealth. He could do nothing wrong — nothing that wealth could not overshadow. He had lived a bachelor life, heedless, reckless, and unthinking. If there was a true, a generous, or a holy impulse in his nature, it was called out by a foster child that had been left by a dying woman to his care.

This child had grown up under his very eye into wild, untamable, but beautiful womanhood. A very tiger in her fierceness, wayward and wilful, to all but him, there was a fascination in her society which, when sated with city fantasies, always drew him to her presence. She had been carefully brought up by a maiden sister of his, who resided some few miles from Boston. The evening after the *denoue-*

16

ment of the last chapter, a little elfish figure sat gazing out into the shadows of her country home. Her eyes were fierce and bright, and her whole face was darkened by most vehement passion. Anna had been there during the day, and had questioned her regarding her husband. A form broke up her musing, and darkened over the chair whereon she sat. "I am miserable — *miserable*," murmured the strong man, bringing his fist heavily down upon the table. The girl looked up with a fierce, dark smile.

"I wish I had never seen her — I do;" and the sated man of many blessings sank sobbing into a chair.

"*Don't!*" said the girl, rising and laying her hand upon his chair. It was the first time since his marriage that she had approached him kindly. "No one loves me — no one cares for me! I wish I was dead," again burst forth from his livid lips.

"*I love you!*" murmured a soft voice in his ear.

"*You?*"

"*I!*" It was a single word, pronounced with an echo of his own wild vehemence, and he believed it. "Do you think I'm not sorry for you? Do you think I would not bring you back to happiness if I could do it by draining my own heart?"

McVernon opened his wide-spread arms, and folded her closely in his embrace.

"You frighten me!" she exclaimed, "you look so wild."

"Don't shrink from me! Don't be afraid of me — I won't harm you — no, by my soul's salvation. Do you not think it is joy enough for me to hold you on my heart, pure and undefiled as you are, without trying to work your ruin? Do you think it is not enough to hold you in my arms — you that no other man's arms have clasped? O, why didn't I know of this before?"

"No matter; we will never part again!"

"*Girl!*"

"*Never!* To watch over you in sickness; to care for you in sorrow; to sit by you while you slept, — what privileges these would be! No, we'll part no more!"

"O, impossible! You do not know what you are saying."

"I know that you are all the world to me. What do I care, so I am with *you?*"

"You *must* care. I'm not a devil, and only a devil could take advantage of such innocence. No, no, no! You can't be my wife; I will not make you my mistress. Here, Amy!" Before the astonished girl could answer, his sister had responded to his call. She recoiled at sight of her young charge thus passionately folded to her father's heart.

"No words, no words," said he, seeing she was about to speak. "Take her; you'll see no more of me till I am free." A flash of lightning showed his features livid and wild with anguish.

"Go to your room," said the sister, with considerable austerity.

The young girl rose and passed on, but with a flush of haughty insolence on her face which defied her frown. A few more minutes and McVernon, with great, hasty strides, was making for the river, which lay like a belt of gold between the town and city. The storm had been rising unperceived by the inmates of the house, and now raged with unbounded fury. The trees writhed and groaned as if in mortal agony; the river, usually so calm and placid, was white with foam, while the waves leaped up upon the high rocks to bound back again with a sudden crash into the arms of the stream. One moment the whole heavens seemed lurid with flame; the next, the darkness was so intolerable that it was positively alarming. On and on strode the heedless man, now stumbling in the darkness, and anon closing his eyes to shut out the horrible glare. Moored among the alders, a little boat creaked and trembled above the maddened waters. None but a madman would attempt to cross the river in such a shell upon such a night. McVernon, now more of a man than he had ever been, was flying from the only danger he could comprehend — the danger, in his own ungovernable passion, of wronging the innocent girl who had given him her pure heart. He would die first. He was only a man, after all — a man that had never stopped for the still small voice of conscience, where there lay before him any thing which could subserve his pleasure. Why should he now, when her soft arms were round his neck — when her warm lips were firing his blood? No! He had guarded her as something holy in its heavenly purity; as something like a saving clause in his life of excesses and abuses. O, how galling now were the hateful chains that bound him to another! — that other that had never loved him, that held him now by a bond of crime. This thought sent a chill over his frame, and he strode on faster than ever, as if to outwalk some horrible haunting memory. This passed, and the image of his beautiful charge came up again in its stead — her passion and her pity, her impulse and her wildness. He could feel her clinging arms as no other arms had ever encircled him — as no arms could ever encircle him again. It was thus that he desired to be loved — 'twas thus he wished to die. His step was wavering — wavering with a resolution half passion, half despair, when a flash of light showed him his boat dancing upon the foaming waves. Was it fancy — that strange, white figure sitting watchful in the stern of the boat? He would not believe it. He stopped to gaze again. There it was — calm, pale, serene; with its long curls drifting on the wind — a human being. It looked up with a loving, resolute smile, and made way for him to take his seat beside her.

"I *will* go with you." It was his loving, reckless charge, who had left the house before him, and sought the river as the way he would return.

"But the tempest ——"

"*No matter!*"

"The swollen river!"

"No matter!"

"The boat might swamp ——"

"I should be with *you*."

He caught her in his arms, and held her in his passionate embrace. A moment more, and the fragile boat shot out into the river, and cut its way through the drifting foam. The storm which had been gathering all the evening now encircled them with redoubled fury.

"You are not frightened?"

"*Frightened!*"

She laid one soft hand upon his shoulder, taking care to leave his arms free to ply the oars. Her face was sublime in its trusting, determined confidence.

"My God! what is this?" exclaimed the startled man, as a low, whizzing sound caught his ear.

"*The boat has sprung a-leak.*"

It was true. A board had become loose, and in the wrenching of the waves it had given way altogether. The water was pouring in — a rushing stream! Another moment the boat would sink from under them. What was to be done? There was no time for thought. McVernon was only a tolerable swimmer, and a long sheet of water lay between him and the land. It was a fearful moment — a moment of strange, wild horror. It was *only* a moment. With the return of self-possession he threw off his clothes, and as the boat went down with a sucking, whizzing sound, he caught the fearless girl in his arms, threw her across his neck, and struck boldly out into the water.

"Hold firm — don't fear!"

The clasp of her soft hands gave him the strength of madness. He would save her — *he would!* Already the countless lights glimmered before him from the city. A few minutes more, and the shore would be gained.

Courage, courage! Fainter and fainter grow the efforts of the toiling man, while the elfin girl loosens her clasp, and endeavors to aid him.

"See, we are almost there."

The voice, the words reassure him, and once more he vigorously battles with the waves.

Fiercer and fiercer howls the storm, while the pitiless rain falls cold and slant upon the daring pair.

Bravo! Another determined effort, and the shore is won.

She folds him more lovingly — womanlike, rains kisses upon his sea-wet hair — encourages him by soft, fond words.

He hears them, he comprehends their meaning, and his eye brightens with joy, although the water shuts them from her gaze.

Bear up — strike out! Life or death is in the effort.

He does not hear her now. There is a rumbling, as of a thousand waves, deadening his senses.

Fainter and fainter plash the limbs of that athletic swimmer. He cannot see the shore, nor the city, nor the lights. The waters rush up around his face, and choke him. He makes one more gigantic effort. He feels a cold, wet face lying close to his own, and he remembers the reward to be meted out for his success.

In vain — in vain! He knows that all of life and happiness is over for him in this world; yet even with his last throb, his heart shivers with delicious joy that no other arms can ever encompass the form sinking with him beneath the waves.

And the loving girl comprehends it all! She utters no scream, no moan, but clasps him more closely, and gives voice to a low, soft prayer: "*Forgive us our trespasses!*" so soft, so low, that the moaning wind scarcely carries the echo to the coveted shore.

"*Forgive us our trespasses!*" It is all of that grand, consoling prayer her scattered senses could recollect.

"*Forgive us our trespasses!*" There is a wilder commotion, a deeper gurgling of the waves, and where the swimmers were the next flash of light shows only a dead, heavy calm.

CHAPTER XIX.

Fashionable Dissipation.

The "at home" evening of the fashionable Misses Pinchin, on Mount Vernon Street, was unusually crowded and brilliant. Lawrence, the mesmerist, was the lion of the hour, and rumor had circulated it about that he was to honor the reunion with his presence.

The Misses Pinchin!

By rights I should devote a whole chapter to their account. It was never quite known what their antecedents were. If *their* word was gospel, the blood of English royalty ran in their veins; yet it was sometimes hinted that their family tree was rooted in a train oil store. However, they kept a very fashionable boarding house, for the sake of *company*, being both of them on the shady side of single blessedness; attended to their own household affairs, for the sake of *exercise;* and kept record of every body's sins but their own, for the sake of employment.

The elder sister, Miss Margaretta, (a perversion of the homelier name of Meg,) was a tall, showily dressed, bustling busybody, very energetic, very decided, and very like her model woman, Mrs. Welman. Of course, she was the head and front of the establishment — paid the bills, did the shopping, (*did* the clerks too, so *they* said,) scolded the servants, and found fault generally. Viola, the younger, was a sweet, drooping flower, as her name testified; not less than twenty, nor *over* fifty—in short, a young old maid, who, having forgotten how to grow old gracefully, was constantly creating food for the ridicule of the gay and the pity of the sedate. There was only one thing that Viola could do better than to fall in love, and that was, to fall *out* of it. If her heart had been broken once, it had been a hundred times, until it would seem to those who knew her, that there was no fresh spot to break out in. In every fresh emergency, a piece of poetry, in which the various stages of the disease called love were amply shadowed forth, appeared in the Poet's Corner, addressed "To one who could understand it," though there is a doubt upon my mind whether she understood it *herself* or not. In a romantic mood, greatly to her strong-minded sister's indignation, she had adopted a most lovely and bewitching girl, who, being an orphan, gladly accepted the post of attendant upon this antiquated specimen of juvenility. Her weak point, at this time, was a young and brilliant poet, who graced their "at home, 8," with his fascinating presence; for they certainly did get brilliant people into their *conversaziones*—did the Pinchins! and as Ida, the adopted, was something for a poet's eye to rest on, he was not so much to blame after all, although people did say he rather encouraged this idiosyncracy on the part of his adoring old flame. To see her sentimental looks, and her corkscrew curls! to see her youthful airs and her withered shoulders! Well, he was only mortal, and there was some fun in it, you may be sure! Not that I think that at any time, or under any circumstances, any one person is justified in encouraging a passion they have no intention of sharing; but there are circumstances in which the ludicrous is prominent enough to afford an excuse, and this was one of them.

Ida was a soft, lazy, indolent little beauty, with hazy blue eyes and long, sweeping curls; just the thing to creep into a poet's heart, and make music of its strings.

If she thought any thing at all about her lover's attentions to the antiquated juvenile, which I rather doubt, she took the credit upon her own shoulders, which were round, and plump, and beautiful enough to bear the burden with becoming honor. As I wrote above, this evening was one of unusual expectancy and excitement at the Pinchins' fashionable boarding house. The double parlors were thrown open, the furniture uncovered, while the brilliant chandelier — the Pinchins' especial pride — flung a subdued twilight over the assemblage, quite dreamy in its softness. Curiosity was upon tiptoe to see the wonderful mesmerist, in whose eye lay such mysterious force; and it is only natural to suppose that the female *spirits* were wondering to themselves if it could affect *them*, and, perhaps, not a little curious to try the experiment of mesmeric influence. Let us peep in upon them in our capacity of clairvoyance. It is easy to perceive that there are but few gentlemen present, the conversation goes on in such quiet whispers. One party is formed in a far-off corner, where characters are being discussed and picked to pieces; for where many women congregate, it is impossible to shut out scandal. Miss Margaretta is sitting bolt against the wall, stiff as a poker, in her lemon brocade, ready to make a bolt at the celebrity the moment he enters the room. The poet is busily entertaining his little world by details of newspaper items. He is the reviewer and puff writer general for one of our large publishing houses, and as such feels invested with a lordly degree of interest in authors that *are*, and authors that are to come. Just now he is especially urgent in the cause of a fair lady, just about making her *début* in the literary field. Of course all ears are open to the wonderful details of the forthcoming volume.

"I'm writing it up famously," he whispers, with a nod of his head. "Uncle Tom's Cabin will be distanced altogether; besides, the work itself is a thousand times superior to Uncle Tom. By the by, have you seen my advertisement? *Somebody* will wince under it. It is a great thing to hold the destiny of authorship in the palm of one's hand." And the poet complacently threaded *his* through a mass of reddish hair, which seemed to defy all efforts at smoothness. No one had read the advertisement; so he produced it for their gratification. By that time nearly all the company had gathered around him, Hagar among the number.

He spread the paper before him, once more petted his forehead and hair, and then commenced reading.

"This story is destined to produce an impression upon

the nation, powerful, far-reaching, and permanent. As a novel merely, it equals in interest the most brilliant fictions of modern times. But it is chiefly in relation to the institution of southern slavery that the book will awaken the deepest interest. The thrilling incidents to which this anomalous institution gives rise, by interweaving the destiny of master and slave in the same web of fate, are represented with wonderful vividness. A calm, inflexible adherence to truth marks every page."

"Arn't you cutting it rather fat for a new beginner?" broke in one of the listeners.

"Don't interrupt me. You haven't got to the joke of it yet," answered the reader.

"Yes; let him go on. If there is any joke about Wimple, let's have it," laughed Ida.

"Nothing of the blue fire of melodrama is seen; nor is the deepest tragedy marred by the *screech* and contortions of a second-rate actress."

"Ha, ha, ha! Do you take? I can imagine how *somebody* will wince over that." And he folded the paper, as self-elated as if he had raised the one and crushed the other by the wave of his pen.

"And will your publishing house sell one more novel for that slur upon a woman, who, if not reaching your range of intellect, at least meets the wants and desires of the average mass?"

It was Hagar that had spoken, and now bent her calm eyes upon him for an answer.

"Sell! Why, no; it won't sell any more copies, that I know of; but it will make some sport, and annoy another writer," answered Wimple, his eyes brimming over with mirth, as if there never was and never would be any thing so funny again.

"But why should you desire to annoy her? Has she ever injured *you?*"

"No; but one must have some fun in the world."

"And this that you call fun is one of those incidents which make those they are aimed at lose all confidence in the kindliness of human nature. Suppose, now, that an accumulation of annoyances had made her especially sensitive just at the time you were penning that article, and that on reading it she had grown dispirited enough to think seriously of self-destruction?"

"I should say she was a bigger fool than I ever took her to be," he answered, laughing.

"I was with her, Wimple, when that notice was sent her. She had been ill and depressed all day; and when she read *that* — so unnecessary — so unfeeling — I trust never again to see a person so utterly reckless and depressed as she was. O, believe me, 'truth is stranger than fiction;' and these little heedless stings do more to break up the heart's love of life than do all the great events which call forth strength to meet them."

"How seriously you take it, Hagar! I didn't mean to injure any one especially."

"I know you didn't; and that is why I speak of it, that

you may restrain your hand when again tempted to do a similar act. What sent the recent suicide, Anna McLain, out of the world, think you, but an accumulation of just such petty annoyances as this? I don't approve of it, mind you, or think that any thing could make me do so rash an act; but there are few of us, I think, that, at one time or another, do not, in contemplation of perverted human nature, ask 'if this be all of life, and nought beyond, O earth!' But what a solemn-looking crowd we are, to be sure! It is all your doings, Wimple. I hope you feel the better for it, for I am afraid none of the rest of us do."

"Hagar, you have read me a lecture that I shall remember to the longest day of my life. I never thought of these things so seriously."

"Come, stir about. Let's shake off this solemnity. We'll install Hagar preacher yet."

But what gush of melody is it that rings out through the hall? and what vision of brightness frames itself in the door?

"Ha, ha! ha, ha, ha! How terribly proper you all are! What's the matter, eh? I should think it was a church, and you all doing penance for your sins."

"No. Only Wimple's got any sins to answer for in this crowd. Eh, Wimple?"

"O, you go to grass, will you?" grunts the poet, in a very unpoetic humor.

"Ha, ha! But what does ail you, eh? and where's the lion? I want to see the lion. I've got myself up at tremendous expense, all for to see the lion. Ah, Western, is that you? How are you, Western? — and how am I looking, eh? Shall I take down the lion?"

O Lizzie! O, bright, saucy, bewildering Lizzie! O, mischievous, merry-hearted, tormenting Lizzie! O, Lizzie of the ringing tone and loving heart! looking so innocent of intention, yet laughing, in those flowing sleeves of yours, to see the wincing of poor Mrs. Western! Was it worth the powder to ruffle the feathers of that jealous, petulant little wife only for mischief's sake? In all that large room, is there nowhere for you to sit but just there, in front of Western, where, every time your laughing brown eyes fly out, they must rest upon *his* face? O, bewitching, beautiful Lizzie! if all the women you torment, and all the wives you tease, knew just how many straws you care for admiration, unless coming from the one legitimate quarter, it would save them an immense deal of bitterness in their cup, and an immense number of thorns on their seat, while you are about with your pretty little ways. O Lizzie! with all your frivolity, you are one of the human books whose leaves are worth learning by heart. But here comes a raft of visitors — Ellen Willard, Mr. Veazie, Walter Meadows. Ah, bright Lizzie! you may well leave Mrs. Western in peaceful possession, and fly off after *him*. He is one of your sort — knows just what you mean, and takes your little coquetries for just what they mean, and that is — *nothing*. I should like to describe Walter Meadows — he being, in a manner, the hero of my story, if he would only stay just long enough for the operation. Without being that despicable thing, a male flirt, he was the most popular man imaginable among the opposite sex. Bright, witty, and keen — full of fun and anecdote — ever ready to do his share in the way of amusement — there was no party or social gathering voted complete without him. With an ordinary degree of personal vanity, he was still a man with whom a woman could dance, laugh, chat, walk, or perform any other familiarity in reason without the fear of being misunderstood, or immediately besieged with a desperate tender of inordinate affection. Handsome he was, too, beyond the usual standard of manly beauty. In fact, those who knew him best asserted that he had a narrow escape from being that horror of society, a *pretty man*. His form, scarcely above the medium height, was rounded in the most perfect mould of artistic grace. His hands and feet were exquisitely small, and bore the same unmistakable marks of Nature's aristocracy. His sunny eyes radiated sunshine; and his expressive face beamed with the genial humor of a happy, noble heart. And noble he was, beyond all precedent. He might be influenced wrongfully by the force of circumstances, for he was sensitive to a high degree; but his heart was in the right place, and no circumstances could long pervert *that*. He was a man that no woman with an artist's eye could pass in the street without turning for a second glance; and he was also one whom no woman could know without instinctively recognizing his claim to confidence and gentlemanly consideration. His refined taste for elegant surroundings, his genial, laughter-loving spirit, and more than all, his open and avowed scorn for what was in the least mean or sordid, rendered him as great a favorite with his own sex as he was with the opposite. And yet, with enough to spoil a pretty sensible man, he had not the least particle of vanity or of self-conceit in his nature. He dazzled without being conscious of it — pleased without effort at effect. His careless, graceful demeanor had a *home* sensation in it which placed every one coming under its influence quite at ease. If there was a stratum of deeper thought, or of wilder power, embedded in his nature, his genuine *sunny side* kept it in shadow. He looked upon the world as it was, rather than as it ought to be — marred by inconsistencies and caprices, yet possessing a bright face for all who choose to look for it. Until of late, his sensations had nearly all been happy ones. To desire, with him, was to have; and that his successes had not made him a coxcomb, was attributable as much to the solid and sterling merit of his nature as to the purity and halo encircling the existence of a first, a true, and an only love. Lizzie Linder had known Walter from childhood, and fully appreciated the nobleness of spirit which a thorough acquaintance so fully disclosed. She knew, though few there were to credit it, that strong and powerful feelings were slumbering beneath a peaceful exterior; and this evening her unerring judgment told her that the dash, the glow, and the sparkle of an unusually brilliant conversation, with which he amused the company, was but a mask which he did not choose the careless eye should penetrate. She had, two or three times, perceived that suffering, care-worn look supersede his joyous gayety; and caring little for conventional reserve, and less for the surmises of the company, she folded her little hand over his arm, and led him out on the balcony.

"Walter," she began, when out of hearing of the crowd; "something ails you, Walter. What is it?"

The question coming from any other quarter would have been met with indignant repulse. But Lizzie — she was an exception every where. Her frank, honest ingenuousness paved her way to immense popularity. Hers was one of those earnest, honest hearts so seldom to be met with, yet so greatly to be revered. There was no impertinence in the open, direct question addressed to Walter, and nothing but the sincerest sympathy in the bright, earnest face upturned for an answer. He tried to shake off the anxious, uneasy expression of suffering, and turn her surmises into ridicule; but there was such an honesty of purpose in her eyes that he could not resist their eloquence.

"Lizzie, I *am* unhappy — miserable. I won't deny it to *you*. But I *am*, and that's a fact."

"What is the matter? Perhaps it's not so bad, after all."

"Bad! Isn't it, though? The fact is, I — I'm not well pleased with Hagar lately. She has turned out different from what I had a right to expect."

"Hagar has been unfortunate, Walter — *very* unfortunate," replied Lizzie, hesitating, as if she was treading on dangerous ground. "But, Walter, it is not for us to say how much of sin there has been in her misfortune. There have been clouds for her, and storms, Walter, such as we know nothing about; and her struggles for the right will redeem her in a mightier eye than ours. I think, if we could have more sympathy — we *women*, I mean — with the unfortunate of our sex, we should appear better in the sight of *Him* who, with all his purity, was not too pure to lend a helping hand, and speak a kindly word, to one who had fallen from her high station amongst those about her. Indeed, Walter, Hagar is a noble woman, 'obscure her excess of glory' as they may. She is worthy even of your love, and that's saying a good deal."

For a moment Lizzie seemed wrapped in her own meditations, and Walter looked in her face, to read there any revelation the bright features chose to make.

The exposition had come upon him so suddenly, was so unlooked for, that he was not prepared to read its knowledge in the faces of those about him. He had forgotten that "ill news flies fast."

"There is no use mincing matters," Lizzie began, again, in a hasty, nervous manner. "Under other circumstances, or to another person, I might have blushed to revert to acts of criminality for which the world has chosen its especial method of retribution. But you are, both of you, dear friends of mine; you both love and are worthy of each other; and you both are struggling with thoughts and intentions, which, if carried out, will ring the death knell to happiness! It mustn't be, Walter! indeed, it mustn't! You must dare the world's sneer, and show yourself above the pool of little prejudices which ingulf so many hearts."

"But it is the hypocrisy, Lizzie! Think of her, in all these years living a lie."

"*Walter!*" It was only a simple word, spoken in a grieved and simple tone; but the blaze of indignation died away before it, and left a sad, thoughtful expression in its stead.

"What could she do otherwise, and retain the least foothold upon that hill she was striving so hard to ascend."

"True, true, Lizzie! If the bitter censors could only hear *you* talk! I wish they could for Hagar's sake."

"Now you are like your own manly self, Walter! When I first heard what you have so recently learned, like the generality of my sex, my *woman's* nature rose in arms against her. I couldn't imagine an excuse for such a degradation. Because I was strong I thought no one else need be weak; and that's the way we all judge, Walter; how rightfully, we shall never know this side of eternity. Well, as I was saying, I too shrunk from her, and passed by upon the other side. I may as well own up to the entire truth while I am about it. It was before I was married, you know — when Hagar first moved to the city — you know she was always popular with your sex; and, somehow, her self-possession, her calmness, her impatient endurance of gentlemanly courtesy and attention, fascinated Linder."

"Jealous — eh, Lizzie?"

"Yes, that was it! I'm glad to see you smile, though it is at my expense. Yes, I was jealous! ferociously so, I can tell you; and so I watched Linder, yielding and yielding, while each step drew him farther from me. I felt as I suppose other women do under such circumstances — that I could kill her if there was no law against murder. Well, to make a long story short, Anna Welman (she was then) saw it all, and, I dare say, enjoyed my misery as much as I supposed she sympathized with my suffering. Thinking, perhaps, that I would then and there confront her, she told me the story. How *she* got hold of it, is more than I can divine; but she did, somewhere, and you may be sure I was horror-struck. Much as I supposed I had reason to dislike her, I was loath to believe her all that Anna insinuated. For the first time in my life I began to reflect. This, then, was the cause of all Hagar's coldness and disdain; this the reason why she so imperatively shut herself from the society of those who would have been proud to recognize her."

"What are you and Lizzie doing all this time, out there in the balcony?" sang out a voice from the party.

"What is that to you?" was her saucy answer.

"Am I tiring you?" she questioned of Walter.

"No! go on!"

"Walter, I had to watch *myself* from that time, as much as I did her; and I fully believe, had I seen Hagar encouraging Linder by a single look, or felt that, in the least, she endeavored to estrange his heart from me, I should have exposed her, and crushed her back into the horrible gulf of infamy from which she had so nobly saved herself."

"Do let *us* have some of that privacy," again called out the voice from within.

"You go to grass! I'm coming in a moment."

"Well," said Walter.

"I don't know *how* I felt when I next came face to face with Hagar. I believe I flushed up, and grew pale again, as if I, instead of she, had been the aggressor. I only remember turning suddenly away, that she might believe I did not see the hand extended for its friendly clasp. I was ashamed that I had ever been jealous of one like her; and yet I couldn't help it. About that time, Linder, I heard, offered himself, and was refused. The same night I met Hagar in the street, and she looked so depressed, so full of care and woe-begone, that I forgot every thing but her suffering. 'If ever you want a *true* friend,' said I, 'come to me. Nothing can make me love you less than I do!' '*Nothing*,' said she, in her low, pitiful voice, and I could see the tears struggling into her eyes! '*Nothing*,' said I, emphasizing the word to its fullest extent. I'm sure she understood me, for she gave me a glance so full of gratitude that if at that moment the time had come to separate from her, and cast her off, or abide with her and share her disgrace, I should have chosen the latter. It might have been wrong for me in the eyes of the world; but I should have been happier for the approval of my own conscience, and you know I don't greatly fear any thing else."

Walter pressed the little hand lying upon his arm with fervent warmth, while she went on.

"From that time, Walter, I watched her with admiration. If there had been any tampering with duty, any swerving from the most discreet path of honor, any specious reasonings, calculated to pervert the minds she taught, any attempt to reconcile wrong with right, I must have shuddered away from her, even if I had kept my reason from all but myself."

"But, Lizzie, it is the hypocrisy I despise; plotting and scheming through all these long years to save herself from the contempt of the good."

"*Walter, what could she do? You,* at least, should have charity for her!"

"She should have had courage; courage to face the punishment of the crime she had found courage to commit. Courage at all hazards!"

"And what would have been the result?"

Walter was silent.

"What would have been the result, even of her having told *you?* Walter, you know that out of the world she has never loved mortal but you. She was crazy — insane when she heard of your purposed marriage. You cannot understand the kind of insanity I mean. Nobody but a woman can understand a woman's grief to imagine the form she loves in the arms of a rival. Like maternal anguish, there is nothing which can be compared to it."

"But why need she keep up the deception? That man is in town — in communication with her now."

"I don't believe it!"

"I have seen him; and more than that, she has appointed a meeting with him."

"I don't believe it," exclaimed Lizzie, with a petulant stamp.

"Here is the letter, containing the request."

Walter produced the letter from his pocket. Lizzie read it attentively and curiously.

"I've seen that writing before. Walter, there is some confounded plotting going on here. This is Anna McVernon's work. Hark! they are calling for us again in the parlor. If Hagar is there, treat her kindly for my sake. She has suffered a great deal more for you than you know of."

"This is the night of the appointment."

"At nine o'clock," said Lizzie, consulting first the letter, and then her little French watch, which hung among other trinkets at her side. "Nine o'clock, and it is now half past eight."

Another call from the parlor, and the sound of approaching footsteps brokē up their consultation.

"What a fiend that Anna McVernon is!" thought Lizzie, as they retraced their steps to the parlor. The company had increased. The lion had come; and there was a very general excitement afloat in consequence of his presence, when Lizzie, like a fresh sunbeam, entered the parlor.

"Here she is," sang out half a dozen voices at once, including Mr. Western. Poor fellow! he could get only a scolding, any how, when he returned; and he thought he might as well be hung for an old sheep as a lamb. Consequently his admiration points were rather luminous during the evening.

"Well, you are not so very formidable, I'm sure," said Lizzie, turning up her saucy, bright face into that of the mesmerizer's. "I'm not afraid of you. Mesmerize *me!*"

It was no place for dignity, or propriety, or conventional manners where Lizzie Linder was. So, in a very short time, the whole party felt as much at home as if they had met on those familiar terms for years. Among other changes which troubled Lizzie exceedingly, was that in the character of Ellen Willard. From the rackety, almost hoidenish girl, she had settled down into the sedate, thoughtful woman. Lawrence had assumed unbounded influence over her. She had become one of his most apt subjects; and, although Mr. Veazie, and in fact all her friends, opposed it, she seemed of a sudden to possess a most indomitable will, which would brook no restraint. It was the triumph of mind over mind; a proof that mesmerism, if not a science, was at least an existence, and a power capable of enormous abuse, if in the nature of a bad man. Strong, powerful character had always possessed unusual fascination for Ellen, and she had often been irresistibly drawn towards her dark, stern guardian by this influence. It was a singular fact, too, that in the absence of Lawrence, her spirits would acquire very nearly their old healthful tone, and she would endeavor to make amends to her guardian for any dereliction from the duty she owed him. She had possessed herself of the secret of Lawrence — knew she had already claims upon his affection which could not be overlooked, and consequently never dreamed of him but in the way of friendship. Veazie had grown more indulgent, as he saw the gradual declension of his power, and more affectionate as he believed her entirely indifferent to him. But Lizzie, she was a regular little plotter, if any good was to come of plotting; and she had already a kink in that curly little head of hers to put a spoke in the wheel of Mr. Lawrence. The serpent glance of his eye fell harmless upon her heedless heart, and he might exhaust his mental resources without opening her eyes a fraction wider for his superior eloquence. Eloquence was no novelty in the history of Lizzie. It was her element. She took to it as naturally as lambs to clover. She had kept the company of superior men from her earliest girlhood, and was rather proud, if any thing, that nature had gifted her with brilliant qualities of conversation, as well as person. There was food for her keen, provoking little ways in the different characters met together on that evening. Viola usually dreaded her approach, for the queer way she had of making her feel uncomfortable; but this evening there was too much serviceable work to be done, to allow a thought for the silly, infatuated old maid. She saw

Hagar leaving the room with a hurried, frightened face, just as herself and Walter entered at an opposite door. She missed *him* a few minutes after, and feeling conscious of his errand, she was abstracted, absent-minded, and any thing *but* Lizzie Linder, till his return. He came in a shade paler than usual, but his laugh rang out more musical than ever. Very soon Hagar returned, and joining Anna McVernon, passed out into another room. The eyes of Lizzie and Walter met — his so bright and fierce, hers so deprecating and pitiful. To change the current of thought, Lizzie proposed going to the music room. It was at that hour in the evening of a fashionable party when wines have done their work in the way of unlocking tongues and hearts. Miss Margaretta talked louder and more peremptory than ever. Viola clung to her idol's *other* arm with sickly sentimentality. Ida, lazy and tired of every thing and every body, (apparently) remained behind, half asleep upon the lounge. But there were a pair of bewildering black eyes, which not all her efforts could shut out from her thoughts. And so the music swells out in rich, harmonious gushes, for Lizzie is an accomplished singer, and she was the musician for the time. Song after song is sung; some sweetly sentimental, some hilarious and wild. Now and then the old, cracked voice of Viola breaks out in chorus, a good deal out of tune, and quite out of words, giving droll little Lizzie a chance to say something funny; something to make Viola grow red and hot, and make the rest of the company to laugh, all but Miss Margaretta, who, having drank wine enough to be sociable, comprehends that there is a meaning in the jokes, which makes her glare at Lizzie with her great, hard eyes; and, walking boldly up to the piano, she stands behind Lizzie's chair, as if to defy her to turn *her* into ridicule. But Lizzie only looks saucily up at the waving plume which decorates her dressy head gear, and bids her look out for the gas light, and not set herself afire; upon which her honor gives a sort of a snort, which sends the feather vibrating, as in a sudden breeze, and marches off to hold converse with Mrs. Welman, under the shadow of the window curtain. Again music drifts up from the heart of the beautiful woman who presides at the piano. "Then you'll remember me," is the song which seems speaking to the multitude, so sadly is it given. It was Walter's favorite song. The evening was warm, and he stood leaning against the doorway leading to the garden. Hagar sat in the embrazure of the window, so near to him that the passing breeze brushed her drapery against his form, but he knew it not. *That song!* All the evening he had been trying to bear, unshaken, the sorrows which seemed piling themselves around him. But as the last cadence of that song died away in echo, a sudden vision of all he had loved in the past, of all he had hoped for in the future, rushed over him in a flood of bitter memory. In that moment of anguish his hand was suddenly clasped with wild vehemence, and Hagar stood weeping by his side.

"Do remember me, DO love, DO pity me," she murmured, through her passionate tears.

The impulse was to clasp her to his heart, and hold her there in spite of fate or any other power that sought to part them; but the revulsion came, and he tore her hands apart and flung them petulantly away.

"Don't be such a cursed actress," he murmured, passing away from her to another part of the room. That moment of passionate grief only Lizzie saw, and her heart bled for them both.

"Command yourself," said she, gathering her arm around Hagar, and taking her into the shadow where no one could see her suffering.

An addition to the company, in the form of editors, artists, and other *late birds*, gave her an opportunity to compose herself before the persons present noticed her excitement. She was not left long in her retirement; for, although she was no flirt, she was very popular with the class of persons comprising the literati of Boston.

Once more all was enjoyment and hilarity. The brilliancy of Hagar's nature stood her wonderfully in hand on this occasion. "*Command herself!*" She followed the counsel bravely. She laughed with the gayest, jested with the wittiest, and argued with the wisest, till even Walter began to think that a woman like her was worth the wearing, even though circumstances so much to be regretted had overclouded her life.

In the very midst of a *fi-yi-yah* chorus, which had been given with more regard to mirth than to music, a shrill scream started the party to their feet, and sent them off on an exploring expedition to the room from whence the sound proceeded. A scene met their gaze so pitiful and yet so ludicrous, that but for hospitality's sake I fear the guests would have indulged in a laugh quite as hearty as any one that had scared the echoes that evening. In the arms of Wimple, poor old Viola lay in a deep swoon. It seemed, from the confessions of the crestfallen, that, missing Ida, he had wandered off in quest of her. Seeing some one lying asleep on the sofa, and supposing, in the dark, that it was she, he had gathered her up by his side, and in all human probability had told his love in rather more vehement terms than came within the limit of maiden modesty, though not quite fancy free. He denies the imputation, however, to this day, and stoutly affirms, if there was any aggressor in the case, it was herself. Ida is satisfied that he neither committed any indiscretion of sufficient weight to make a butterfly faint, or, what's more, had any intentions in that quarter that were not the most strictly honorable. However, he bears the weight of the joke very good humoredly, and has his own ideas of love-making in the dark. Of course the *contretemps* broke up the party; but from certain loud laughs which startled the sleepers from their dreams, as the male portion of the company threaded the deserted streets, the presumption is, that a pretty considerable of a *roasting* was going on among them.

CHAPTER XX.

THE POET'S CAPTURE. — HAGAR.

"Now, that is very pretty," said lazy little Ida, as she sat in her favorite attitude by Wimple's feet, with her arms supporting a book upon his knees.

"What's pretty, Ida? Those pictures are all horrid nuisances to me!" he replied. "What's pretty?"

"This cottage furniture, and this pretty French bedstead."

"We will have one like it when we are married," he answered, while a roguish smile played about his lips, in which there was a tinge of mischief.

"So we will!" exclaimed Ida, quite innocently.

Wimple flung the book to the farthest corner of the room, saying, —

"Well, you are the most unaccountable girl I ever did see! Do you know I've said something impertinent to you? Do you know you ought to blush and look annoyed? Why, any other girl would have boxed my ears soundly, and have served me right."

"Would they?"

"*Would they?* Of course they would."

"What for?" she innocently asked.

This was a poser for Wimple. Ida was too thoroughly indolent; so perpetually calm, and so beyond or beneath a sensation of any kind, that he was beginning to feel a little doubt about her capability of loving. Her very calmness had amused him at first, and her quietude had been the oil to still the waves of his more tempestuous nature. This apathy had provoked Lawrence to try his skill upon her; but he was equally a failure, for when he would imagine her safe in a mesmeric trance, a nearer examination would find her dozing off into a natural sleep. To Wimple's interrogations as to the state of her affections, she would invariably answer, "I love you better than I love any body else." Sometimes this honest declaration would satisfy him, but of late he was beginning to feel as if his nature would require some demonstration more positive than this.

Ida was crossing the room to recover her book, when she caught the glimpse of Lizzie, cantering up alone to the door. Without dismounting, she motioned her out, and called for Wimple to follow her.

"I want the loan of Wimple for an hour or two," said she, laughing and tossing away her curls. "I ordered a horse at the stable, as I came along. Ah, here it comes now."

"But where are you going, Lion?" That was Ida's pet name for the poet.

"O, only out to Burlingame's," Lizzie answered for him. In a moment after, the two were cantering off over the pavement, making it ring again. It was a prerogative of Lizzie's to pick up any of her friends at any time, and press them into her service. She was so generally understood, that even the most inveterate gossip failed to make food for scandal out of any such material.

"I want your aid," said Lizzie to her companion, when they were well out of hearing.

"In what manner?"

"There is a breach between Hagar and Walter, which must be healed. It is all that Anna McVernon's doings. By the by, they say that McVernon has eloped with that adopted daughter of his. They have neither of them been heard of this three days. I don't much blame him, for that wife of his is an awful wretch. She imagines herself to be in love with Walter; as if *she* could be in love with any thing! She knows that in my heart I have sworn to defeat her. It is woman against woman, and you must help me."

"But what am I to do?"

"She has somehow got hold of some secret about Hagar. You know we all have our faults, — too many, I think, to be hard upon the faults of others, — and it seems that a great many years ago, when Hagar was quite a child, in fact — well, I can't tell you. You'll hear of it soon enough, for ill news travels fast. Now, what I want of you is, to keep some trace of her. I have reason to believe there is a place here, no more respectable than it ought to be, where Anna picks up all the disgraceful items going. If you could find out where it is, and outbid her, I have hopes that all will be well — between Walter and Hagar, I mean. Of course, the good opinion of those whose friendship is worth the having, will not be shaken by the rumor about her, for every one knows that Hagar has been before the public for many years immaculate, at least as nearly so as a woman in her position can be. It seems this secret was what kept her from marrying Walter years ago; and gossips, of course, have seen great impropriety in their close intimacy under the circumstances; but if her name has been mixed up with his in all these years, it has never for a moment been associated with that of any other man; and that's more than many of our sex can boast of."

Lizzie laughed her low, sweet laugh, which seemed to say that scandal didn't spoil her appetite.

"You see," she went on, "Hagar is a sort of public property. Men that *were* men would scorn to persecute her; and she takes good care that if women patronize her, it shall be of their own accord. But there are little gadflies, things sent into the world to fill up the chinks and crevices of society, that have no occupation so tasteful to them as that of stinging. It is these which will fatten on the discovery."

In low, earnest conversation they at length reach their destination, and, alighting, they appropriated a parlor, while Wimple ordered one of those capital dinners for which Burlingame's hotel is so famous.

For a long time after they left, Ida wandered restlessly

through the rooms of the Misses Pinchin. It was "take care," and "get out of the way," and "do go to your room," from all quarters. Never before had she felt so alone, so uncared for, so in every body's way. Then she began to miss Wimple, and to blame Lizzie for taking him away; and at last she did what would have rejoiced her poet-lover exceedingly — worked herself up into a desperate fit of jealousy, rang the bell furiously for the servant, and before it could be answered, seized her bonnet, and, in her haste to escape, nearly ran into the open mouth of Miss Margaretta, who was coming up stairs with an inglorious slop pail, — *only for exercise,* — and I should be the last one to doubt it. This fashionable boarding house keeping is a great institution. I tried a spell of it once. Paid enormously for nothing to eat; found the guests in my private store of luxuries *without* my permission, and swapped off a darling little gold repeater with the *elegant landlady* for a galvanized bit of trumpery, — my first and last attempt at *swapping,* — only to be told, when I accused her of the imposition, that she "didn't know the difference between one and the other," — and I don't think she did. Any one wishing to see the elephant can't do better than take a week or so of a fashionable boarding house. In less time than it has taken me to make this digression, Ida had chartered a horse, inquired her route, and put for Brighton, at a gait which would have astonished the owner of the horse. It certainly astonished Wimple and Lizzie, who caught sight of her, footing it down the hill, and for a moment they feared her horse had run away. Not so, however; for, with a pretty piece of management, she brought him quietly up to the door, flung herself from his back and the reins to the hostler, and confronted them with a flushed and angry face, which had the effect of a comic almanac upon Lizzie.

"Well, I *would* laugh if I was you," she retorted. "I won't stand it — *I won't!* You have no business to coax Wimple off in this manner. It is too bad of you. I wonder how you would like it." Wimple tried to put his arm about her. "Let me be; let me be, I say! You are a false, bad man! I'm going home again right away, and if you are not there in half an hour, you'll never see me again!"

And out she bounced, leaving Lizzie convulsed with laughter. The next moment she might have been seen making the same speed towards home which had characterized her coming out, never once looking behind her to see if her injunction had been carried out. If there are any lovers reading my story, I needn't say to them that Wimple wasn't a minute over his half hour behind her, or that from that day he never had occasion to complain of too much calm; for every look he gave any other woman, he had to pay toll of many promises, which, from my experience of human nature, I'm inclined to think was any thing but agreeable. Such quantity of fibs, though very white ones, must have troubled his conscience considerably. However, sometimes he let her have her own head, and say and think just what she pleased; at other times, when his temper was a little crabbed, or when by accident he had got out of bed head foremost, (the wrong way, sages say,) he would take her up so shortly in the curb that only a good crying spell would render her at all comfortable in her gait. This, together with the spoiling she got from other quarters, went near to undo the work of Dame Nature, who had voted at the onset to make her a very lovable, amiable, lazy little item among the steadier items of society.

CHAPTER XXI.

Lizzie the Medium.

"I'll give you up, Hagar, I certainly *will*, if you don't come down off of that high perch of yours, and be a little more reasonable. Come — come down with me into the parlor before the company have time to discuss you. I never saw such a firebrand! You'd keep me in hot water from now till next day after never, if I humored your caprices. Come!"

"*I won't!*"

"Why not, Hagar? I declare you are the wildest, the most inconsistent, the most incomprehensible creature I ever did see; there's no method to *your* madness — I'll take my oath of that. I'm discouraged — I certainly am."

"Why don't you leave me, then? Why don't you go down and amuse the company? I shall be better without you, any how."

"There's gratitude for you now — after all the battles I've fought for you too! I shouldn't think you would treat *me* in this manner. Hagar, indeed I shouldn't."

"Forgive, Lizzie — dear Lizzie! I wonder you don't get discouraged. I should; but you can't think how I suffer!"

"Can't I though! But that's no excuse for shocking the whole company; let alone piercing Walter's arm with that confounded dagger! What the old boy you wear it for I don't see! I should serve you right to have you arrested for carrying concealed weapons;" and Lizzie laughed through her tears; for she had been crying through her anger.

"I was wrong, Lizzie; I know I was! but I couldn't help it. To see him promenading the room with *that woman* on his arm, carrying her shawl and her bouquet; and then to have him smile in my face so audaciously — Lizzie, I *couldn't* help it; you would have done the same under the same circumstance. I didn't think I ever *could* have been so angry with him, and he to take it all so coolly. As for shocking the company, that's nothing new for *me*, you know; I wish I could have shocked *her*. I would have galvanized the triumph out of her by a shock that she wouldn't have forgotten in a hurry. I shall do something horrible some time, I know. I wish Walter wouldn't tempt me so — I get so, *so* angry."

"Angry indeed! It is madness, Hagar — perfect madness. No lunatic ever needed a strait jacket more than you do at such times of frenzy! As for Walter, you can't stir him with your passion any more than you could stir a mountain."

"It is that which exasperates me so."

"His calmness is his great point. Catch *him* in a passion — why, I have known him for years, and never saw him ruffled in the least. I do believe a mine might explode beneath his feet, and not disturb him in the least. And the worst of it is — yet, no! *not* the worst! nothing could be worse than your ungovernable passion — but every inch of ground which you lose by your impetuosity, *that woman*, as you call her, gains. She is free now — handsome, cunning, and shrewd enough to see the points you overlook; and has duplicity enough to make them *tell*. Walter loves you, but you must tame that lion heart of yours before he trusts his to your keeping. Walter dislikes conflicts, and always did, while you — *you* —— "

"Well — I *what?*"

"Why, there is no medium to your temper — that is all. You are frantic in every emotion; extravagant in every impulse; impetuous in every thought. Walter is the boundary of your religion; which is the first error, and the greatest. When there is peace between you, the bliss of paradise would pale before your extravagant joy; but when your wills clash, flint and steel are nothing to the sparks of temper which they fling out. This evening for instance."

"I can't help it."

"You *must* help it, Hagar, or make up your mind to lose Walter altogether."

"Better lose him altogether, Lizzie, than to bear what I bear."

"Well, whose fault is it? Only see the absurdity of the thing! There is hardly a day passes that something does not occur to offend you, and off goes a letter full of bitterness, telling him never to come again. He keeps away, as of course he will, till you send another letter as passionately humble as that was passionately defiant. And then, when he answers it in person, his calm, comfortable *nonchalant* manner enrages you to madness. No wonder he calls you Tempest! you are a tempest — an imbodied storm — and the worst of it is, you are beating your hail-stones in the face of your own destiny."

"You point out the disease minutely enough; why not say something of the remedy?"

"That must lie in your own hands. If you would really think seriously upon the subject, you would see as I do how necessary for your happiness it is that you curb your wild impulses. All the wrath in the world would never impress Walter so much as one gentle word; while it keeps him from your side, and makes you suffer as you are suffering now. O Hagar, if I *could* only break you of this unwomanly habit, there is no sacrifice in the world I would not be willing to make. And people all along have thought you so calm and self-possessed! But it is not what *the people* think; it is your own peace that is at stake. You know, Hagar dear, I'm not one of the counsellors who continually preach the duty we owe to the world; it is the duty we owe to *ourselves*, and to *Him* who gave us tempers to subdue: that's my argument. But we stay talking here, while the company wait and wonder below."

"But, Lizzie, only tell me what to do."

"Do! Why, your own heart, if you consult it aright,

will tell you what to do. For words, give him works. He must *see*, before he believes; but no frenzy of passion ever can convince him. By the by, what were you doing at the judge's this evening?"

"I wanted to ask Walter about that. Anna said he was arrested for some paltry sum, and was detained there till he could get bail."

"Who? Walter?"

"Yes!"

"Ha, ha, ha! That *is* funny. You didn't believe it — you couldn't have been stupid enough to believe it! Well, well, well, well — after *that* nothing will surprise me. Some time — I have not time now — I'll tell you why I asked. There are wheels within wheels sometimes."

"Perhaps you would have had no occasion to find fault with Walter's coldness, had he known the truth of it. All's well that ends well; and if that woman don't find she is 'heaping up wrath against the day of wrath,' I'm mistaken."

"But he had no business purposely to torment me. I should have had more confidence than that in *him*. He don't love me; there's the truth of it. I'm fierce and exacting, I know, but never to *him*."

"I tell you he *does* love; but you must yield obedience to his dictates: you must learn to take his little peculiarities as a matter of course."

"O, yes! look calmly on, and see him smiling up into the face of every woman he meets — give him my exclusive devotedness, while he returns me lukewarm love, or, perhaps, no love at all! If I do, I hope he'll appreciate it — that's all!"

"There — there you go again — flying off at the handle like a hatchet! Now, what is to be done with such a fire-brand? If I hadn't sworn to defeat that woman at the cannon's mouth, hang *me* if I wouldn't let you break your heart your own way; for that will be the end of it after all, I believe!" And Lizzie for a moment ranted up and down the chamber, quite as much in a passion as it was possible for her to be. Her lecture on mildness and sweetness of disposition was so nearly "preaching without practice," that even Hagar took up the cudgel where she had laid it down, and whispered, —

"Whose in a temper now, Lizzie?"

"You are enough to provoke a saint. Any how, it isn't so bad as your jealous fracas just now!"

Hagar's face darkened again with the sad thoughts which crossed her memory; and before she had time to reply, Lizzie had left her to answer some call from the crowd below. Long after the room had been vacated, she sat growing more and more sad over what seemed to her accumulating misery. She knew there was a crisis coming, and she had made up her mind that certainty was better than suspense, though that certainty shut her out from the pale of society. The party at which she had intended to come out boldly with her life's history had been broken up by the sudden death of McVernon. And now weeks had lengthened into months, and Anna was once more on the flood tide of fashionable society. Cautiously she ventured at first, as if feeling her way, then audaciously flashing out with sails full set to catch the breeze of happiness, regardless if beneath her bark went down a high, true heart, love-freighted, into the waves of despair. Most ingenious were the devices by which she contrived to keep Walter by her side. The explanations which she knew must ensue if confidence was once restored, would not only thwart her designs upon Walter's hand, but render her an object of disgust and loathing.

"Once mine," she would say to her fears, "and then it will be my fault if he ever listens to Hagar's reproaches or explanations!" and then she would dreamily count upon the weeks and months which must ensue before it would be prudent, or even decent, to change her weeds for the dazzling garniture of bridehood.

Hagar was taking no note of aught but her own dreary thoughts, till a light crossed her vision, and Walter stood beside her. She had grown wretchedly pale, and her whole manner betokened weariness and languor, as much of body as of spirit. Walter must have noticed it, for he at once took her two thin hands between his own.

"Now *don't* you torment yourself needlessly, Hagar?" he said. She looked up, dolefully enough, into his face. "I'm weary of it, Walter — weary of it all! Weary — O, *so bitterly* weary of struggling for that which I never can gain; weary of this strife, and toil, and misery; weary of watching the crumbling away of *my* kingdom into the possession of another; and I'm not sure that I'm not *most* weary of *myself!*" She withdrew her hands from his clasp, and pressed them upon her burning forehead. The look of fatigue and helplessness by which her words were followed touched a kindly chord in the bosom of the man before her.

"What do you want, Hagar?" he urged, again possessing himself of her truant hand.

"Nothing *now*, Walter! Whatever I may have wanted is nothing to me now! I am weary of it all."

"Weary of *me?*" he questioned.

"I believe I am weary of *life*, Walter! I'm afraid I am! I am afraid it is this sin I'm punished for — or if I'm not weary of that, I *am* of being repulsed and purposely annoyed and insulted. It is nothing new to me to feel that we must part. If *this* did not part us," — and she glanced at his wounded arm, — "something else *would!* It is better as it is — better at least for *her*, and I wish her joy of her success."

"Which *her* do you mean, Hagar?"

"Why, Walter — I loved you before she knew of your existence. It seems to me that I have loved you more years than she has days; at all events, I have felt what it would be to lose you before her fatal beauty tempted you to win it. O Walter, you try me too much — I am weary of the struggle — it is beyond my power of endurance." Her face was again becoming indifferent and abstracted in its expression.

"Hagar, you seem determined to misunderstand me; you are foolishly, *needlessly* jealous of Anna McVernon. If it was not *she*, it would be some one else."

"No, no, *no!* Walter."

"It *would*, Hagar! You love me *too* much; it is not often one has to prefer a charge of this kind, but, Hagar, it is the truth, and nothing but the truth. You are passionately jealous, and ever have been since your impulsive child's heart folded itself over the careless boy who came to your rescue in years agone! Do you remember it?"

"O, do I *not!*" With her quick impulse, she would have flung herself into his arms; but he held her firmly, steadily away from him.

"No love scenes *now*, Hagar! I want to talk with you reasonably. Suppose now we were to marry; what chance of domestic happiness should we have while this restless, jealous state of dissatisfaction lasted? Why, just none at all, Hagar; and I should be crazy to risk it. You might have killed me, Hagar, just now, instead of wounding my arm."

"*O Walter!*" Hagar shuddered, and would have clasped him again, but that she feared a second repulse.

"Well, lay it there," he said, drawing her head upon his shoulder. "But, Hagar, though I neither spoke of nor looked my dissatisfaction, you hurt my heart more than you did my arm. The pain is there yet, telling me that though I love you, I love my own peace of mind and my future comfort better. And yet we might be so happy if you could — if I was *sure* you could — restrain that fearful temper. Try, Hagar, for my sake, for both our sakes — won't you?"

"O, I think nothing would be too hard for me to do if you would speak to me as you do now. Yes, if you would only keep away from that woman ——"

"I cannot, Hagar — at least not now. After what has just happened, people would say you forced me to give her up."

"Why, Walter! do you think what people said would have any influence over me where *your* happiness was concerned?"

"But you are a *woman*, Hagar, and judge these matters with a woman's judgment. A man's heart is naturally too proud to indulge the supposition of its being ruled. It is a weakness, I suppose — a greater one than woman's rashness, I suppose; but so it is. Now, you say you will overcome this impetuosity for my sake. I am going to put you to the proof."

"Speak kindly to me as you do now — only let me feel that I have still a corner in your heart — and I will overcome any evil you object to in my nature. What proof?"

"Anna wants to pass the holidays with you. I wish, to silence blabbing tongues, you would invite her."

Hagar bounded from his arms, and stood erect and firm before him.

"*What!*" she exclaimed.

"Invite Anna to pass the holidays with you."

"O Walter, how cruel you are! — how cool, and calm, and deadly cruel you are! So handsome and so cruel! Who would believe that beneath that earnest, honest face such a mine of cruelty lay! Ask Anna? yes, I *will* ask her; I *will* have her before me, day after day, knowing that I am an obstacle in her way, which she has determined to remove, and which she WILL remove; I will see her day by day engrossing, absorbing, bewildering away from me the life of love, the holy life that God gave me before fate singled me from all the world to kill — *to kill!* O, never fear me; I will ask her, as you desire."

"You will?"

"*I will!*"

"When?"

"To-night."

"That's well. Now smooth your hair, and try for once to believe that I am acting for your future good, and ——"

"*My future good!* Well, go on."

"Come down with me into the hall; act as if nothing unusual had happened."

Hagar obeyed mechanically; bathed her eyes, smoothed her hair, and would have taken his arm; but he held her at arms' length, that he might take a survey of her features.

"You are looking wretchedly ill to-night, Hagar, truly," he murmured, with more than usual fondness.

But the memory of recent disclosures — of the visit to Justice A——'s, which was still unexplained, and of the numberless trials to which she had unconsciously subjected

20

him, stepped between him and the real affection which, after all, still lived for her in his heart. And Hagar went down with Walter to the crowd below. Laughing back defiance to their questioning eyes, she sent out flash after flash of fitful mirth, belying the previous gloom, and gathering about her those who revelled in her power to charm, and who pronounced her the quaintest morsel of oddity and eccentricity extant. Walter scarcely left her side, and for once seemed proud of his position as the lover of one so brilliant. It WAS something of a triumph to be loved exclusively by such a spirit, and to have the world aware of such love. And she, for the time at least, was wildly happy.

"I believe Walter belongs to me for this set."

The low voice broke in upon some very sweet and soothing words; and, looking up from the window where they sat, the form of Anna McVernon stood before them. Hagar's eyes flashed fire, and her lips sprang apart, freighted with some insolent words; but the warning pressure of Walter's hand arrested their utterance.

"You are *not* going, Walter — surely you are not going," she whispered between her closed teeth.

"O, never mind, never mind," laughed Anna. "Fortunately you are not the *only* man present. I can find a substitute, I fancy, unless all the men are prisoners, as you seem to be."

"O, no; I bar that. I don't relinquish *you* so easily." And Walter sprang up, with his light, gay laugh, to join her.

"Go! and, so help me Heaven, I'll never speak to you again!" hissed Hagar, livid with anger.

"No, I won't have it. I won't be the cause of trouble to you, Walter," said Anna, moving away.

"*Trouble!* Not the least. If people will be ridiculous, I don't choose to take the responsibility of it;" and, shaking Hagar off, he was soon engrossed — heart, soul and sense — by his fascinating partner.

"What a pity Hagar will be so jealous!" said Anna, as they moved away. "It makes you look stupid as well as herself."

Anna had touched his weak point; and, by the sudden flush which lit his face, she knew that she had sprung a mine between the two over which he would not care to pass, for that evening at least.

CHAPTER XXII.

THE STRAWBERRY VENDER.

"STRAWBERRIES! straw*berries!* straw*berries!*" The unusual cry proceeded from the lips of a pretty, brown-eyed little girl, whose curly head poised itself first on one side, then on the other, graceful as a bird's, while the brown eyes roved up and down the street, to arrest customers for her luscious merchandise.

"Strawberries! straw*berries!*" It was a sweet, timid voice, which rolled over her lips with protracted melody, causing many a passer-by to turn for a second look at the sweet face, warm from unusual exercise, which shone out through the drifting curls that shadowed it.

"Strawberries! straw*berries!*"

"Here, girl — thing — you strawberry seller!"

The round, sunny face of Ida peered from the window, distorted by most extraordinary grimaces, by which she was endeavoring to gain the attention of the fruit vender.

"Strawberries! strawberries!"

"Here, you girl! Why, you ridiculous little mouse you, are you deaf or blind?" This last remark followed the capture of the girl, which had been made by Ida's hopping out of the low window, and as rapidly hopping back again, upon remembering that her dress consisted only of a petticoat and a loose gown. The galvanic shock which had startled Ida into life had made her the busiest, brightest little creature imaginable. The great disappointment consequent upon the dereliction of her poet had sent Miss Viola Pinchin to a camp meeting for consolation, where she contracted religion and an inflammatory rheumatism, which, between the two, gave her plenty to occupy her mind, without allowing it to rest upon her aggrievances. Sometimes, to be sure, she would sit gazing at Ida with a sort of ludicrous gravity. Ludicrous it must have been; for Ida had a persistent horror of turning the peculiarities of her kind friend into ridicule; yet, under such inspection, and knowing its cause, her little heart would run over with its mirth, and finally explode in a gush of laughter. And very red and angry Viola would become at such times, and quite forgetful of her religion and its teachings. However, these were rare occasions; and, on the whole, the two got along much more nicely together than persons are apt to where one has eclipsed the other in the matter of affection.

"What a noise you are making down there, Ida!" called out Viola from the chamber; "you make me quite nervous." And a bundle of something that looked like burdock leaves and flannel came slowly creeping down the stairs.

Ida was on her knees over the strawberry basket, enjoying to her heart's content the luscious fragrance which drifted up from the fruit.

"They are too good to eat — they are, indeed!" and her

plump little fingers rested one after another upon the tempting fruit. A shadow falling upon the basket started her to her feet. "*Why!* Now just go up stairs this minute! I never saw any thing like such a careless woman; and the doctor expected every minute! Now go, or I'll leave a chink open in the window, and let a draught in on you, now see if I *don't.* After all my care!"

"But what are you doing? and why don't you dress yourself?"

"I'm going to make some tarts for dinner; and I don't dress myself because I'm more comfortable as I am. Now *do* go up stairs, that's an old dear, and I'll make you a flipper, and bring you up a cup of coffee that you can see your face in for clearness."

Whether it was the promise of the coffee or the threat of the draught that had the most effect I'm not prepared to say; but while the little merchant sat astonished over her basket, Ida was toiling up stairs with the almost helpless Viola in her arms.

"Now don't let me see you out of bed again for a month," said the puttering little nurse, putting some warm clothes upon the invalid's feet, and tucking the bed up like a matronly body as she was. It was worth all the medicine in the world — or would have been to a bachelor — to have that soft, sunny face glinting like a sunbeam about the room. Nobody's hands were so soft and cool to the invalid's head; and nobody could arrange the pillows and assist her generally so tenderly and with such unwearied care as did this sweet *foundling*, who had indeed grown to be a foundling to both the old maid Pinchins. By the time she was down stairs again, another person had joined the strawberry girl, who, with an artist's eye for beauty, and a poet's heart for incident, was endeavoring to draw her out and learn something of her history.

"Now do let the little toad alone!" exclaimed Ida, with just the ghost of a pet in her voice. "Put her down, do. She's half crying now with your teasing."

"It's not him at all," replied the little girl. "I was thinking of my mamma. I must make haste home, for she is sick, and *so* white; so please buy my berries, and let me go."

"What's your mother's name?" asked Ida.

"I don't know."

"You don't know! Why, what a Hottentot she must be to bring you up in such ignorance!"

"No, she isn't a Hottentot; she's a washerwoman, and I'm a secret."

"A *what?*"

"A secret, so she says. I don't belong to any body now but one of these days, if I'm good, I'm to be a great lady and have plenty of money to buy candy with, and ride in a big carriage with fourteen horses, and see all the circusts that come along."

"What's a circust, for goodness' sake?"

"Why, didn't you never see one?"

Ida shook her head in astonishment; but the little merchant had mounted her hobby, and her timidity had taken French leave.

"Why, you never see a circust, nor a helephant, nor a rinocerious, nor an ingirubber man, nor a cat with two tails, nor a gianter, nor a ——"

"Why, gracious me, the child's crazy!"

"O, I've seen all of them, and a great many more curiosities; and when I grow up I'm going to larn to ride in the ring with shiny dresses on."

"Mercy on us, to hear the child talk! and did you ever see such a likeness? There, turn up your face so." Ida took the brown little face between her two palms, and held it up to her lover.

"Well, there is a likeness, certainly."

"Why, Anna McVernon's real self couldn't be more like her than this child."

The poet thought for a moment, and then questioned the child more attentively. Nothing was elicited, however, but that she was a secret; so, clearing her basket of berries, they sent her home, promising to call and bring some nice thing to cheer her sick mamma.

I'm sorry to say it, for the sake of romance, but this poet lover of Ida's had a narrow escape from being disgustingly rich. As it was, he had just as much money as he could well get rid of, and was, moreover, pet nephew and heir to a most aristocratic and tonnish elderly lady, who, overlooking his morals and his pockets, took care that neither should ebb very low. It took him a long time to decide in what manner best to break the news of his engagement with a nameless, portionless girl to this stickler for family distinction. But it was done at last; and this morning he had in his pocket an answering letter, demanding him, on pain of her august displeasure, to return at once to safety and her arms. No wonder the poet's brow was clouded. To give up Ida was not to be thought of for a moment; and to offend his aunt smacked so greatly of ingratitude that he shrank from such a step.

"I have it!" he thought at last. "I'll get Ida *up* for the occasion, and take her with me." Nobody could resist Ida that had half a heart; and so *she* should intercede for him in person. Her own winning ways would be excuse enough for his affection, and her beautiful face prove more eloquent than family rank and title, which, after all, were only nonentities in the cup of happiness. Having settled it to his satisfaction, his spirits rose proportionably high. In his mind's eye he already saw his sweet wife domesticated in the old family mansion, like a gentle violet in the shadow of some great tree. Already the tones of her voice were mingling with the rippling fountains that lent their freshness to the conservatory, while little footprints in the garden mould showed what fairy spirit reigned queen of the flowers. His dream was broken by the voice of Ida calling to him from the kitchen.

"Never mind the door," she said; "let it stand open; it will cool the house. Mind that flipper while I pick over the berries," said she, laughingly handing him a knife to turn it. The poet was in too merry a humor not to indulge her fancy.

"Here; put my apron before you, to save your clothes. O, how awkward you men are! let me try it."

With mocking gravity he suffered her to tie her apron about him; and, to complete the picture, he said, he had jocosely fitted Miss Pinchin's turban upon his head, and saddled his nose with her spectacles.

"Now mind the flipper. I'm sure I smell it burning. Come in!" The last part of her speech was addressed to some *outsider* who was knocking at the door.

"Don't let any body in!" exclaimed the (for the nonce) cook, looking very red with his fiery exercise.

"O, it's nobody you care for; the wood man, I guess. Aunt Margaretta said she would send for him. Do come in! That flipper is certainly burning. Why, for mercy's sake *do* come in!"

Out of all patience, Ida jumped up and flung open the door to confront, not the wood man, but an elegant, stately-looking woman, whose manner at that moment suggested the idea of her doing the freezing for all the country round. Without noticing Ida in the least, this grand apparition sailed in, and sank leisurely down into a chair, and as leisurely surveyed the scene through her jewelled eye glass.

"My dear aunt! — Curse the apron! — My dear aunt!"

"I beg your pardon."

The air with which this simple sentence was pronounced

forbade all further familiarity. As for Ida, she had disappeared much in the manner of Gabriel Ravel, and quite as mysteriously.

"The cook, I presume," surmised the frosty lady, indicating with her fan the place where Ida had been seated.

"Dear, bless me! no; the most ridiculous affair!"

"That turban is not the most becoming headdress for a young man."

The turban went into the stove in haste.

"And now I suppose you are ready to go home with me. Such tom-foolery is not what I might expect from you."

"But, aunt, —— "

"No words! If that was 'the gentle, lovable Ida — the soft, delicious Ida,' of your letter, the sooner you are away from her influence the better."

"But, aunt, —— "

"No words, I say! I have been used to obedience. If you choose to remain here and help about the kitchen, well and good. You can't expect me to recognize you."

"If you would only see her —— "

"I think I *have* seen her. A short gown and petticoat may grace a kitchen, but it would be rather a novelty in our parlor, and among our *set*."

The stately lady rose to go.

"But, aunt, —— "

"You will find me at the Revere. There is no occasion for further explanation. You desired me to see your intended; I took you at your word. I have seen her, and must express my unbounded surprise at your choice. However, I trust it is only a passing infatuation, which a little wholesome advice will cure. As I said before, you will find me at the Revere, where I shall expect you immediately."

The stately lady sailed out in the same gorgeous manner that marked her entrance. As the door closed upon her, Ida tumbled sobbing from the closet into her lover's arms.

Of what came of the *escalade* we shall hear all in good time; for the present we can only say of the poet that if he had not loved wisely, he had loved well; and that is more than his class always do.

CHAPTER XIII.

THE JEALOUS WIFE. — THE UNWELCOME SURPRISE.

WHILE storms and calms had alternated, there had been a "terrible tempest in a teapot" at poor, jealous little Mrs. Western's. It seems that, proposing to pass a few days with her relatives in the country, she had left home with her three little ones, her husband seeing her safe off, and out of sight, in the cars. On arriving at a depot about half way to the place of her destination, she had met the party on a visit to *her* in the city. Full of glee at the happy surprise she thought to give her husband, she persuaded the party to return with her, instead of continuing on, as at first intended. Mr. Western happened to be *out* on her return, and what was worse, not being aware of the *treat* in store for him at home, he happened to *remain* out till the sun was up a foot or two the next morning. Mrs. Western was in despair. Every conceivable resort of the rather flighty husband was canvassed in vain. Every club room, every billiard saloon, every restaurant was scoured by scouts of the enemy, in shape of paid emissaries of Mrs. Western; but no truant husband could be found. Her company, feeling themselves *de trop* under the circumstances, took French leave during her absence on an exploring expedition. There was no sleep for Mrs. Western that night. Wardrobes and closets were disgorged of their finery, and trunks packed with their contents. Every movement betokened a desperate determination on the part of Mrs. Western not to give it up so. About breakfast time the unconscious husband let himself in with a night key, and was brought up all standing by the sight which met his astonished eyes.

"So!" exclaimed the aggrieved wife. "So! I've really caught you, at last. I hope you have had a pleasant night of it!"

"Why, Lily——"

"Don't Lily *me*, Mr. Western. You have Lilied me once too often, Mr. Western. I've done with you forever. You can't have *me* and a dozen other women besides, I can tell you." And down went the lid of the trunk with a crash that awoke the baby, and sent him off into a luscious cry.

"You'll let me explain, I suppose?" said Mr. Western, assuming to be particularly indignant at the charges which were hurled thick and heavy at his head.

"There can be no explanation, Mr. Western. Do you suppose if I had been thought at home you would have been absent all night? The least you say for yourself, the better it will be for you."

Mr. Western looked as if he thought she was right. Just then his partner was seen approaching the house. With an uncommon sprightly step he hastened to admit him.

"I was at your house last night looking over the books," he whispered, in an under tone. "You understand. Trouble in the camp up stairs." And with a comical face, he preceded his partner to the parlor.

Mrs. Western was on hand as soon as either of them. He should have no mercy shown him. He should have no chance to hatch up an excuse behind her back. No, indeed. She knew Western too well for that. She had caught him out and out, and he should have the benefit of it, or she was not the Mrs. Western she believed herself.

"Ah, madam," began her husband's partner, as she entered, "you are looking blooming this morning — better than you would have done had you been where Western and I were last night. Eh, Western?"

"There; stop, now, stop!" exclaimed Western, theatrically waving his hand. "She has condemned me without a hearing. I just want her to find out of her own accord."

What a persecuted victim Western did look! But Mrs. Western had seized his partner's hands, and was imploring him to proceed.

"Why, our books got into a devil of a snarl, and we took last night to set them right again. Eh, Western?"

"O, my poor Western! And me abusing you like a pickpocket, and you working all night long."

"You haven't half my constitution, Western. You *show* the effects of your night's labor. Look at *me*. I'm as fresh as lump butter."

Western *did* look at him, but, as it nearly upset his gravity, he turned away again.

"Tompson's people are up this morning about that bankrupt stock. So, get your breakfast, make your toilet, and come down to the store."

"O, you abominable rogue, for getting caught!" exclaimed his fun-loving partner, as he attended him to the door.

If Western had been in *very* bad company, I would not have let him off so easily; but his misdemeanor in this instance consisted in his having met a clique of friends, with whom he passed the night. But Mrs. Western was one of those unfortunate women who think their husbands should have no amusement in which they do not share. If she knew him to go to a theatre, or a concert, even, unattended by her, it was the occasion of at least a day's lecturing and tears. The consequence of this injudicious treatment occasioned numerous deceptions and misrepresentations on his part, which, coming to light sooner or later, bade fair to destroy the last grain of confidence between them. If women would only learn the folly of this ridiculous restriction, the happiness of married life would soon cease to be a jest. To my mind, no man deserves the name who would allow himself to be tied to his wife's apron strings. The more a woman exacts, the less obedience is rendered to her wishes. The very nature of man prompts him to use the freedom of his sex. He cannot find that calm and rest perpetually in his wife's society which she does in his. A woman's passion goes with her love. Let a man be sure of *that*, and he may be sure of her fidelity; but with a man, variety is the charm which leads him into temptation. For my part, I contend that a man's infidelity has no more to do with his love for his wife than it has with affection for its object. I have heard women say, time and time again, "If I could only *catch* my husband, it would be the happiest day of my life." Now, how absurd is such a wish! "What the eyes do not see the heart does not grieve at." The very peccadilloes which, if they were known, would possibly destroy forever domestic happiness, in nine cases out of ten render the perpetrator more gentle, more tender, and more thoughtful for the comforts of the wife which conscience tells him he has wronged. It is only your termagant, shrewish wives who drive their husbands to other women for the associations which they miss at home, who need fear the estrangement of their liege lords, even if they do occasionally stray from the fold. Now, had Mrs. Western learned to *manage* her husband, instead of *forcing* him, she would never have had occasion to mourn over his conjugal delinquencies. And there are more Mrs. Westerns in the world than there are sensible wives, by a long odds. Forbidden fruit is always tempting to masculinity; but let a husband have his full swing, unmolested and unwatched, and the odds are ten to one that he finds his own home the most agreeable shelter after all. That's *my* experience. Those who don't relish its freedom are not obliged to subscribe to it; but take my word for it, there is nothing made by jealous, peevish surveillance, unless it is the assurance of perpetual deceit and insincerity.

Need I say that Mrs. Western is a living reality, having a "local habitation and a name" within the limits of circumspect old Boston? However, no one need fit the saddle to their own backs, unless particularly anxious so to do.

Among the apers of fashionable life, Mrs. Western was a showy, fussy, under-bred woman, whom the chances of fortune, and the benefit of a pretty face, had given a husband of shrewdness enough to pass for rich. Of course, this was enough to gain a passport to the margin of society, though, to the utter discomfiture of *the madam*, it failed to secure for her the countenance of those who deemed education and intellect matters of something more than minor importance. In vain the St. Martins, and the Greys, and the Welmans smiled upon her ostentatious display; while the lip of the haughty, aristocratic Mrs. Miles Scammon curled in disdain. Her diamonds were immaculate, her dress unquestionable, her equipage the envy of the lower million; but there was still an aching void which nothing but the recognition of Mrs. Miles Scammon could fill. She was a constant visitor at the various watering-places, patronizing alternately the Springs, Cape May, Newport, and sometimes condescended to astonish the *parvenus* at Long Island — not "old Long Island's sea-girt shore," but our tiny speck of an island in Boston Harbor. At these places she would flourish largely — talk of her dear friend Mrs. Miles Scammon — display her jewelry, as being selected for her by Mrs. Miles Scammon in Paris — flaunt her costly brocades, as being the exact pattern of those worn by Mrs. Miles Scammon; but, as Moore so beautifully wrote of the broken vase, in the midst of all her glaring finery — the prestige of old time — ignorance and vulgarity would cling round her still. Once, to the horror of Madam Western, and the amusement of her auditors, Mrs. Miles Scammon absolutely did alight at the door of the Ocean House, just as her admirer was descanting upon some lovable trait in her character. Of course Madam Western was seen no more at Newport that season. Mrs. Miles Scammon, however, was well aware of her constant endeavors to reach the altitude of her circle, and as sedulously shook her off, and kept beyond her reach. Her husband, who was really, in all other matters, a sensible man, inherited her desire for plebeian display, and consequently furnished not only the means by which his wife became the laughing stock of the city, but allowed the most lavish expenditure upon household adornment. A pretty cottage in the suburbs of the city not being considered *genteel* enough, it was exchanged for a palatial mansion in a most fashionable street. But Mrs. Miles Scammon frowned alike upon palace and cottage; and, to say the truth, poor little madam was quite losing heart at her ill success in that particular.

Summer had passed, with its out-of-town flitting, and winter had come, with its long evenings. There were costume parties, and *soirées*, and concerts without number;

and as Madam Western had climbed tolerably high in the social scale, she was permitted sometimes to gaze upon her brilliant luminary.

"I wonder that you tolerate that ignorant, vulgar Western!" exclaimed Mrs. Miles Scammon, one evening, to the lady at whose residence they were jointly assembled.

"O, she's a harmless little thing enough! Besides, I don't know what we should do for a scape goat if we were to lose her. Why, she is invaluable. The way in which she breaks the neck of the king's English is curious in the extreme. I should think, while her husband is lavishing his money upon her dress, he would try what a little teaching could do for her. He is quite a presentable gentleman *himself*."

"Of course *that's* not the inducement," laughed Mrs. Scammon.

"Well," replied the lady, "if the truth was known, I'm afraid about all *her* associates are owing to the companionable qualities of her husband. Who in the world would chaperon *her* for herself alone, I should like to know? Ugh! the very idea of hearing her talk gives me the fever and ague. How, in this enlightened age, a woman could grow up in such utter ignorance I can't conceive."

"Their prestige is not a very lofty one, I believe."

"But he is rich; and money covers a multitude of sins."

"It would take something more than money to make *me* recognize them. He is well enough, as you say; but there is scarcely a moment of the time that he is not subjected to her *snappings.* He can't be very manly, or he never would allow it."

"*Allow!* Talk of *allow* to Mrs. Western! Why, she thinks she has done him a lasting favor by allowing *him* to marry herself and her entire family. *Allow!* I like that."

After a few more such remarks, the parties separated, one to recline in superb indifference upon a *fauteuil,* the other to chatter and flirt with the handsome Mr. Western.

CHAPTER XXIV.

A Dramatic Scene, not in the Bill.

"Scenes from the drama!" "Scenes from the drama!" "That will be capital," shouted half a dozen voices at once.

"Well, scenes from the drama be it," lazily drones Mrs. Miles Scammon; "only don't think to drag me into the arrangement."

The evenings had been long and tedious, and almost every style of amusement had been exhausted, when the above happy suggestion gave material for talk as well as active exertion to a little world of pleasure seekers. Mrs. Scammon, at whose house the party was to come off, gave her niece, a bright-eyed little girl of sixteen, *carte blanche* for the preparations.

"Whom shall we invite?" That was the next question of interest to be debated. For once, Mrs. Scammon didn't care, and Madam Western, to her enthusiastic delight, on returning from a ride in her superb carriage, found a card of invitation to the long-yearned-for mansion of Mrs. Miles Scammon.

"Who in thunder is Mrs. Miles Scammon?" abruptly questioned Job Thornton, the uncle of Madam Western on her mother's side. "Derned if I've heard of any thing but Mrs. Miles Scammon since I came home. Can't you vary the tune, and harp upon Mrs. somebody else a bit?"

"How vulgar you are, uncle! You would mortify me to death, if any one should hear you use such low-bred language. Suppose Mrs. Welman should hear you!"

"Mrs. Welman be hanged! Who is *she*, I wonder, to turn up her aristocratic nose at her betters? Mrs. Welman, whose father used to carry parcels for me when I kept the little grocery at the corner; and as for her, many a time I've seen her scrubbing the floor of the old Tremont! I wonder if she remembers it."

"Why, uncle, how can you talk so absurd! They lead the ton now, and bygones ought to be bygones."

"*You* may well say that, niece. I dare say now, you don't remember when you used to pick up shavings and sell them to the highest bidder. *I do!*"

"Uncle! uncle! I never *did — never!* What would Mrs. Miles Scammon say!"

"Mrs. Miles Scammon again! You must eat, drink, and sleep with the fear of Mrs. Miles Scammon before your eyes. If this is what you call being fashionable, thank my precious stars, there's no danger of my catching the disease."

"Mr. Western," said the amiable niece a few hours after, "we must get rid of uncle Job, by hook or by crook. He'd ruin us, if Mrs. Miles Scammon was to see him."

Mr. Western, being quite as much gratified at the invitation of the aristocrat, although showing it less boisterously, fully concurred with her in the expediency of giving their whole-hearted, but rather rough, uncle a gentle hint to find quarters elsewhere.

"O, certainly," said he, when the intimation was made, "certainly. I only hope you will find happiness enough in your high-flown life to make amends for the loss of a sound heart. You're a clever boy, Western, only a trifle too much led by the nose for an independent man; but you are a good boy, and if ever you want help, — the best of us *may* fall, you know, — remember old uncle Job has a little pile of California, which is at your service."

For a moment there was a dewiness about the old man's eyes, but when Western looked again it was gone. It was something more than the formal clasp of fashion with which he grasped the horny hand of his uncle.

"No, don't go, uncle Job; don't go. Something tells me I may want a true friend yet. *I'm* not ashamed of you, *hard* as you look. Stay with us, and let wife pout if she will. I can afford to be snubbed for such an honest friend as *you*."

"No, boy, no! I should only be in the way here. Besides, I feel like a cat in a strange garret, any how, among your crincums and your crancums, and your Mrs. Miles Scammons. No! I'm content as it is. You will always know where to find me."

With another clasp of the hand the old man departed, muttering to himself, —

"This comes of being fashionable. As good a boy

spoiled as ever came from the hand of God. O fashion! fashion! you have much to answer for."

The night of the party came, and at an early hour carriages landed their freights of beauty at the dwelling of Mrs. Scammon. Probably there never was a greater collection of youth and beauty at any one party in Boston. Mrs. Scammon was more than ever superb in a black velvet dress, studded with diamonds. Mrs. Welman was among the *wall flowers*, stiff with brocade. Anna McVernon, Hagar, and Walter Meadows were there in characters, they having been coaxed into the arrangement by Mrs. Scammon, who was a stanch patron of Hagar's. At a late hour, before the scenes commenced, however, Madam Western arrived, loaded down with finery. All the colors of the rainbow were blended in her drapery, and more diamonds sparkled about her person than could be found on all the other dresses present. Not even the courtesy of hostess could *quite* prevent Mrs. Scammon from indulging in a quiet smile at her expense.

The rise of the curtain in an alcove attracted general attention, and a series of paintings were represented by the active participants of the scene. First came "Ivanhoe and Rebecca." The Rebecca was represented by Ida, whose great dark eyes and long black curls corresponded gloriously with the picturesque costume. Of course, her poet lover was the Ivanhoe. She would agree to no other arrangement, although it was suggested that Michael

Lawrence would better *look* the character. Next came Falstaff and sweet Mistress Page, giving the crowd something to laugh at as well as admire. Then came "Romeo and Juliet;" Romeo by Walter Meadows, and Juliet by Anna McVernon. Every one dissented from this tableau. It would be hard to find a more exquisite Romeo, but the Juliet was entirely out of place with Anna as its delineator. However, she had requested the character, and it was not an easy matter amicably to refuse her.

Poor Hagar! Ever since this fiend had become established in her house, there had been a series of persecutions almost unheard of carried on. Her health was suffering from it, and it seemed as if she had no longer any spirit to resist, or any desire to counteract the pernicious influence. She still wrote at intervals, but her verses were so tinged with the gloom of her mind that she wisely refrained from their publication. She had never fully understood Walter, and now his manner had become more perplexing than ever. Sometimes she would look suddenly up, and catch his blue eyes, moist with tears, mournfully fastened upon her face. Yet, if she thought to treat him with an old-time familiarity, he would put her away gently at times, and at times roughly. Lizzie was still the guardian angel of the house, and kept some little restraint upon the machinations of Anna. Report was now current that an engagement subsisted between Walter and Anna.

"It is hard to bear, and still treat her with the courtesy

due to an invited guest," said Hagar to Lizzie, when she first heard the news. "It is very hard to bear."

"But you will bear it?"

"Yes, patiently as I can."

And she *did* bear it; but day by day her efforts for calmness and self-possession showed more visibly. Decay was stamped upon her features, and the short, hacking cough sounded harshly upon the ears of her friends. Anna was always at hand to nip in the bud any appearance of returning tenderness, and thus far her efforts at estrangement had been met with most positive success. Hagar sat like a statue while the tableaux were in progression. The next was a scene from "Love," in which, with her accustomed cruelty, Anna had suggested that Hagar should appear. The three characters, the Countess, the Empress, and Huon, were to be rendered by Hagar, Anna, and Walter. Mrs. Scammon, who was a dear lover of poetry, expressed a desire to hear the language of the scene, as well as to see the tableaux. Hagar was a fine reader, and moreover was conversant with the poetry now committed to her care. Commencing with the fifth act, all went smoothly enough, until the words seemed to Hagar as part and parcel of her own thoughts. As speech after speech called forth its answering one, she grew excited, passionate, and wildly conscious of the adaptation of the words to her present position. The audience was hushed into silence. Not a whisper, not a flutter of a fan broke up its depth. All eyes centred upon the stage, while Hagar, forgetting caution, prudence, every thing but the woman before her, thus hurled the language at her baffled rival: —

"How couldst THOU love him?
How couldst thou steal a heart thou knew'st to be another's?
Thou knew'st he loved me, and did covet him — covet a heart at second hand.
His heart was mine till thou didst rob me of it.
Not of it all, but of a part! Yet if a part is gone, go all! 'Tis
Gone! my peace, hopes, every thing along with it.
What then? Would I have it back? No! I would
Sooner die! Its worth was its fidelity. That lost,
All's lost! Thou coveted'st a faithless heart!"

Hagar had grasped Anna by the arm with such force that a slight scream betrayed to the audience how much of reality there was in her most natural acting. With a simultaneous rush the spell was broken, and Hagar, looking first to one and then to another in a bewildered maze, finally caught the eye of Lizzie, who was struggling to get to her friend.

"O, take me home — take me home! Never let me go out again till I'm *carried* out; never, never!"

"Make way there! Clear the passage! Throw up the window!" exclaimed Walter, catching her in his arms in time to prevent her falling to the floor. "My God! you have killed her!"

A small stream of blood was issuing from her mouth, and lay in crimson stain upon Walter's bosom. They bore her to the window, where the light breeze swept in from banks of snow. At first resuscitation seemed impossible. By degrees, however, her eyelids unclosed, and her respiration renewed its gasping sway; but there was no sense in the glimmering of those wild eyes, no discretion in the words which occasionally fell from her lips. Her sun had gone down into a night of insanity.

CHAPTER XXV.

THE MESMERIST AND HIS VICTIM.

THE winter was setting in, and balls, parties, sleigh rides, lectures, and theatres gave excitement enough to the circle in which our characters moved. The home of Mr. Veazie alone retains its sombre hue. Stern and cold to every one else, Michael Lawrence seemed only to live in the presence of Ellen Veazie. There was a thoughtful, loving care, so acceptable to a woman's heart in every act regarding her; a gentle, observant tenderness, so unlike the harshness of her guardian, that no wonder she received it with gratitude, and endeavored to repay his attentions by constant and untiring devotion. But hours of loneliness would come — times of deep thoughtfulness, when every kindness of her stern monster, every self-denial of his strange life, every gentle word would flash with lightning swiftness over her impressive fancy. Then would come thoughts of the long days and years when, spite of his singular habit of contradiction, he had tended her with more than a father's fondness. Did she not owe him something for the watchful solicitude with which he carried out her father's will? — a solicitude which certainly seemed at times unnecessary harshness, but which at that was more palatable than the eternal deference of Mr. Lawrence. It was only in the presence of the mesmerizer that his influence was at all decisive; but that determined, wilful glance, those thrilling, shivering eyes, there was no escaping their influence or evading their power. They had uprooted the honor of man, and the virtue of woman! They had incited masses to rebellion, and raised revolt where peace had ever lain with folded wings. Should he give up the conquest, more than half won, of a girl so full of generous impulses, of high and noble resolves, as was Ellen Willard? — a conquest that at their first meeting had seemed inevitable. It was not to be thought of.

Among the fashionable families who were vying with each other in point of exclusiveness and frivolity was that of a Madam Monpensieur; a lady, American by birth, but whose Puritan prejudices had been washed out by many years' contact with, and observance of, the levities and inconsistencies of Parisian life. The indiscretion of parents whose greatest care was to see their daughter at the head of fashionable life, had given her an education at one of the prominent French seminaries, which, with the after addition of a French husband, initiated her into the infidelities which, with the nation, pass as lighter crimes, and rendered her the last person in the world to have the care of a young and impressive mind. Her apparent frankness had rather favorably impressed Mr. Veazie, and her seeming interest in all that concerned Ellen had awakened an almost sisterly regard in the bosom of this impulsive girl. She, unknown to Mr. Veazie, was an earnest partisan of Lawrence, and one of his warmest patrons. Wherever Madam Monpensieur was, there too was Lawrence. So great, indeed, had become their intimacy, that scandal was beginning to meddle with their names, and mix them up in no enviable manner. To counteract this error, it might have been, which caused her so strenuously to plead his part with his Ellen. The most dangerous sophistry, the most bewildering arguments, were used to pervert her mind, and prevent her dwelling too deeply upon the situation of Lawrence, as the husband of a woman he detested.

"Will the utterance of a few meaningless words, the sanction only of a man after all, though bearing the robes of priesthood, make you dearer to each other than you are now? Will you be truer to him, or expect him to be more faithful to you, because you have blazoned your love to the world at the altar — a very indelicate proceeding, by the by. The heart is the criterion. If that remains firm, you will never separate, though your vows have only been sanctioned by the love you mutually feel; and if it changes, surely you would not desire to retain the person, when his thoughts had wandered from you!"

With such specious reasonings did the reckless woman of the world strive to undermine the purity of a soul all spotless in its impulses. Some said Madam Monpensieur had herself been a victim to the wiles of the mesmerizer, and that with her easy and convenient ideas of morality, she hoped, by creating pleasures for him, even though conflicting with her own happiness, to secure some portion, if not of his affection, at least of his gratitude. Many and many a time, after listening to her arguments with flushed cheeks and flashing eyes, Ellen would decide to tell her guardian all; but the native delicacy of her mind revolted against the subject, and so she listened and reasoned, and in the end came near enough to conviction to lose her own true sense of the brink upon which she was standing. But good fortune was with her, and she was not allowed long to pervert her pure mind with such distorted philosophy. The charm was broken by the arrival from New York of a gay party, on a visit to the Monpensieurs. Among them was a young lady of peculiarly fascinating appearance, although the closest observer could not tell in what that fascination lay. She was not handsome, — her warmest admirer could not lay that flattering unction to her charge, — nor gay, except at fitful intervals. Her eighteenth summer had scarcely ripened the bloom upon her cheek, yet no one placed her age at less than twenty-five. There was such a sedate, sorrowful air, amounting at times almost to melancholy, that it was next to an impossibility not to speculate upon its cause; and with the spirit of exaggeration which always imbues gossip, it was soon currently reported and generally believed, that Esther Milroy had, at some period of her eventful life, been the victim of an unfortunate love affair. This, however, was far from the truth. No girl in the circle which owned her as a star had been more fortunate in heart matters than had herself. Her parents were, it is true, an ill-matched pair, — vulgar, showy, and ill bred, as two thirds of the *ton* leaders inevitably are, — with only one point of interest, and one fact to be agreed upon between them, and that the beauty of their only child. To rear her in every extravagant expense; to bestow, what they so greatly needed, an education of rare and thorough mint; to dress her in the most luxuriant style, — these were the daily cares which agitated with like strength the minds of the adoring parents. And amply had they been rewarded, by seeing her grow up into refined and polished womanhood, alike the envy and the emulation of the society into which wealth had thrown them. Every available method had been tried to banish the feeling of languor and *ennui* with which she seemed to regard the excitements of the circle in which she moved. An air of superb haughtiness frightened away from her the mass of men who would gladly have supplied the void so palpably expressed. Her disdainful eyes took in at a glance all the little arts and coquetries of her sex, and in her heart she despised what seemed to her so frivolous. Her perceptive qualities were vigorous in the extreme, and in proportion to their strength was her contempt of those to whom admiration seemed such a necessary ingredient. It was seldom that she warmed into admiration of any thing or any body, but when she did her conversation was brilliant and inexpressibly engaging. Between her books and an invalid cousin her time was chiefly employed; and when, as in the present instance, she had been over-persuaded to join a lively circle, it was more to superintend the nursing of said cousin than for any purpose of pleasure to be derived from it. Go when or where she would, he was her companion. If in doors, her hand was clasped between the thin, shadowy ones of the fragile consumptive; if on the streets or in the cars, his pale, spiritual face was as a foil by the side of her more animal one. And dearly he worshipped the brilliant woman who guarded him with such care, and dearly, after her fashion, she loved the stricken flower thus withering day by day from her embrace. Nothing this side of heaven could be more pure, more holy, more saint-like and angelic than the affection which linked its golden chain around these gentle cousins. If she had a passion, it was her love for music. In this she revelled and excelled. A voice clear, full, and musical as a bird's, had been cultivated with a patience and an assiduity that had left all competitors far in the rear of her excellence. This was her resource from all annoyance and fatigue. No invitation was ever refused by which she could amuse others, or gratify herself, in this capacity, and no one ever heard her thrilling voice to forget it, or blend its memory with that of any other songstress. In this regard she was alone, exclusive, unapproachable. It was in the midst of a most thrilling sonata that Michael Lawrence first caught sight of this strange being, whose utter indifference to admiration or affection had already been poured into his ear with many exaggerations. Madam Monpensieur was upon the point of interrupting her for the purpose of introduction; but a signal from him kept her quiet.

"Miss Milroy will pardon my presumption," he said, courteously advancing to the piano, "but after that song it would seem of 'the earth too much earthly,' to come down to a common introduction."

The lip of the proud girl curled with scorn and impatience, and she raised her eyes for the purpose of returning some curt reply, when they met a glance at once so thrilling and so respectful that the words remained unsaid, and her eyes, late blazing with defiance, drooped down upon the sheet of music before her.

"If I could ever think of heaven and the angels, it would be under the influence of music like that. Would it be asking too much to desire another song? — something sad or plaintive — something suited to a heart that has known little else than suffering," he murmured in a low tone, designed for her ear alone.

Whether it was the tone or the glance which she met at that moment that troubled her, I know not; but with a flushed cheek and a quick, embarrassed manner, she went on singing song after song, till the madam's parlors had grown alive with spell-bound listeners. But the most rapt and absorbed of all seemed Michael Lawrence, the mesmerist.

"Do you sing Italian songs?" questioned one of the company.

"No," she replied; "I sing only what I feel."

"And what you make *others* feel," again murmured Lawrence, in his deep, musical whisper.

In a moment Esther was herself again — haughty, superb, and majestic. Other songs were sung, and many performers, if not as artistic, equally brilliant, tried their skill during the evening; but not one of them elicited a word of praise from the usually voluble Lawrence. For once Ellen Veazie was passed unregarded. She had lost her power to please him. Like champagne, while the sparkle lasted she amused him; but the sparkle had gone, and the wine lay unheeded in its goblet. No less a child in years than she had been a child in the facility and readiness with which she yielded to his ideas and desires, it is not wonderful to those who have learned their lessons in the book of life that he longed for any change, and most of all for some new object upon which to try the power of his *science*. O, diabolical science, that was to be fostered and proved by the life blood of bruised and aching hearts! Where was it to end, if victim after victim was thus to become distasteful after serving the short term of interest to which its master subjected them? But here was a child that was more than a woman in her deep, self-calculating knowledge of the world. If he won her heart it must be with open eyes and soul conviction. And yet she had trembled beneath his burning glance, and in time incredibly short her eyes roved restlessly round the crowd till his step sounded at the door. She might avoid him; it was evident she did; but worse symptoms had been overruled, and these must be in this instance; besides, she knew that his attentions were the right of Ellen Veazie, and she was not artificial and fashionable enough to desire any pleasure from the torture she was inflicting upon another. That Ellen had become dejected, dispirited, and unhappy, Esther was the first to discover.

"I have come to talk with you," said she one day, soon after her first knowledge of Lawrence.

Ellen was standing in the door as she approached, and, with an impulse half of dislike, turned abruptly, for the purpose of shunning her visitor. They were closeted for several hours; and when Esther came out again her eyes were red, and her cheeks bore evidence of tears.

From that time there was a marked avoidance of Lawrence, although when they did meet he contrived to give her food for anxious thought for many an after hour.

There were gay times indeed after the arrival of the New York party, and their delay had extended many weeks longer than at first it had been proposed. From the ardent admiration of Lawrence he had become as haughtily indifferent as Esther herself. He even went far enough in his indifference to chatter gayly and noisily while she sang her most brilliant songs. A contraction of the lips and a moisture about the eyes showed how much Esther felt this marked and painful rudeness. One evening, after a more than usually positive demonstration, Esther had wandered off into the conservatory, which skirted the parlors, and filled them just enough with exquisite fragrance. Leaning her head against a frame of honeysuckle, she gave entire vent to the feeling which was overpowering her. She gazed upward to the cold, bright stars; but even their glittering beauty could not still the proud, passionate thoughts which were coursing through her brain. "And this is my philosophy," she muttered, with a bitter smile. "I love him; deny it as I may, I love him, — that cold, proud, cruel man — that tempting, tantalizing, dangerous man — that man of nerve, and power, and will, whose smile is fatal as the Upas's breath! *Love him!* I that have hitherto been ice to his sex — that have ridiculed and defied them — that have never tolerated the society of one except my poor cousin. Ah, poor, poor Edward!"

The sigh was echoed, and, starting up, she encountered the mournful gaze of her invalid cousin.

"Can I escape you nowhere?" said she, petulantly; for that he, of all others, should have witnessed her emotion annoyed her beyond reason. The sad glance which was the only reply cut her to the heart.

"O, forgive me, Edward! I didn't mean that — not that to *you*, Edward — my poor, afflicted boy, my only friend on earth; but I have been very unhappy of late, and I want to go home."

Edward took her hand, which was hot and feverish.

"We will return to-morrow, Esther. There is no peace here for you, nor for me. I only regret that we ever came."

"But the change has brought quite a bloom to your cheek, Edward."

"And bleached *yours* to the pallor of snow. O, do you think I have not seen it all — the trial and the temptation? Who would have thought it of *you*, Esther? I will not reproach *him*, at least not just now; but it is said that his life has been one of heartless cruelty; that he has tried his powers of fascination, first as a profession, till it has become a second nature to him. An unhappy marriage rang the first knell to his happiness, and from that time, as a sort of revenge for the wrong done him, he has lost no opportunity of adding conquest unto conquest. You, with your palpable indifference, awoke his slumbering nature, and in his own heart he has determined yet that nothing shall thwart him of his prey. For your own sake, dear cousin, let us return to-morrow."

After a short consultation it was agreed upon that, without previous announcement, they should prepare for their journey, and take a formal leave of their host and hostess in time to depart in the morning train. As her cousin left her, happier in spirits than he had been for many days, his place was supplied by another, and the eyes of the mesmerist were burning into the brain of his designed victim.

"*You* here!" she exclaimed, in startled wonder. At the same time a thrill of triumph flashed over her, that she had won him from the crowd of worshippers who circled round him in the parlor below.

"Frown on me if you will; I cannot resist the impulse

which bids me seek you. Kill me — still my last words must be of the passionate devotion with which your impressive manner has inspired me." He had taken her hand, which she haughtily withdrew.

"Insolence!" she said, scarcely deigning to raise her eyes.

"No other woman has so imbued me with that fervor of passion, that religion of the senses, as you have done. No other woman has ever filled the restless void within my heart which you *can* fill by allowing me to worship at your shrine. O Esther, if you only knew — if I dared tell you — what a life of storms mine has been! how every good and generous resolve has been turned to clouds and darkness by adverse fate; how, with capabilities for loving, with inordinate desires for love, I have still lived on, unblessed by the sweet companionship of affection! When your glorious voice first thrilled to my soul, my heart exclaimed, There lies your fate. I have watched for you at every turn. I have listened to your voice, till its melody has become part and parcel of my being. I have studied your face till each feature is engraven on my heart. O Esther! have you no word of hope — not one?"

By degrees he had gained possession of her hand. The moonlight lay calm and clear upon the thousand homes of the city, and upon the pleading face so sorrowfully upturned. The spell-bound girl trembled in every limb. With a last effort she again withdrew her hand, and motioned him to leave her.

"Be it so," said he, slowly passing to the door. "I might have known that fate had only bitterness in store for me. Forgive me, and forget that one so unfortunate ever crossed your path."

He was passing away, with his eyes still riveted on her face. One moment of intolerable bewilderment, one thrill of overwhelming passion, and his name, soft and sweet as music, passed her lips.

"*Michael!*"

It was the first time she had ever called him by that name. In a moment he was at her feet, covering her hands with passionate kisses.

"Leave me now — leave me. Let me think."

He did not obey, however; but, after a protracted interview, in which the whole soul of the impulsive but heretofore unimpressible girl went out in *abandon* to her lover, they left the conservatory together, and proceeded to the parlor.

"*Father! mother!* why did you not take *me* with you?"

It was a wail wild and bitter as the last lay of anguish; and with its utterance, Ellen Veazie, who, tired and weary, had dropped asleep among the flowers, and thus unintentionally became a listener to the above declaration, fell as one dead among the vines borne down by her fall.

CHAPTER XXVI.

THE CRISIS.

RESTLESS, jealous, and discontented, Madam Western wandered about the rooms of her superb mansion. Since the evening of the costume party, Mrs. Miles Scammon had ceased to show the least knowledge of her existence. Her brief dream had been but a ripple upon the ocean — past and forgotten. The same teachers who taught Mrs. Scammon's children's young ideas how to shoot overlooked the education and mental culture of Madam Western's; but although the world knew that the representatives of a "first family" were sedulously cautioned against associating with the plebeians, and although the children knew the distance between them, and although *she* knew that the world knew her struggles and her disappointments, she still hoped on, struggled on, determined to remember no such word as *fail.* Virtue is its own reward, however. In good time, the carriage of Mrs. Miles Scammon drew up before the lordly door of Madam Western. Much as she desired it, and proud as she was of the honor, the visit was very inopportune. Madam Western, having sat in state for so many mornings to no purpose, had begun of late to lounge away her minutes in rather an untidy wrapper. See her she would, come what might of it. The chance was too good to be lost; besides, those odious Peepengers were glaring through the blinds opposite, to see if Mrs. Miles Scammon alighted. Madam Western *was* at home, of course, and so impatient was she to greet her guest, that she followed her servant to the door, and amid apologies for her careless dress, and blushes and stammerings at her too evident sentiment of pride for the honor shown her, she clasped her hands, and *would* have kissed her, had not the aristocratic head negligently moved away from a juxtaposition so disagreeable, to say the least of it. This kissing of women don't amount to much in a long run. Judas betrayed his Savior with a kiss, and when he died, he left a long list of relatives. Besides, it is an unnatural act, savoring greatly of indelicacy. No *natural* impulse draws women's lips to each other, in close clasping; and when witnessed by the opposite sex it invariably calls out some comment which a true woman would blush to occasion. No! there is neither taste nor delicacy in the kissing of women, though, I am sorry to say, it is a habit disgustingly prevalent. But to the subject. The difference between a well and an ill-bred lady never was more apparent than during the interview of the two ladies in question. Mrs. Miles Scammon was quiet, graceful, *nonchalant*, yet perfectly familiar and at her ease. Madam Western was restless, fluttered, and evidently not at home.

There is one woman in the world in whose presence I always feel uncomfortable; and I have often thought, when seeing people striving so hard to arrive at positions which they could not fill, and associate with persons whose habits and associations were in all regards calculated to unsettle one's natural elegance, how ridiculous it was to bear so much inquietude for so little honor. I presume Madam Western, on this occasion, felt about as I do when encountering the cold gray eyes of Charlotte Cushman.

After half an hour's chat, in which the guest, by her own elegance, quite charmed her hostess into forgetfulness of her awful presence, she prepared to take her departure.

"You will call to see me very soon, I trust, my dear," said the patronizing Mrs. Miles Scammon.

Of course nothing could make her happier, and she said so.

"Say to-morrow evening — for a quiet time by ourselves. Bring your husband; Mr. Scammon will be at home; and while they immerse themselves in business topics, we shall have the chance to improve our acquaintance."

Gracefully as a swan, Mrs. Miles Scammon sailed out of the room, down the hall, over the steps, into her carriage. *That magnificent sweep!* Madam Western practised it for months afterwards, an hour every morning before her mirror; but what was so perfectly natural in the one failed to be acquired by the other, and only rendered her more than ever ridiculous by her assumption of foreign airs and native graces.

Could the madam have heard the private conference of Mr. and Mrs. Miles Scammon the evening previous to his lady's call, something of the exultation with which she poured the happy tidings into her husband's ears would have been lost in secret misgivings.

The evening came tardily enough for Madam Western. Never had the day seemed so long, or the hours so tardy in their flight, and never, in her most extravagant display, had she come from her robing room such a mass of glittering gems. The mirth flashed from Mrs. Scammon's eyes, and as hastily withdrew, as she took in the ostentatious bundle of dry goods and jewelry paraded before her. Her own dress was, like every thing associated with her name, elegant in the extreme. There were no ornaments of any description, but fold after fold of snowy tarleton draped around her like a cloud, and fell in graceful wreaths quite to the floor. A tiny foot, encased in a shoe which Cinderella might have envied, peeped out from the mist of muslin, and kept time to thoughts which, had they been the property of any one but the envied Mrs. Miles Scammon, would have seemed any thing but happy ones. Her long black hair was wound in a massive braid around her head, from which struggled out a single curl on either side of the neck. Madam Western felt more uneasy even than usual in her presence; for there was an occasional contraction of the brow, and a sigh strangled in its birth, which had never before marred the handsome face so often studied.

"What can the men find to talk about, I wonder?" queried poor Madam Western, sitting more and more on thorns, which the increasing abstraction of her hostess created.

The question caused a start, and a deeper flush upon the cheek of Mrs. Scammon; but she was too well accustomed to regulate her emotions not to retrieve herself at once.

"O, these men! Only let them alone, and we should be the last of their thoughts," replied the hostess.

"Wrong for once, Mrs. Scammon," said a voice, which brought the smiles to poor madam's face.

"You would be vain to know how much you have had to do with our confab — wouldn't she, Scammon?"

Mrs. Scammon bit her lip, and flashed out that strange glance upon her husband which often before had characterized her expression. Refinement was so much her element, that she found it hard to recognize the well-meaning but rough merchant, although persuaded that it was a necessity which knew no law.

"Scammon and I are partners," exclaimed Western, as soon as they were out of hearing of their new friends.

"You *don't!*" replied his wife, gasping in her astonishment.

"Yes, but I *do,* though. A cool hundred thousand invested in railroad stock, on the —— Road. We'll see *now* who'll turn up their aristocratic noses."

"A hundred thousand dollars!"

"A hundred thousand dollars! quite a little pile, isn't it? Old Scam rather opened his eyes, when I planked for such a sum."

"A hundred thousand dollars! Are you *sure* it's safe?" questioned the wife, her pocket, after all, weighing more in her estimation than the friendship of the Scammons.

"*Safe!* Mr. Miles Scammon *safe!* Why don't you ask if the moon is made of green cheese, or if the earth revolves on its own axis or somebody's else, or any other stupid question, after *that!* Mr. Miles Scammon *safe!*" and a laugh rang out quite merrily at the precaution of his little wife, who could even ask if Mr. Miles Scammon was *safe!*

"Any how, I'm glad them Peepengers will hear of it. Only think! they never returned my call, nor card, nor any thing, till they saw Mrs. Scammon's carriage at the door. Then the first thing I knew, over came a monstrous bouquet, with the Misses Peepenger's compliments. Perhaps I didn't show them what's *what!* Perhaps I didn't send it back to them with my compliments, and that Mr. Western could afford to buy all the flowers he wanted. They will send me no more bouquets — now mind that! Though vulgar things, like them, are forward enough to do any thing."

Highly elated were the worthy couple at the occurrences of the evening. Not so the Scammons. As the door closed upon the visitors, the smile faded from the aristocratic lips of Mrs. Miles Scammon — the brightness from her eyes; and holding off the offending hand that had returned the parvenue clasp, with a gush of tears she sank down among her muslins, as miserable as if her husband was *not* the millionnaire.

CHAPTER XXVII.

THE DYING STRAWBERRY GIRL.

A MESSENGER stood talking with Ida Chiffering in the doorway — the little strawberry girl was dying. The woman who brought the message was a dark, stern-looking creature, whose eyes seemed to have grown unnaturally bright through her tears.

"I was loath to come," she said, in a tone which explained more than words the condition of her life. "Such as *I* have poor welcome at the doors of the pure." And she cast her eyes down, sweeping them over her person, as if she would gladly scath out the stain upon her life.

"She desired so much to see you once again," she went on, still drooping her eyes to the ground; "and I love her — O, so dearly! *You* can never know how dearly the poor and the depraved cling to that they love."

"Wait a moment for me, and I will accompany you," replied Ida, in her gentle, pitying tones.

The eyes of the strange woman were lifted now, and searching into Ida's face.

"*You* accompany me! No — no — no; that would *never* do. There is a distance between you and me that all the speed in the world cannot make shorter — there is a difference between us that could not be greater if I was black and you the white angel that you are! No; I will leave my address, and you can follow at your leisure."

Placing a card in Ida's hand, she withdrew, and passed rapidly down the street, turning neither to the right nor the left, till a low, neat little house was gained, into which she disappeared.

"In a brown study, Ida?" said her poet, as she stood gazing too intently for seeing upon the street whereon she last caught a glimpse of her visitor.

"You remember the little strawberry girl, don't you?"

"Yes; she that was a *secret.* By the by, I intended to know more of her."

"She is dying, and has sent for me."

"I will go with you; for I am mistaken if it is exactly the place for you to go alone."

Half an hour afterwards the two knocked at the door of the strawberry girl. The same woman who had brought the note to Ida came to give them admittance. She was evidently unprepared for the visitation of any one but Ida, and for a moment seemed undecided whether to admit them.

"*She* was not over chary of *my* peace or good fame — why should I be of *hers?*" at length she murmured, as if answering to her conscience for the step she was taking. With that she motioned them in, and then threw another door open, which communicated with the child's bed room. Though every ray of light was excluded from the room, it was easy to perceive that they were not alone. Low sobs came from some one kneeling by the side of the bed, and once a fair jewelled hand brushed away the hair lying loose upon the child's forehead. They were about to retreat, being unwilling to disturb such apparent grief, come from what source it might; but the woman who had admitted them stood in the doorway, and seemed to bar their passage.

"She should have been *human* while humanity would have been of service," she murmured.

The sound of voices disturbed both the dying child and the weeping mother, for she it was.

"It is an old story, rife since the world began," said the woman, in answer to Ida's question of the occasion of her illness. "I was poor, and she too feeble for the employment forced upon her by unnatural parents."

"Cruel, cruel!" murmured the voice at the bedside.

The eyes of the speaker glittered like daggers drawn from their sheath; but she went on.

"I knew how it would end. I sent till I was tired of it for the means to save her life."

"Cruel—*how* cruel!" again came from the sick room.

"Were you ever kind to *me*, Anna McVernon, that I should show *you* mercy? Ask your own heart. She is reaping the reward of *her* system of torturing now," said she, addressing herself to Ida.

Anna rose from the bed with every trace of emotion removed. Calm as if in her own house, she motioned Ida and her companion to the bed.

The child, who had seemed sleeping, opened its eyes, and held out its arms to Ida. And how pale she was! — how thin and worn!

"I'm going to heaven," said she, in her childish whisper. "Mamma says I shall not be a secret there, nor have to work when my head aches, nor feel sorry, nor sad, nor any thing but happy. O, I wish I was in heaven!"

"Poor, poor girl!" said Ida, bursting into tears.

"Don't cry. There are no more tears there. Shan't *you* be glad when you go to heaven? I shall look for you every day."

"Poor child! There are no days in heaven, darling."

"And shan't I know *you* and mamma there?"

"Don't ask me. I don't know. We don't any of us know, darling. It is to be with God and the angels. That is all we know."

"Did you ever see an angel?" said the child, gazing upward with that holy, reverent look which all dying persons wear.

"No, darling."

"How do you know, then, that they live in heaven?"

"I *don't* know."

"Then I don't want to die — I don't want to die. Pray God not to let me die!" And the pale face grew paler with terror.

"O God!" cried Ida, gathering her in her arms. "I have deprived her of her beautiful faith, and I have none left to give her in return!"

Beautiful faith!

Ida said truly. The sweet, trusting faith of childhood *is* beautiful. Pity the taint of earthly knowledge should ever mar its holiness and truth.

Slowly and by degrees the look of terror gave place to the old holy expression of trustingness.

"O, there *are* angels there! I can see them now. I know them for angels. Yes, there *are* angels in heaven, and I am going to them. *Mamma!*"

Anna rose to speak to her.

"Not *you*, lady. My *other* mamma."

The woman who had been quietly weeping under the cover of the window curtains came slowly forward.

"Kiss me, mamma! Good by! Good by, sweet lady."

The sun came slanting in through the window blinds, and lay in little golden pools upon the bed; the breeze crept in, and lifted the matted locks carefully as a mother would have done; while the rustling of the vines over the window, the stifled sobs of the party present, and the labored respiration of the little sufferer, were the only sounds that disturbed that chamber of death.

"I'm going to sleep now," she whispered in the ear of the woman whom she called mamma. "Say Our Father who art in heaven, for me. I'm going to sleep!" And so she did; but it was the sleep from which she would wake no more but in heaven, among the angels whom she recognized on earth.

CHAPTER XXVIII.

The Wealthy Parvenus.

"Now that is what I call slap-up and tidy," soliloquized uncle Job Thornton, turning himself round and round before the glass, scrutinizing each new point of excellence, and practising such airs and manœuvres as he thought best adapted to his new character.

"If this here harness don't please Becky Western, then I'll never bet agin, and that's a fact. But it can't help it; no, it can't possibly help it. My hyes, Job! but here's a go, at your time o' life! I arn't quite sure but you're a precious old fool, Job; but time'll show, time'll show." This last bit of argument was addressed to the Job in the looking glass, who, it must be said, looked rather thoughtful and very uncertain.

"There's no time to be lost. I'm tired of this here shut-off life. Old Job never was made for single blessedness, and he can't stand it, not that he knows on. Why *shouldn't* he be fashionable? that's the question. If mopusses will do it, he's got a cart load or less. If there is any peculiar hang to it, he'll get it in no time. My hyes! but won't Becky stare?"

The very idea sent uncle Job off into one of his *immense*

laughs, which was brought up of a sudden by the entrance of the waiter.

"Did you ring?"

"Did I ring? Well, yes; I guess I *did* ring. Why don't you look sharp when a nob is to be attended to? Who am I, I should like to know?"

"Old Job Thornton, I believe, sir, though no one could ever know you in that rig."

"Mr. Obadiah Thornton, Esq., and nothing shorter. And as to the knowin', that's just what I don't want. Of course you never saw me before."

"Sir!"

"I say of course you never saw me before. Isn't that as plain as the nose on your face? You never saw me before — you wouldn't know me if you was to see me agin. That's what I want to get at. If I should happen to drop in with a party of ladies and gentlemen as *is* ladies and gentlemen, you wouldn't remember ever to have seen me. You understand."

"Well, I don't — know — as I could *help* knowing you."

"Do you know a golden guinea when you sees it?"

"O, *don't* I neither? Don't ax me; you hurts my *feelin's.*"

"Well, here's one on 'em. Just you pocket that. Now, that's my argument. For every time you *don't* know me you shall have its feller; for every time you *do* know me I'll take you by the scruff of your neck and the seat of your trousers, and pitch you out of the winder! That's my argument. *Now* do you think you could *help* knowing me?"

"*Me*, sir! I wouldn't know you from a mutton head if I met you in my porridge dish, as the sayin' is."

"It's lucky for *you* that it *is* a saying—that about the mutton head. Well, now, the next move is, I want a pair of carriages and a hoss."

"A what, sir?"

"A pair of hosses and a carriage, stupid! And, look ye! I don't want none o' your spavined, knock-kneed, creepin' animals; now do you understand that?"

"Well, I don't know as I do, quite."

"Here; do you see this here list of *goold?*"

"I don't see nothin' else. Criminy! you're a buster of the first water!"

"Well, pocket it. *Now do you* understand?"

"*Don't* I neither? and won't I *keep* understanding, from this day till next day after never, while you hold out such wery stavin' arguments as these ere. I don't think I could forget it if I was to try—I don't. You shall 'ave the 'osses, sir;—dashin' ones, sir;—'osses as has got plenty of *go* in 'em;—'osses as shall be proud to carry you, sir. O, I've got a memory like a meeting 'ouse, I have." Bowing himself out, and stopping in the passage to take a loving peep at his gold, the servant left uncle Job more than ever elated.

"If such as *he* gets stunned with this rig, what *will* Becky Western say?"

"Carriage at the door, sir; 'osses champin' the bit with impatience, sir."

"That's the ticket. Now hand me my tile. How do I look?"

"Why, I — don't — know as ——"

"Do you see that gold piece?"

"O, criminy! don't I?"

"Well, pocket it. *Now* how do I look?"

"*Magnifferous*, sir! There's not a snob in all Bosting can hold a candle to you, sir. Perfectly beau*ch*iful, sir! You'll cut such a swell, sir, as was never cut before, and as will never be cut again, sir."

"You're a sensible feller, Bill — leastwise what's your name — and I'll reward you yet."

It would have been worth something to a fun lover to see uncle Job, in his new-found dignity, strutting loftily to the carriage. The servant had told him the truth about the "'osses."

"They are hard 'uns to look at, but good 'uns to go," said the driver, mounting guard upon the box. "Where now?"

"To — Mount Vernon Street, quick as the Lord will let you."

In five minutes more, Madam Western was greatly surprised, in the midst of her morning levee, to see a hackney coach stop at her door; more greatly surprised to see uncle Job Thornton alight; and most greatly surprised to see him swagger into her parlor with the rakish sort of swing which he fondly imagined was tip-top fashionable. A pair of black pants, a trifle tighter than the law allows, a black coat, the waist being next thing to limitless, a white vest, an eye glass, a pair of lavender gloves, and an Ellsler cane masked what was once — alas the day! — old Job Thornton. Had the ghost of Hamlet's father walked into the room it would have created less consternation in the mind of Madam Western. There was no help for it. Mrs. Miles Scammon sat scrutinizing him through her eye glass, evidently expecting an introduction. If wishes had been horses, uncle Job would have found himself floundering in the fountain under the window; but as it was, only a torn rosebud went out in his stead, and lay floating for hours afterwards among the gold and silver fishes.

"I say, Becky, ain't this fly, eh?" whispered uncle Job to his discomfited niece. "You needn't faint; I know how to come it. I've been practising as you used to do before the glass. Introduce me. Why don't you introduce me? Don't you see that old lady with the eye glass is a-waitin' for an introduct?"

"*Do* go — for Heaven's sake, go!" implored the mortified madam.

"Go! I guess so, after all this rig up! Do you think I'm a fool? If you don't introduce me, I'll do it myself. Mrs. ——"

"Hush! I'll do it."

"Well, then, *cut* — and blamed quick, too. You're ashamed of me — that's what it is. As for that, I can buy and sell old Mother Thing-em-bob, as little as you think of me. Go, indeed! Not by this light."

Seeing there was no other alternative, Madam Western took his arm, and led him into the room.

"My uncle — Job Thornton. He's an oddity," she whispered in an undertone to Mrs. Scammon, "but immensely rich."

"You may well say *that*," broke in uncle Job, who had only heard the last of the sentence. "*Immense* is no word for it. The mopusses I've spent upon this ere rig up would be a fortin' for some folks. Only look at *that*, and weep!"

Uncle Job drew a large gold watch from his pocket, to which was suspended what he called "two stunning seals."

"Look a here! two bobs and a sinker! Eh, what?"

This last exclamation was elicited by seeing Madam Western's lips moving behind the window curtain. As no further information came from that quarter, he went on as if no interruption had occurred.

"There's a bosom pin, too; the mopusses I paid for that! Eh, what?" Again the mysterious lip movement arrested him.

"What's that you say? Ain't I doin' it brown? If I ain't, spit it out, and done with it. If there is any thing I *do* hate, it is to be mumbled at, and not know what it's for. Eh, what's that?"

A low, plaintive voice was heard under the window.

"We have nothing for you; go away; go away. If we

encourage beggars we shall have the whole town at our door," urged Madam Western.

"O, come now; you're not going to send off the old woman in that ere fashion. Say — you — old woman! here! come back here!" called out uncle Job, leaning half out of the window. The beggar thus importuned turned and answered to the call.

"What's the difficulty, old woman? Where's the pain, eh? What'll ye take? I mean, what's the trouble?"

The usual story was told, with the usual emphasis, which sent uncle Job's hands down deep into his pockets, from which they returned laden with small change for the beggar.

"There, take that, and be off with you. Don't stop to thank me; I can't bear thanks. I tell you to *cut;* do you understand *that?* For *sissy's* sake," pleaded uncle Job, as he met the angry eye of Madam Western. *Sissy* had been the pet of uncle Job's family; his sister, in fact, who had early fallen a victim to consumption. Whatever good deed or generous action he might have done, it was ever prefaced or followed with the pleading "for sissy's sake."

"Well," said Madam Western, "I never encourage beggars. There is not one honest one out of ten."

"But suppose," said uncle Job, "it should be that one honest one that you had said *no* to. Suppose that one honest one was poor, and sick, and starving, and you had sent him away because of the nine dishonest ones. For my part, I don't care how much I believe, if I don't believe too *little.* I had rather that *nine* dishonest ones should say, 'I took him in,' than that one poor and honest one should feel that I held back my little utmost from his starving mouth. That's *my* argument. It mayn't be a very popular one, nor very popularly expressed; but there it is, and them as has a better can hold to it, say I."

"I like you, uncle Job."

"Sakes alive! where did you come from?"

"I like you, uncle Job."

"I'm glad on it; I don't know who you be, but you're a sweet one to look at, and you like uncle Job, and you ain't afeard to say so. That's enough for *me*. Sakes alive! and don't she look like sissy?"

"And who was sissy, uncle Job?"

The small, white hands rested in the horny palm of the old man, while the soft, brown eyes went up in sympathy to his face.

"Who was sissy?"

"She was an angel, if ever an angel lived in human form. She was too good for this earth; she couldn't stan' it; though, if I could have saved her, there is not a stone on earth I'd left unturned. There is not a trouble or a sorrow I wouldn't have borne for her sake. All the causes that carry grief to the heart I would have defied or shared, or taken 'em to myself, if I could have saved one blessed tear from spoiling her bright eyes. I couldn't do it, lady; I couldn't do it. There was nobody could help being kind, and good, and affectionate to her; but I think there came one that couldn't love her just as she loved him — I think there did. She would have been torn to pieces before she'd have said so; but I think there did, for after he was gone she pined and pined, as I have seen a flower as didn't get the sunlight it wanted. Bimeby she died. It wasn't much; hundreds of people die every day; but it was every thing to *me*. I was poor then as any body need be, and so I went off to Californy. I made a heap of money there — nobody but me knows how much; but I'd give every blessed cent, and beg my bread from door to door, for one of her lovin' smiles and lovin' words — I would, *I would!*"

The tears were running down over uncle Job's face faster than the bright little thing who stood by his side could wipe them away. There was a misty look about Madam Western's eyes, and even Mrs. Miles Scammon swallowed a sigh which sounded very like a sob. Only the still, fair girl who seemed most interested in the story retained her usual calm.

"I've nobody, nobody now! What's the use of my mopusses, and *she* dead and cold in the ground?"

"*I like you, uncle Job!*" said the soft, still voice.

Bless that sweet, sympathetic tone! The world cannot be all bad while simple, gentle hearts like hers beat for sorrows not their own.

All through that long morning, helping him out when he floundered in the sea of small talk, defending his absurdities upon the plea of his goodness, standing in the door of ridicule, and shielding his mistakes, was this sweet young girl, who never in all her life had seemed to care for any thing or any body enough to interest herself as she was now doing. Her cousin, the superb, and her invalid brother alone occupied her thoughts. But now it seemed as if a new existence was open to her as an existence of usefulness. She had been serviceable to a human being, and the deference and the almost ludicrous trustingness with which he appealed to her to unravel some knotty point, proved that it was not unappreciated. The conversation again took a lively turn, just lively enough to bring out uncle Job's odd sayings. Finally, to cap the climax, when Mrs. Miles Scammon rose to go, he had offered her his hard, horny hand, for a parting tribute. Of course, she was too fashionable to see it, or to observe Madam Western's embarrassment in consequence.

"You can shake hands with *me!*" said the little fairy, coming back to him from the carriage.

"O, bless you! bless you! Just for all the world like sissy used to do. If you *had* no objection, I should like to kiss you — just for *sissy's* sake."

She *had* no objection; so uncle Job very gingerly lifted the bright face up, and touched the red lips with a gusto worthy of a more practised hand.

"I like you! I *do* like you, uncle Job!"

The next moment a fair hand flung him a kiss from the carriage, which was just turning the corner of the street.

"How *could* you!" exclaimed Madam Western, the moment her fashionable friends were out of sight.

"Why! How could I do what? Didn't I do it up tip-top?"

"To come here at all in *that* trim, was perfectly ridiculous! And then to go on as you did! If I could have sunk into the earth, I should have been glad. What on earth Mrs. Miles Scammon *will* think, I don't know!"

"Think of what?"

"Why, the way you acted! And then to blubber about sissy so! Why, it was ——"

"Stop a bit now! Stop a bit! Abuse *me* if you like. My shoulders is broad enough to bear it. But when you speak of sissy, there's a pint as I won't bear to have touched with disrespect. Mind that, now, Becky Western as was; Madam Western as is. Let's come at it logically. Suppos'n I did blubber!"

"Do you suppose Mrs. Miles Scammon would have betrayed her feelings in that way?"

"Why not?"

"In the first place, it is not fashionable to show any emotion! Why, if every friend in the world that Mrs. Miles Scammon has was to die, you would not see the slightest quiver of the lip, no more than if she was bidding them good night!"

"Then *hang* Mrs. Miles Scammon — dern and thunder, Mrs. Miles Scammon! I thought I was lonely away in a hotel by myself, and so I took it into my head to get this ere rig, and come back here and play elegant with you. You know you wasn't once any more at home among the snobs than I am now; but I thought, thinks I to myself, I'll see how *she* piles it on, — meaning you, — and perhaps

I can get the hang of it in time, — *but* — I've had enough of it. If fashion breaks the neck of feeling, I don't want to be fashionable. If one must nod and smile when one feels more like bustin', to be in the style, let it be long years before I'm in any such fashion. I thought fashionable people were like other people, with this exception of the mopusses; being kind to each other, and affectionate to each other, and drawing nigh to each other in the thousand ways which bring folks to an understanding like; but I find it is all a mistake — mistake that has been growin' and increasin', till bimeby — mind my words — there'll be no more likin's nor affections, no drawings together like one human family, as God designed us to be, nor any thing but cold, selfish, calculatin' critters, with no more to do with happiness than the *automaters* that shake their heads and nod in the window yonder!"

All the while he was speaking, uncle Job had been divesting himself of his finery, putting it away from him as if it was something loathsome, from which he had a narrow escape.

"The great, lonely, solitary life of livin' for one's self!" he went on, as he deposited his heavy watch with other trinkets upon the table. "Afeard to speak to this one, leastwise they was a step lower on the ladder than themselves; and passin' that one as if he was the dirt upon the ground, because he was born with nothin' but a sound heart and a clear conscience. Passin' with the crowd, and not being of the crowd — no! before I'd do that, I'd go down to the Frog Pond some night, when there was nothing but the stars to see me, and go to sleep there forever and forevermore, amen! There, take them all, — watch, pin, rings, seals, — a precious heap of old Job Thornton's folly! I've had enough of fashionable life for one day."

Without another word, or another look, he darted out into the street, and walked straight to his hotel. At the door he met the obsequious waiter, whom he seized by the collar.

"You old fool, you! how do I look *now?*"

"Magnifi ——"

"You lie, you rascal! That's one of the fashionable dodges, eh? I look like a thunderin' old jackass, that ought to be sent up, and fed on porridge the rest of his life! I say I look like a blasted old hunker! You know I do! and if you don't tell me the truth, I'll break every bone in your hide, you cheeky scoundrel! What do I look like, I say?"

"I — I — don't know — I ——"

"Here, here's *another* guinea! *Now* what do I look like?"

"Like a sensible man ——"

"You lie, you villain! I'll take every blessed guinea away from you, if you don't tell the truth!"

"Well, you won't hear me out. I say you look like a sensible man, that came within an inch of makin' a precious noodle of himself."

"That's it! You'll do! You'll rise in your perfession!

Now just hand me over them ere old clothes I gin you this mornin', and take these fly traps in exchange; and if ever any body catches me up to this dodge again, they may say as how old Job Thornton hasn't got sense enough to go to bed when it's dark!"

It didn't take long to effect the change in uncle Job's costume; and, for once, he seemed fully to appreciate the comfort of his former suit.

"Now, this is what I call easy," he said, turning round and round, and working his limbs in a strange manner.

"Why, would you believe it, Bill, when I had on them other gimcracks, I felt afraid to move about leastwise I had busted, or should bust through somewhere as wouldn't be delicate to mention. Why, they pinched like the old Harry! Now, these wouldn't be hired to play any such tricks upon travellers. Now, then, this over, let's have a bottle of the best Otard, and then we'll straighten things."

Uncle Job Thornton sat and drank, and drank and thought. The sun drooped down through a wreath of autumn clouds, and his last smile flickered in a thousand sparkles upon the homes lying all around him. The golden ripples glided up and down the steeples of the churches, and drifted backward and forward upon the glittering house tops. He sat and drank, and drank and thought, till the darkness lay on the earth like a curtain; till the stars came out in troops upon the blue sky; till the moon lay looking at him with her calm, quiet glance; till the noises had all died out of city life. Sometimes there were dreams, —

sweet, confused dreams, — from which he awoke with sorrow; for the angel of them all was a fair, bright girl, who whispered ever and anon, "I do like you, uncle Job!" And so he sat, and thought, and dreamed, till the moon, tired of gazing at him, had moved on, and was gone; till the weary-eyed stars had blinked their last blink; till the broad sun lay warm and golden upon his silver hair.

With a quick start he awoke just in time, as *he* thought, to see the trailing of white garments going out at the door, and the murmured sound, "I do love you, uncle Job; I do love you!" And while he dreamed in his chair by the window, a fair, bright head, nestled down among its mass of curls, was brimming over with visions and fancies almost as wild as uncle Job's had been. With her it was, "Poor sissy, what a pity she died!" with him it was, "I do like you, uncle Job; I do like you."

If I could only follow up those dreams till they ended in reality; if I could only describe how he watched her day by day, patient, loving, and always gentle to her consumptive brother; how she grew step by step to do *more* than like the honest old man who was so considerate for her, so anxious to serve her; how he brought himself to think that in *her* God had sent him his darling sissy out of heaven; how she, young as she was, became his instructress; how he improved under her care; how she stood between him and ridicule, in the circles where they were wont to meet; and how, in the end, she stood with him at the altar, a gentle bride, prouder of the gray hairs of her noble husband than ever she could have been of one whose youth had less need of her! But there are few pens in the world that could do justice to this course of true love, which *did* run smooth. There was no one to oppose her, even had it not, in a worldly point of view, been considered a good match, which it was. Descended from a family of unmistakable aristocracy, the lack of positive wealth had been no drawback. Until her singular infatuation for the mesmerist Lawrence, her cousin had devoted herself to her invalid brother, and she had been their attendant. There might have been a selfish point in the early portion of her intimacy with uncle Job, — the desire to make a home for her brother, — but if that had been the early inducement, long enough before the marriage was consummated it had merged into grateful affection for the man who cared for every breath she drew, and who, to use his homely idiom, loved the ground she walked on.

There were wise people to shake their heads and predict a future of misery and discontent; but she only laughed at the prediction, and clung the more fondly to her good old man. Her home was the picture of comfort. Refinement and elegance were visible on all sides, while uncle Job could not be grateful enough for the windfall of fortune which enabled him to gratify her every desire. If ever it came into his head that a younger or a more comely man would better correspond with the homestead and its pretty wife, he discarded it upon the instant, as being an insult to her.

"Why, she might have married enermost the king on his throne, if she had liked. She needn't have married me; and she wouldn't if she hadn't seen somethin' in me worth while. I deserve to have my head punched in tryin' to think it possible that ours wasn't a tip-top love match."

This was always his argument, when any thing like doubt arose in his mind as to her sincerity. The gossips might watch her every turn, might twist and distort every circumstance of her life to suit their views, but with all their sagacity, the clear, open, happy disposition of Mrs. Thornton completely balked their designs. There was no guile in that sunny face; there was no deception in those radiant eyes, and nothing but purity, gentleness, and angelic goodness in the character which was daily developing some fresh trait of excellence. The poor had in her a constant friend. Like her husband, she chose rather to believe too much than too little; and although there were, as there always will be, instances in which their bounty was abused, as a general rule their charities brought them in tenfold in the barter of money for gratitude. While occasionally mingling in the pastimes of their circle, the larger half of their time was devoted to the promotion of usefulness. About twenty times a day old Job would say to himself, "If there ever was an angel on the earth, that there wife of mine is one;" in which belief all who had the pleasure of her acquaintance cordially assented.

CHAPTER XXIX.

The Foiled Intrigant. — Mother and Daughter.

> "What is love but another word for pain—
> For an aching heart and throbbing brain?
> What is love but another word for tears —
> For the death of hope — for tumultuous fears?
> 'Tis a fragile bark on life's troubled sea,
> To be wrecked by its false intensity."

A day of unusual brilliancy had gone down upon a night of storm and darkness. The sleet and rain chased each other over the hill tops and around the corners of the streets — sometimes running against hurrying pedestrians, and in their haste bearing away with them luckless umbrellas, hats, caps, *et id genus omne* — sometimes leaping down chimneys with a rush which sent the smouldering embers whirling about the room. The awnings creaked and groaned in their affrighted loneliness, while the clashing blinds and the rattling windows suggested all that such a night would suggest of discomfort.

And discomfort there was, perhaps, if the city could have been unroofed, in every dwelling wherein the spirit of the storm strove for admittance. And discomfort there certainly was in the dwelling of the superb and fortunate millionnaire, Mr. Welman. From the grand assembly, where she had shone in all her regal beauty, the envied of a thousand hearts, Anna McVernon had returned to droop down in all her finery, a statue of misery and despair. There she lay, as if every nerve was prostrate, that regal woman, who, only an hour before, had turned the heads and hearts of a crowd of followers. Flowers, crushed and broken, were matted in among her long curls, sending out a faint perfume — a dying moan, as it were, that they should thus have served the purpose of a woman's vanity, to fall a victim to a woman's woe. Jewels flung out their radiant gleams from folds of brocade, and clasped, as if in mockery, the round, white arms, which were folded above the head of her who lay crushed, moaning, and despairing, mingling her wail with the storm cry that assailed her dwelling. Were there thoughts *there* of the hearts *she* had broken? — were there memories of the miseries and despairs that *she* had created? Alas! no. Her own grief, her own sorrow, and her own despair had shut her senses from all external things. Her demon projects were failing her when she thought them most secure. She had seen Hagar, in her quiet insanity, unlinking knot after knot of her tying; she had seen her restored, not alone to reason, but to the affection of her beloved; she had seen her that very evening, radiant with happiness, leaning on the arm which she had sworn to secure; she had seen it all, calm, seemingly joyous and rejoicing, till the mockery of the ball was over. Her laugh was loudest at the door of the hall, and was heard even amid the murmurings of the crashing storm, as the superb carriage, into which she had been literally borne by her admiring followers, wheeled away, and sped along into the sombre darkness. At her own door, even, her calmness remained to support her. Giving some slight command to the servant, she sprang lightly up the marble steps — up the tufted stairs — into her own solitary room. A large astral lamp filled the chamber with lustre, for Anna was a connoisseur of grandeur, and loved brilliant surroundings ever around her. After closing the door, she stood for a moment gazing upon her dark prototype in the pier-glass. Dark, and regal, and splendid were the face and form which her mirror reproduced. Could it be possible that *she* could love in vain? Could it be possible that a heart cased in gorgeous beauty could throb and ache with the misery of unrequited affection?

How the wind howled and the rain pattered against the windows of that splendid abode of sorrow! How the storm shrieked and clattered for entrance, as if to answer the moanings of the stricken woman!

How long she lay moaning upon the soft lounge it was impossible to say. Its very softness and sense of rest annoyed her. Her sobs must have penetrated beyond her own locality, for very shortly a side door, communicating with her mother's, opened, and Mrs. Welman stood haughtily in its frame.

"*Anna!*"

"*Mother!*"

In both exclamations there was a haughty defiance — a

superb indifference, and reckless carelessness of what might follow. Anna had risen upon her elbow, while the snake, which wound its coil around her arm in the form of a bracelet, seemed to undulate and emit sparks of rage and hatred. Her long black hair escaped from its bondage, and, with broken flowers clinging here and there amid its blackness, it swept over her shoulders, over her disordered dress, and lay in inky quivers upon the carpet by her side. Every motion of her arm sent the scales of the serpent into sparkling contortions horrible to contemplate. The same style of ornament had bound her hair, and in its escape seemed crawling down the long curls to hide itself from danger.

"*Anna!*" again broke forth the mother, gliding along the floor to lay her hand heavily upon the bared and polished shoulder. "Where is your *womanhood?*"

"*Gone!* — lost! — bartered forever and forever! *You* are my *mother*. You have taught me, led me, *forced* me, and here is the wreck of my womanhood."

The miserable woman had shaken off her mother's hand, and now stood recklessly defiant, in the full glare of the lamp.

"This to *me* — *to me*, Anna!"

"Mother, it is time we understood each other. It *was* time for that years ago. We *should* have done it, before, in *your* school, I had unlearned all that nature, innocence, and purity taught me; we should have come to an explanation before my whole nature was black and putrid with deformity."

"I will not say you are *mad*, Anna. I will leave you to your own thoughts. Perhaps to-morrow ——"

"No, mother! not to-morrow, but to-night! I have been an obedient daughter to you; have I not? When you saw me as a girl, stooping to what you thought an unequal love, you said, '*Be a woman!*' You inoculated me with pride — with vanity — with self-esteem. You taught me that only knowledge was power — that only evil existed where it was palpable — that only *position* could be made an available weapon in the battle of life. There *was* a time when I could have married the man of my choice, and have been happy. You treated the subject with scorn, and combated it with a wealthy suitor. That suitor became my husband! Did you, for one moment, believe I *loved* that man? Did you care whether I did or not? Did you care if the next hour found me pillowed in the arms of a criminal passion, so the world saw it not?"

"These are strong accusations to bring against your mother, Anna."

"Strong, but true! My life has been a lie from the beginning to the end of it, and you know it. There is nothing that ever lived so utterly false — so utterly saturated with degradation — as myself. False to my nature — false to my friends — false to my husband."

"Anna — Anna! You do not know of what you accuse yourself."

"Are there no crimes but the actual, mother? Is imagination nothing? Is desire — will, nothing? It matters little now, mother. Time was when the mistake of supposing only happiness could arise from position might have been rectified; but it is too late now, mother — too late — too late!"

Anna had lain down again with her face half buried in the pillows, while the serpent tangled itself among her curls, and seemed ready to spring out upon the self-convicted mother.

"Can I help you to redeem what you have lost in that — that — man?"

"Something must be done — I care not what! He has owned my influence — he shall again. *She* must be disgraced. He must be separated from her. It is too late now to stop at means. There have been times when I might have felt humbled down to own to you how entirely he has brought me to worship him. Those times are past, with much else that should never have been. I have tried 'to be a woman,' and have made a failure of it — a magnificent failure, hidden from the knowledge of all but myself and that I own it to you now, is because I demand that you should help me in breaking the tie that binds him to Hagar Only one thing can do it — her disgrace! Drive her from society, and you drive her from him. In the first place, she would not suffer him to share in her downfall; in the next, he is too sensitive to stand alone in her defence."

"But her position is too firm now easily to be shaken. Her only misfortune is an understood thing in society, and yet she has its recognition."

"Because it *is* an understood thing. Rake it up — blow it into life — discuss it as something but now having reached your ears — that is the part I would have *you* play; while my passive silence shall convince *him* that I am not the instrument of her disgrace. If you recede from her, leading the fashion as you do, there is not one person out of ten that will dare uphold her."

"This it is to have daughters!"

"This it is to have mothers who teach their children every thing but what they most need to learn! If you had taught me to pay that deference to worth which you have to wealth, this horrible episode never would have marred my existence."

More bitter tears, more anguished sobs, and the morning sun, all the brighter for the night's storm, crossed the still burning lamp, and fell upon the swollen eyes and flushed cheeks of Anna McVernon.

Mrs. Welman had retired to her chamber, but not to sleep. There had been too much truth in Anna's ravings not to disturb the calmness which usually reigned in her bosom. She would gladly have escaped the alternative; but Anna's happiness demanded it, and that decided her. Perhaps the knowledge that at the feet of her deleterious system of education lay the evil which had resulted, and was still likely to result therefrom, aided her desire to see her child once more free and happy. Disgrace Hagar Martin! All the long hours it rang like a doom upon her brain, which not even the languor of sleep could overcome.

It echoed in the shivering storm, and in the pitiless wind. Disgrace Hagar Martin! Fall gently shadows upon the closed eyes of the happy sleeper, for the short season of peace which fortune has allotted thee will soon melt away into suffering and dismay.

CHAPTER XXX.

THE DISAPPOINTED OLD MAID.—THE OLD MAN'S DARLING.

AMONG the most bitter and sarcastic of all the bitter and sarcastic persons who reviled the marriage of uncle Job Thornton with the youthful Genevieve Conant was Miss Margaretta Pinchin, the fashionable keeper of the fashionable boarding house. I don't say *she* had any positive designs upon him. To be sure he had been her most profitable boarder for the six months following his return from California. His room was the pleasantest in the house, his wardrobe always in good repair — his appetite was consulted every day before the regular market-house visit — if he wanted pork nobody else had chicken, and if he wanted chicken nobody else had pork — his cup of coffee was the first to be poured from the shining urn. The bath was saved till positive information was obtained from uncle Job that he could dispense with it. It was, "Ask Mr. Thornton," and "If Mr. Thornton desires it," and "Just as Mr. Thornton pleases," from morning till night. In fact it had become rather a standing joke among the boarders, that Mr. Thornton ruled the roost; while he, good simple soul, saw only a kindliness of feeling which he flattered himself was extended to all the establishment alike. Had he imagined that there were any designs upon his liberty in that quarter, any man traps concealed beneath the roses of good humor, he would have been the first to beat a retreat from the dangerous premises.

It was with very fierce eyes and a very bitter heart that Miss Margaretta looked on the manœuvres of "that artful little minx," as she called Genevieve, and with a very praiseworthy view of saving him from the clutches of a designing girl, that she *re*doubled her exertions to make him in love with his present quarters, and unwilling to change. How her head throbbed and leaped when he nudged her arm and winked in his old awkward way for her to follow him into the library!

"I want to consult on a matter as requires a previous deal of judgment," he whispered, as she passed him in going out.

He wanted to consult her; and upon what other subject could he possibly require her judgment? After all that had passed, he never could have the face to mention any other person to her as his intended. No, indeed! The time had come for which she had hoped so long — the fish was caught for which she had angled with all sorts of bait — Miss Margaretta would be Miss Margaretta no longer. With a step springy as a girl's, she started to obey his request. Womanlike, she gave one look at her mirror, settled her cap into more becoming form, and tucked away a lock of sprinkled hair, which had crept out from under her false front.

"I'll not give in too soon," thought the venerable spinster.

"He shall not find me too easily purchased. Let me see — shall I go in sort of abashed, as if I knew he was about to propose; or pretend that I've no suspicion of his intentions in that regard? I'll take the chances — follow his suit — that will be the safest way. Ah, ha! I wonder which side of the mouth people will laugh from now;" and in imagination she had already cut some of her acquaintances who had presumed to joke her upon her predilections for the bachelor.

"Miss Genevieve shall keep her distance; but I've determined! I know what men are too well to throw temptation in their way; and she would wheedle a saint with her airs and her make believes."

On entering the room she found uncle Job restlessly looking out at the window.

"That's the ticket," said he, presenting a chair for the pleasure of his guest, while she inwardly owned that, once married, she would break him of such vulgar expressions.

Although trying to seem at his ease, it was some time before he could fairly launch out upon the subject for which he desired her presence.

"You know from experience," he began, patting his left knee, and disturbing with his pocket handkerchief the domestic arrangements of a family of flies who were domiciled on the table where the sugar bowl had been. "You know from your own experience what a lonely, half-way sort of a life this livin' alone is."

Miss Pinchin proceeded to know immediately, and of course shook her head and sighed.

"Now, I am not much of an argufier; but I believe when God said, 'It is not good for man to be alone,' he meant it — and furthermore, that a man livin' till my time without doin' somethin' for his country can't begin too soon to make up his mind in that there regard." To all of which Miss Pinchin replied by a sigh, and a blush of conscious acquiescence.

"Now, from what you know of me, Miss Pinchin," — here he took her hand within his own, which she modestly withdrew, although it was an old way he had of emphatic argument, ——

"From what you know of me, I think you'll say a woman who didn't expect too much of her husband, and was willing to allow for short comin's in case there should be any, might get along pretty snugly — in fact, Miss Pinchin, might do worse than to hitch on to an old feller like me."

Miss Pinchin, feeling that she was expected to make a speech, hemmed and coughed, and finally got as far as "Mr. Thornton."

Here she stuck dead, and as there was no prompter, uncle Job kindly came to her aid.

"I know what you are, Miss Pinchin, and if you really thought 'no,' you could not but help say yes. I've had reason to say that your name stands for kindness, and goodness, and sensibleness, and so I come straight to you at once; before — before ——"

Here old Job floundered.

"I thought it was best," he went on almost immediately, "to make a clean breast of it to you, and, if you approved, to do the chore right up — parson, bridecake, and all — *you* understand."

Miss Pinchin *did* understand, or fondly imagined she did, as a firmer compression of the mouth, and a keener flashing of the gray eyes, attested.

"Now, am I right or am I not right?"

"Right, I think, Mr. Thornton. With *you*, I believe we have a mission upon the earth which extends to the more than living for *self!*"

"I'm certain of it! To be sure marriage is a thing which shouldn't be did without proper reflection. It is an easy knot to tie, but, as the sayin' is, it takes more than teeth to untie it. And as for some of the wives I've seen, I'd sooner go into the cage with a lion, and put my head in his mouth, knowing for certain he'd bite it off, than get bedevilled up into a snare with any of their kidney. But when people affectionate each other, there is kindliness on both sides, and forbearance on both sides, and happiness on both sides. That's the kind of marriage state I hope to enter. Now, tell me candidly and truly, what you think of it?" Uncle Job, in his eagerness, had again secured the venerable spinster's hand.

"Since you have been so open and frank with *me*, it's

only fair that I should deal as candidly with you. To say that it is unexpected to me, is only what you may premise!"

"Of course — of course — I haven't given the subject more'n a century's thought!"

"You have been one of the family, as one might say, so long, that I think I know all your wants and necessaries; and if I have tried to meet them when you were nothing but a boarder, like the rest of my establishment, as a wife, I should be still more anxious to contribute to your comfort."

Here Miss Pinchin pressed the hand which had held her own, and tried to look sentimental.

"I — I — beg your pardon, Miss Pinchin! I hope I've not made a meddle of what I intended to say; I hope I've made it clearer than I'm afraid I have."

"Had I been foolishly young and sentimental, I might have affected not to understand you; but when a woman verges towards thirty, (she had been towards thirty for fifteen years at least,) sentiment becomes sense; therefore I say again, that as your wife ——"

"*Miss Pinchin!*" exclaimed uncle Job, bounding from his chair, "do you mean to say that you have imagined me proposin' to *you* all this time?"

"Certainly, Mr. Thornton — *why not?*"

"*Why not!* Because I'm not a fool, Miss Pinchin; that's why not! and because you are old enough to be my *wife's* grandmother, Miss Pinchin; that's why not! and because, when I want a Molly Coddle, I'll hire a nurse, Miss Pinchin; that's why not!"

"*Sir!*"

"I can't help it; I'm up! and when I'm up there's no controllin' of me. To think that you could be stupid and ridiculous enough to think I meant *you!* I'm sorry if I'm onmanly, Miss Pinchin, but I know as well as you do that there's no love lost on either side; that you would have married my mopusses, and not me; and that you would have led me by the nose like a caged babboon, Miss Pinchin, allowin' it had been you, which it wasn't. I hope you'll forgive me for speakin' *plain.* I thought that was what I was doin' all the time; but as you didn't understand the aforesaid talk, it is necessary to be plain now, that there may be no more mistakes."

"And may I ask who *is* the *happy* bride, Mr. Thornton?"

"Certain, certain. Miss Genevieve—pretty little Genny Colten."

"I trust you may be happy, Mr. Thornton. Let the mistake pass as if it had never occurred. I trust she will make you the good wife you deserve. You have said some severe things, but I forgive them; and if ever it lies in my power to serve you, command me." A great tear glittered in the spinster's hard eyes, and, rolling down over her nose, dashed itself to pieces on the table before her.

"O, come now, none of that; I'm really sorry I said any thing about it."

"It is better as it is. If it must be, I could hear it better from your lips than from those of any one else. I trust you may never regret your choice; but I fear it, I fear it."

With an ominous shake of the head, Miss Pinchin hurriedly left the room, uncle Job thought, to indulge in the feminine luxury of a good cry; but if he could have peeped in upon her a minute after, and seen with what ferocious hatred she ground the daguerreotype she had coaxed from him under her foot, the twinges of conscience which occasionally stung him on her account would have grown "small by degrees, and beautifully less." From that period, under the garb of friendship, Miss Pinchin became the inveterate enemy of pretty Genevieve.

Newport was in its glory, and, of course, to gratify his young wife, uncle Job allowed himself to be borne off on the whirlpool of fashion which set towards that place. Had he consulted his own happiness, he would have selected some quiet spot, unknown to fashion, wherein to have evaded the city's summer heat. But Newport was the vote, and to Newport they went. The jaded old hack horses were switching their tails lazily under the shadow of the elms when "our party" alighted, amid a wilderness of baggage, at the door of the "Ocean House." The balcony was filled with young men indolently smoking their cigars, to whom sensation was a thing unknown. So large a party could not help attracting their attention, particularly when its chief elements were youthful bloom and beauty. The undisguised admiration which followed Genevieve greatly annoyed her husband. It was his first admixture with fashionable condiments; and the long-levelled eye glass, the bold stare, and the liberal praises bestowed upon her seemed to him unbearable impertinence; and it was only the sweet unconsciousness of admiration with which she met the adulation of the crowd that saved one or two of the most forward youths a journey over the balcony into the long grass. Of course he was spotted at once as a victim for the quizzical powers of the reigning set at the hotel. The youth, the intellect, and the beauty of his surroundings, however, soon turned the scale in his favor; and before he had been there a week, an introduction to Mr. Thornton, and through him to his party, was one of the most desirable things imaginable. The Westerns, no longer ashamed of the relationship, since Mrs. Miles Scammon patronized it, were his stanchest defenders. There were *men* there, few and far between, shining out from the effeminate, enervated mass like diamonds in a circlet of paste, to whom uncle Job adhered, and from whom he strove to fashion his own ideas, and bring into something like polished form the strong good sense which had lain *perdu* under its crusting of ignorance. At first, the bold, free manner of the men had something wrong in it; but when he saw that it was not only tolerated but encouraged by the women, he began to think that the wrong lay at the feet of fashion, and desired more than ever to withdraw from its influence. An overpowering mania for notoriety was the prevalent disease of the season of which I write. No matter how vulgar in manners or position; if the word notorious could be tacked to a title, that was enough to pass the magic boundary which separated the commonplace from the fashionable. Women dressed for notoriety, talked for notoriety, and flirted for notoriety. To be followed by a gaping crowd, to hear the musical "That's she — there she goes — that's the celebrated So-and-so," was inducement enough to make any sacrifice short of positive crime. This is no libel upon fashionable society at crowded temporary resorts. For many years I have been a constant visitor at some one or other of our fashionable watering-places. Having neither wealth nor notoriety, I have been *in* the crowd, but not *of* it, and, consequently, have had no difficulty in achieving my purpose — that of *studying* the different phases of life. Under the influences and excitements of *ton*nish life, it is impossible that society should retain its nerve and muscle of independence. This evening, Mrs. Highflyer is the belle of the hotel. She is handsome, brilliant, intellectual, (as times go,) and gorgeously dressed. A dozen coxcombs follow her steps, as she floats up and down the hall, too happy if only to catch a stray glimpse of her splendid eyes. Now and then such exclamations as the following reach her from the envious wall flowers, upon whom she curls her lip in ineffable disdain: —

"I didn't know that *flirting* was among Mrs. Highflyer's accomplishments;" and "Her husband must feel gratified;" while Mrs. Topnot, who was the star of *last* evening's assemblage, denounces in the harshest terms the shamelessness with which *married* women — meaning Mrs. Highflyer — throw out their lures to catch soft-pated young men. From that moment Mrs. Topnot and Mrs. Highflyer are rivals for the ridiculous honor of *belleship!* If Mrs. Highflyer dresses four times to-day, Mrs. Topnot will beat her time by at least *one* to-morrow. If Mrs. Highflyer wears her dress ridiculously low necked to-day, Mrs. Topnot's plump shoulders will glitter at least an inch more in the sunlight to-morrow. If Mrs. Highflyer's soft glances turn the brains of softer men to-day, Mrs. Topnot will employ something *more* than glances to-morrow, but that her rival's followers shall remove their allegiance to her shrine. And so they go on, from bad to worse, until their own purity is questioned, their husbands' name compromised, and *they* further from happiness than ever. I have always observed, too, that the fiercest antagonisms are those carried on by *married* women. Men are more susceptible to their loves, from the very *impossibility* which hedges them round; and if the heart is sometimes caught in the rebound, and if the happiness of a lifetime is sometimes the forfeit, at the feet of fashion must be laid the fearful charge.

CHAPTER XXXI.

The Waterwitch.

> "She was a creature strange, yet fair,
> First mournful and then wild —
> Now laughing on the clear bright air
> As merry as a child —
> Then melting down as soft as even,
> Beneath some new control,
> She'd throw her hazel eye to heaven
> And sing with all her soul,
> In tones as rich as some young bird's,
> Warbling her own delightful words!"
>
> Mrs. Welby.

Such was Genevieve Thornton as child and woman. Strange — was it not? — that she should have laughed all the handsome young admirers out of their love, and taken to her pure heart the honest but rough adventurer! And yet had you seen her flitting around from object to object, remaining at any one thing just about as long as a butterfly would hover round a rose, you would have said at once that she was only fitted to be what fate had made her — the old man's darling. Not that uncle Job was so *terrifically* old, either; only old in comparison with the years of his child wife. Forty — it might have been one or two — *three* was the utmost stretch of years that the most illiberal planked down on the chessboard of curiosity. Genevieve was a practical little body with all her childishness. Such a little old woman, at times, with her ancient ways; such a substantial, material, every-day wife, that the pity is there are not more after her pattern. Romance passed her by with disdain; one look at her husband settled *that* question. No one would have looked, had they only her childish face for an interpreter, for such a mine of sense and discretion as lay *perdu* under those little winking curls of hers. No one would have suspected wisdom's lurking-place in that exceedingly old head on young shoulders; but there it was, ready for action on any case of emergency.

If I were to say that she really enjoyed herself in the turbulent, excitable routine of Newport's fashionable society, I should write what was false. She did not see the necessity for so much parade — to dress a dozen times a day, more or less, would have given her the *fidgets*, as *she* said — and I am bound to record her words. In vain the more ambitious members of the party would urge her to follow their suit.

"I'll have my clothes all out where every body can see that I've *got* them," she would say, laughingly, "and if that won't do, I'll give my maid an inventory, and have it pasted up among the notices at the office door, with N. B. over it." And away she would fly to uncle Job for his sanction, sometimes in her eagerness taking half his chair, to the immense danger of upsetting his highness; sometimes helping herself to one or *more* of his knees, but always with successful termination to her argument. Please herself, and she would please uncle Job. He didn't want her dressed up like a doll for every body's gazing, and then again he didn't want people to think she hadn't as much *flimflams* as any other body's wife. Uncle Job was *human* after all. If there was one thing more than another that Genevieve did enjoy, it was the bathing. And the old Atlantic seemed to share her enjoyment, and do his best to make her in love with his caressings. He seemed to have a tone and a murmur for *her* unlike his usual thunderings.

"I don't know whether I will or not," she would say sometimes, when, like a bird, she would pause for a moment listening to the eternal roar.

"Will *what*, pet?"

"Why, don't you hear the ocean? He's coaxing me to come and have a frolic with him."

And I half believe she thought what she said, for soon as she could get to the beach after these impulses she was sure to be there; and then such a game of romp as there was! Her little, naked feet upon the sand must have been the funniest things in the world, — by the way, uncle Job laughed at them, — and how daintily they pattered down into the water! putting to shame the crested foam which drifted on to kiss them! And how they shout, one against the other, the waves and their pet! The waves have the best of it, inasmuch as they have never ceased their shouting since the world began. Far away comes rolling in a troop of waves. Genevieve plants her feet ready for the attack. The leader, in his hurry to embrace her, runs himself all to pieces, explodes with a disappointed cry, and silvers her shoulder with his sparkling ruins. Hurrah! for the remaining ones. With a clear laugh, which rings out over the hills, Genevieve plunges headlong into the bosom of her ocean lover, and lays with outspread arms upon his beating breast. The next seen of her is a curly little head, which might be a crest of foam, away out on the far side of the breakers. The thousand and one bathers pause in their own sport to see the agile swimmer drifting like a lily beyond the space allotted to their wildest imagination. The timid ones, who hop up and down in the shallow waves along shore, forget the rolling surge, to gaze, and wonder, and envy, till some heavily charged breaker takes them unawares, and *souses* them head and ears into the briny flood. Even uncle Job begins to get uneasy in his carriage, (for he has too much good sense to disguise himself in a bathing dress,) and to think of cramps, and spasms, and what not, that are associated in his mind with bathers. She is so far away that even his anxious eye can hardly distinguish her. At length, however, when uncle Job has exhausted all the horrors of his imagination, the lithe little figure is seen drifting towards the shore. Uncle Job orders the coachman to drive nearer the waves, that he may guard her more vigilantly with his eyes.

"I shall have to scold her," he thought; "she mustn't do it. Bimeby I'll lose her."

The little swimmer, however, came out of it bravely, and landed upon the beach, — glowing, dripping, palpitating, — a very naiad in all but exclusive *water privileges.*

Of course, she had to peep into the carriage, and say "Booh!" to uncle Job; the result of which was, that the scolding was forgotten, and she coaxed in all dripping as she was, and driven to the very door of her dressing car. I wouldn't like to deprive uncle Job of his laurels, but I'm afraid the idea of his wife trotting up through the crowd of starers, with her finely developed form sacrilegiously exposed by the clinging drapery, had something to do with it. By the by, that has been one of the fashionable mysteries to *me*, how ladies, delicate and sensitive, who would faint at sight of a nude statue, can boldly parade in front of the artillery of eyes marshalled on the beach for the express purpose of satisfying their curiosity, by discovering how much there is of the reigning belles that isn't cotton. Of course, individually, I go in for all the good things going; and I only speak of it as one of the mysteries worth solving. Small blame to uncle Job for secreting his treasure from the curious eyes. Miss Margaretta Pinchin, for reasons of her own, had accepted uncle Job's invitation to make one of their party: with what greedy eyes she followed the movements of Genevieve, and how she longed to overtake her in some act of wrong doing, only those can imagine who have themselves been cursed with some such officious friend.

"Job Thornton!" she exclaimed, one evening after a

week's residence among them. "*Here!*" It was a single word, but her eyes told a volume of mystery.

"*Hush!*" Placing her hand within his arm, she led him unresistingly into the shadow of a window, opening upon the balcony.

"*Look!*" Miss Pinchin dealt in monosyllables, but her eyes blazed out with gratified malice. Uncle Job *did* look, and there, sure enough, was his darling, not arm in arm with a gallant, but with her pretty waist familiarly clasped, and her short curls mingling with those of one to whom he had already conceived a dislike too strong for comfort. They were engaged in low and earnest conversation, were the youthful pair, and once uncle Job saw Genevieve wipe her eyes as if in affliction.

"I'll not watch her — *I won't!* If there's any thing goin' on that concerns *me*, she'll tell me! She *will*, I'm certain! Don't stop me; I won't listen! If there's wrong going on, which there *isn't*, I shan't thank you for the information — mind that! But there isn't; there isn't! I couldn't bear it if there was!" And uncle Job tore himself away, and went in to wait her coming in their private parlor. "She'll tell me — she certainly will! and yet what business had he with his arm around her waist? If I thought — but no, *no*, I don't think! she will make a clean breast of it, whatever it is."

An hour passed, and nothing but the echoing music broke the silence of his thoughts; another hour, and a tripping step passed through the parlor and into the adjoining bedroom. He knew the step too well not to be aware that she had returned. She had never done so before — never passed him without a kindly word. To be sure it was dark, and she might not have seen him. Full of this hope, he passed into the chamber where she was already feigning sleep. He knew she was only feigning, and that more than all the rest began to unsettle his confidence.

"Have you nothing to tell me, dear, before you go to sleep; nothing that I ought to know, or that you would feel more comfortable to have me know?" said he, half kneeling by the bed, and gathering her little head to his bosom.

"Why, what should there be to tell ——"

"Stop, stop, darling. I couldn't bear it, indeed I couldn't bear to be deceived by *you!* I've trusted you so, and loved you so — I shouldn't be hard with you, whatever it was! I know I'm old and rough, and not like what you ought to have had for a husband — I see it now more than ever! and if my loving *you* has made you unhappy, why, we must mend the matter some how. Now tell me, dear, what it is; and what can I do to make up for the past? — only don't let people make a handle of it. You've been so perfect and so spotless that I could not bear to see you ——"

Genevieve gulped down a sob, which she converted into a groan.

"I'm so sleepy — do let me go to sleep!"

"O, darling, there's a hard, cold world before you that you have never tried; there are trials, and temptations, and sorrows, which you can't always shut away by sleep. In memory of the love which *would* have shielded you, tell me what there is that I ought to know, and that I must know sooner or later, from lips that I could less bear it from!"

In his energy he had dropped down on his knees by the bedside, and placed his ear to her mouth to catch the faintest intimation of an answer — but no answer came; only the still, suppressed sound of silent weeping.

"I won't trouble you any more to-night — only promise me that you'll do nothing rash! Promise me *that!*"

Genevieve did promise, and then sat up in her bed till the last echo of his footfall was lost in the night's silence.

"Noble, generous to the last! He will never believe that if I could have a sorrow it would be caused by the thought of having pained him."

When uncle Job returned to the balcony, he found it still in possession of the strange young man to whom he owed his recent sorrow. This person, calling himself Mr. Pearson, from Tennessee, had appeared at Newport on the same evening that the Boston party arrived. He attached himself to them at once, with such tenacity, that now, as it all lay before the memory of uncle Job, there seemed to have been a preconcerted plan to that effect.

"I must see the ending of it," murmured uncle Job. "This may be some old lover come back to her, and she'll break her heart trying to do what's right. But she shan't — no, she shan't! I'll have a talk with *him* to-morrow, and if he wants to go to England, or any where else, and she wants to accompany him, the money shan't be wanting!"

Comforting himself as well as he could with this decision, uncle Job fell asleep in his chair, and woke no more till the sun was up in the east, and the birds breakfasting in the willows.

CHAPTER XXXII.

NEWPORT BEACH.

A STORM had sprung up during the night, but, as is often the case in that locality, its fury had died out with the coming light; and by the time the bathers were ready for the beach, the sky lay broad and blue as the ocean, with no fleck nor cloud to mar its purity. It was indeed a jubilant morning. The birds sang louder and longer-metred hymns, as they rocked themselves to rest in their leafy cradles. Every wave of the ocean seemed to have caught its own particular sunbeam, and to be hugging it with rapture. The very sands upon the beach seemed laughing with the sunshine and the waters. The infectious gayety spread from party to party; and never had the broad ocean caressed such gleeful sprites as this morning trusted themselves to his embrace. Genevieve was the gayest of the gay. She had avoided her husband as far as possible since the events of last evening, for which Miss Pinchin could have kissed her. Instead of paying their accustomed visit to the beach in their own carriage, as usual, she insisted upon going with the crowd in an omnibus. The idea of thwarting her in any way had never entered uncle Job's mind; so, with no word of reproach, he assisted her in, packed her little basket containing the bathing appurtenances under the driver's seat, and turned to his own room in the hotel; not, however, before he had seen the obnoxious rival snugly ensconced by her side. Uncle Job did what I suppose any other man would do under the circumstances — indulged in innumerable moody thoughts, and finally ordered his carriage to drive him to the beach. He arrived just in time to see his wife's party — consisting of Lawrence, Edward Colton, her invalid brother, Esther Milroy, herself, and the stranger youth — tripping gayly down to the water. As usual, Genevieve darted off beyond the wildest daring of her companions, and uncle Job had the satisfaction of knowing that his rival couldn't follow.

"He can't swim no more than a fish," was his inward reflection. O, how *she* luxuriated in the rich surf which came tumbling in from the sea! What fun they had, and what pranks they played upon the timid ones! How their shouts drifted out on the wind, and came back again with the echoes! How the very waves seemed doubling themselves up with the exertion of laughter! and how the cowardly persons envied the sport which was productive of so much pleasure! But hark! there was a shout of fear clashing rudely against the sounds of mirth. A man is drowning! a man is drowning! How the news flew over the waves, and was repeated by the echoes! Every limb of the bathers seemed paralyzed. Was there no one to save him — *not one?* Yes; Genevieve sees him; Genevieve sweeps through the waves to his rescue. Uncle Job looks on, now thoroughly excited, and praying, although it *is* his rival, that his life may be spared. He has no fear for Genevieve. He has seen her battling with the waves too often to fear harm for *her*. The water, which but a moment before was agitated by the pranks of a thousand human beings, is now deserted by all but the drowning man and the intrepid woman. She has gained his side; she has wound her arm around his waist; and now they are both safe upon the shore, while cheer after cheer rings out into the solemn distance. But what a *metamorphosis!* In the struggle for life the tightly-secured oil cap has wrenched its fastenings, and in tumbling off has borne the crisp black wig of the stranger far away, to surprise the water sprites. *But,* streaming down over his neck and shoulders, half shrouding his pale face, a flood of golden curls flutter and ripple in the sunlight!

"*Norah!*"

"*Michael!*"

"*Genevieve!*"

"*Uncle Job!*"

It was as good as a play. With these simple exclamations, the two parties, regardless of the wondering eyes of the crowd, were clasped in each other's arms. And then such a world of explanations as there were to give! — how Genevieve had known Mrs. Lawrence ever since she knew any thing; how she had sympathized with her from the first, when it was found that in the mesmerist's love for novelty his young wife was neglected; how they had always corresponded, with the hope yet that when satiety came, the husband's heart would return to its first love; how, at last, desperate and hopeless, she had disguised herself, to be near him; how the secret was one that wouldn't keep in uncle Job's possession, and so she had concealed it; how she felt sorry at first to give him anxiety, but how she thought he deserved a little punishment for doubting her under any circumstances; — all of which was so satisfactory to uncle Job that he proceeded immediately to set himself down to the lowest mark of humility. Had he deserved all the names he heaped upon himself, the gallows would not long have groaned for a victim.

The explanations between Lawrence and his wife were equally satisfactory, though rather more private in their details.

Esther Milroy, of whom the vacillating nature of Lawrence had already wearied, was that season united to the invalid cousin, to whom she gave her unremitting attention. Of the Newport party I need only say that Miss Pinchin left in the first boat, after the failure of her dearest hope; that Lawrence, thoroughly tired of his wanderings, became devotedly attached to his splendid wife, thereby repaying her for her endurance and suffering; and that uncle Job, more enamoured than ever, paid such heed to little Genevieve's teachings, that by the time they returned to Boston he could pass muster in any society, without betraying the rough angles of his education. Genevieve was so thoroughly a home body, that, so long as her sphere of usefulness was open for her, she cared but little for the interests and excitements of the fashionable world around her. "The poor have ye always with you," was her motto, up to which she still lives, although years have silvered the hair of uncle Job, and swelled her own luscious plumptitude of person into positive *dumpiness;* but there are plenty to remember her when her waist could have been spanned by a half yard of ribbon; all of which her husband recounts day after day to their friends.

CHAPTER XXXIII.

Turning the Tables.

Disgrace Hagar Martin! Now that the hour had come, Mrs. Welman sat in her lonely chamber, and *thought.* What had she done that revenge so horrible need be meted out to her? Was it *her* fault that a lifetime had been devoted to the man her daughter loved — to the man her daughter had determined to conquer and wear in her bosom as a trophy of triumph? No matter — the die was cast. There was but one road to the accomplishment of her desire, and that she determined to take.

"Let this be the last crime, and the last accusation!" she said to Anna, who, all flushing with anticipation and triumph, had left the crowd below to tell her mother that Hagar had arrived.

"I promise you, mother. Only aid me in securing that man, and I promise you that my life shall be as pure, as exemplary, and as immaculate as you could wish."

There had been a large party invited — the first reunion since the return of the fashionables from their summer retreat. Mrs. Scammon was there, subdued, but not humbled, by misfortune. Madam Monpensieur rattled away, voluble as ever, to the little clique who owned her sway — Mr.

Veazie and Ellen; Lizzie Linder and Hagar, with Walter as companion; in fact, all the persons who were wont to figure in the Welman clique. The first cotillon was just forming, and the music already sounding through the halls, when the haughty form of Mrs. Welman appeared in the drawing room door.

"*Stop!*"

Every eye was turned upon the speaker, while a thrill of dread ran through the assembly. Perhaps each one there had a secret of their own, which they feared had reached the ears of the merciless woman. Hagar had instinctively risen up, and standing alone in the crowd, like some wild beast of prey, looked back the scorn and defiance which flashed upon her from the eyes of Mrs. Welman.

"What is there," Mrs. Welman went on, with her eyes still glancing at Hagar, "what is there in the world — what sin, what crime more demoralizing to society, more dangerous to principle, more fearful in its depravity, than impurity of a heart burnt and blackened by wantonness?"

Mrs. Welman's eyes swept round upon the wondering group, until they again met those of Hagar.

"I need not tell you to whom I allude. Look at that woman, whose pale face and trembling limbs —— "

"*Trembling!*" repeated Hagar, with sharp scorn, standing, as she had risen, with one hand pressed upon her bosom, to still its tumult.

"There have been years of hypocrisy and wantonness — years of impenitence and recklessness, too open for the deception of any but persons deluded by her seeming talent, as we have been."

Ellen had left the side of Veazie, and now stood with one arm around her friend.

"Of course there will be plenty to defend her — plenty, like that misguided *girl* now clinging to her, who will blame me for the duty I must discharge, and perhaps cling all the more closely to *her*. That sin such as hers is fascinating — that sin such as hers is bewildering — it is not only *now* that we have come to know ——"

"But what does it all mean?" broke in the voice of uncle Job. "Of what do you accuse Hagar?"

"First, of wantonness, at an age when other girls are children; secondly, of deceiving us, of mingling with us, and of poisoning the minds of her companions."

"*False!*" cried Hagar; "false from beginning to end. I stand here alone ——" There was a stout arm around her waist, and turning her eyes, she met those of Walter, kindly encouraging and affectionate.

"Not alone, Hagar; never more alone."

It was the second time she had met that gentle, protecting glance; once when as a child he defended her from the cowardly boy, and now in his determination to defend her from the crowning sorrow of her life.

The crowd began to gather around Hagar, and prepared to hear her defence. Mrs. Welman was exasperated beyond all prudence.

"Did I not say so? Did I not tell you that vice was

bewildering, and could wear the mask of innocence? I tell you there is contamination in the very air she breathes. There is hypocrisy in every thought of her heart. Be warned in time. Crush her — disgrace her — shake her off!"

"Hoity toity, old 'oman! who put you in spokesman, and never cropped your ears? I guess you'd better let somebody else get a word in edgeways, hadn't you? Speak up, Hagar. We an't any on us perfect, unless its old mother thingumbob there; and if she isn't she'd ought to be," laughed uncle Job, while his little wife nodded her approbation.

"Come, speak out, Miss Martin. Are you so very wicked?"

"*Yes!*"

"Yes! O, don't say that, looking so sober! *Don't.*"

"Had Mrs. Welman thus publicly assailed me for any purpose of duty, or of kindness to those about me, I would have borne it all, and felt that it was merited; but persecution like hers bears the stamp of insincerity upon it. From my youth upward Anna McVernon has been my direst foe. She loved where I loved."

Walter's arm tightened around her waist.

"You have all known me for the past fourteen years; I have been before you, daily and nightly, as a woman and as a writer; and I ask if, in those years, beyond the love for my childhood's friend, which I have been too proud to conceal, I have evinced any disposition of wantonness in my daily walks? Have I tinctured my writings with contaminating doctrines? If so, discard me."

"No, no, no!" rang out from the interested group.

"If I desire to veil the incidents of years agone — incidents which I know, and *have* known, were familiar to you all — it is because I do not choose to pain my friends with their recital. I have sinned, and I have tried to atone. You cannot know how grateful I have been, and *am*, for the consideration you have shown me — for the helping hands which have been offered me. *That* woman there has meditated this exposure, thinking to scare from me all my associates — as if I could care for friends who would turn their backs on the struggles of a woman really repentant, and desirous of atonement. No; and if I speak of it now, it is with the experience of *my* life before you, telling you that there *is* redemption for the sinning Magdalen, that you may hereafter deal less harshly with the erring portion of womanhood, believing that charity can harm no one, and may be the means of restoring to society, the world, and herself some erring woman, whose greatest fault, like mine, was her youth and inexperience."

"Bravo, bravo!" shouted uncle Job; "bravo — several times bravo! *Mind*," — and here the smiles faded out of uncle Job's face, — "mind, I don't say there should be no dividing line betwixt virtue and vice; I don't contend that a person, either woman or man, should go agin the laws of a Christian land without the punishment they deserve — that's not my argument; but when one's down, and shows a penitent desire to get up agin, I say, don't pass by on the t'other side, nor refuse the helpin' hand to lift 'em up. The Bible says there is more joy over one sinner that repenteth than over ever so many just ones that need no repentance. They make that *last* class of people nowadays. We are all born with a spice of the old what's-his-name in our hearts, and what's misfortune to somebody else now, may be to *us* before we die; so ——"

"Will that man have done his ——"

"You shut up, and clear out! *That man* won't, and if he don't put a flea in your ear before he's done ——"

"Don't, Mr. Thornton! I don't deserve your kindness," murmured Hagar, more thoroughly subdued by it than she could ever have been by harshness.

"As I said a moment ago, you all know the history of my life; you have all seen my efforts to retrieve the past! If you deem me still fit ——" Hagar could contain her grief no longer, but sank, sobbing, on Walter's shoulder.

"Miss Martin," uncle Job went on, having voted himself spokesman for the whole company, "Miss Martin, one must winter and summer you to understand you as well as we do. There's *too* much of you — that's your only fault, as I know of. There ought to have been a dozen children by when you was born, to have shared your individuality. You are independent, and can't help it; and if every body else tried as hard to be *themselves* as they do to be one among the million, the world would be the better for the exchange, and we should at least have the gratification of knowing that people were in earnest."

Uncle Job's oration — *ovation* Mrs. Welman called it — was interrupted by the opening of the door, and the entrance of Ida's poet, with a strange woman on his arm.

"What brought that woman here?" almost screamed Anna. "Hide me from her! O, hide me! Who has thus betrayed me so cruelly?"

"Was it cruel for *you* to betray one who had never wronged you?" questioned the intruder. "Anna McVernon, before Heaven and these witnesses, I accuse *you* of the same crime which you have brought against Hagar Martin. The child of *your* shame faded out in my arms, the innocent victim of its mother's neglect."

"*Anna!*" exclaimed her mother, white and quivering with emotion, "*Anna!* disprove this wretch's word; you surely are *not* guilty of such a crime!"

But Anna's only answer was a sob.

"For Heaven's sake answer me! or *if* guilty, when and where was your crime committed?"

"*I* will tell you," exclaimed the intruder. "Years ago, while passing a twelvemonth in New York. You should have been certain that there was no stain on *your* garments, before crushing a struggling woman like that."

"Who brought her here? Never let them darken my doors again! Call the servants, and have her hustled out. I don't believe a word she utters! *Her!* The common street walker, the trull that comes and goes at every one's bidding, that can be bought or sold for sixpence of any man's money, to dare denounce *my* daughter!"

"I'm afraid '*my* daughter' will have to cry guilty, Mrs. Welman, or I'm no judge of countenances," said uncle Job, with a flourish of his hand towards the sofa, where Anna lay trembling and confused. At the insinuation, she started to her feet, and beckoned forward a member of the party, who, from the unknown stranger, had grown to be the most ardent admirer of the proud beauty.

"You have not triumphed *yet*, let me tell you. You have begun your rejoicing too early altogether. This gentleman may have a word to say on the subject." Waving her hand towards the person designated, the eyes of the company all turned in his direction; but instead of the handsome, dark-whiskered, and dark-mustached gentleman, who had circulated through the city for some months as a southern planter, there appeared a fierce-looking, gray-haired ruffian, holding his wig, whiskers, and mustache loosely in his hand. Hagar neither screamed nor fainted; but after gazing a moment, fixedly, into his face, she pronounced the name *Laird*.

"O, you *do* know him, then; and perhaps you will recognize *these* gentlemen," laughed Anna, as two officers, equally well disguised, approached, and laid each a hand upon her shoulder.

"Stand off!" shouted Walter, wrenching her from their clasp. "Stand off, villains, fiends! What is the meaning of this outrage? Stand off, I say, and answer me!"

"She is my slave!"

Horror stricken indeed seemed the friends of Hagar.

"Your slave!"

"Whom I demand at your hands. I come prepared to claim my property."

"*Your* property — Hagar *your* property?"

"'Tis too true, Walter — I have expected this for years. I should have told you, but I had not the heart."

"You a slave, Hagar! O, impossible, impossible!"

"Come — no more fooling — time's precious, and I must be off." Laird, (for he it was,) who, under the influence of Anna, had gained entrance into the house, advanced to seize Hagar; but before his hand touched her arm, he was sent by a well-directed blow of Walter's, reeling to the floor.

"*She* shall pay for this!" he muttered, as he gained his feet; but his prey was not quite within his grasp.

"Michael Laird!" exclaimed the strange woman, who had first confronted Anna, "do you know *me?*" She had been pressing closer and closer to Hagar, with looks of unutterable love and sorrow.

Laird returned her gaze for a moment, and then faced round to Anna with a whisper. "It is all up — *that's* Hagar Martin's *mother.*" The whisper was caught up, and circled from mouth to mouth, while the confused woman stood glaring into the face of Hagar, to see how the news would affect her.

"O my darling — my beautiful Hagar — my own, *own*

child!" she burst forth at length, prostrating herself at Hagar's feet, and kissing the hem of her garments.

"If you knew how I have watched over you, and followed your footsteps, and tried for *your* sake to be what you would not blush to recognize, should the knowledge ever come to you that you were a child of crime and remorse, you would not wholly despise me — you would at least pity me."

During this speech, while the party were engaged with this singular scene, Laird had crept away unnoted, even by the tiger eyes of Anna.

"My head is wool-gathering, I do believe! It seems like a dream! What does it all mean? You Hagar's mother? Come, sit down and tell us all about it."

"There is not much to tell! It is an old story — old as love, and suffering, and sorrow. I was the sister of Alva Martin — Hagar's supposed father — his youngest sister, and — O, spare me the shame of a recital. Enough that there came one that the family opposed — prayers, entreaties, all were vain; he was forbid the house — and I — I fled with him. Hagar was the offspring of that sinful attachment. Time proved that my friends were right in their opposition; for soon after her birth he left me to seek some newer fancy, and to add another link to the chain of his crimes. I sent Hagar, with a letter, to my brother. He adopted her — his wife became a mother to her; and I — I became an outcast. Judge of my surprise when I met Hagar, my child, in the streets of Boston.

I knew her, for I had made yearly pilgrimages to the south to see, at least by stealth, the object of my mother love! O, how my heart yearned for her! but I knew it was wisest and best to leave her in the hands of those who were willing and able to do well for her. I traced her here, to the house of her uncle, in Charlestown. Since then I have been her shadow. I had Anna Welman's child to bring up; and through its mother learned much that was likely to affect Hagar's peace — amongst which was the supposition that she was the child of a slave. Laird knew me when a girl, and somehow became acquainted with the fact of Hagar's birth. I will not tell of the acts of extortion he performed to secure his silence. Until to-night, I did not dream he would dare lay to her charge that of being a *slave!* And now, O Hagar — *my* child — one kiss, and I will never again intrude upon your presence. It was only to save you that I have done so now."

"O, never — *mother* — for my heart tells me you *are* my mother! Never! My home shall be your home. Walter will not object, I'm sure."

"Not he — not he!" exclaimed uncle Job. "If he does, I'll object to him!"

To do him justice, he was as anxious as Hagar to save her mother from further care. It was an excited party that left the mansion of Mrs. Welman that evening, but few of whom questioned the truth of the story, or the policy of Hagar in at once adopting her new-found mother into the heart of her home!

The last guest had departed from the brilliant mansion of the Welmans! Two forms alone gave life to the lonely rooms.

"Daughter!"

"*Mother!*"

"The game was a deep one!"

"*And is lost!*"

Neither Anna McVernon nor her worldly-minded mother ever appeared in society again; but a few months after there was a bill of sale in the windows of their once magnificent home.

CHAPTER XXXIV.

MILES SCAMMON'S CRISIS.

THERE came one day a dismal morning for the Westerns. State Street was full of it, and the papers were full of it, and the private circles were full of it.

Miles Scammon had failed!

Had the sky fallen it would not have created greater amazement.

Miles Scammon! After that, who could have credited the wealth of any one? "Who could have thought it?" was on the lips of every one; while not a few gloated over the discomfiture of Mrs. Miles Scammon in a manner which proved that envy could become a guest even among the "*tons*" of society. More calls were made on that particular morning than ever before, and more scandal and illiberality disseminated than would have stocked a country village. Mr. Western came home pale and trembling, as if an ague had seized him.

"What is it, Hiram?" questioned Madam Western, winding her arm about her husband's neck; for, with all her faults, she was an affectionate wife and mother.

"I am ruined — undone! That villain Scammon has

failed, and broken me down in his fall!" and Western buried his face in his clasped hands.

"We will be happy in spite of it, Hiram. We haven't been half as happy since we tried to get into fashionable society as we were when we were contented with our little country home. O Hiram, I must say I'm not a bit sorry, only for *you;* and you've got me, and the babies, and the little farm of *mine*, and we will go back again, and be as comfortable as the day is long."

"But to think how he took me in! Curse ——"

"No, no, *no*, Hiram! Don't curse him. He's miserable enough without that, you may be sure; and as for *her*, I certainly do pity her, from the bottom of my heart."

Little Madam Western pitying *Mrs. Miles Scammon!* After *that*, there was no knowing what might happen in this world. Western took the advice of his wife, arranged his affairs to the best of his ability, and was once more the inmate of his own quiet country cottage.

"Every thing is for the best," one day burst forth Madam Western, from the cloud of her musings. "I never was happy till I got into big company, and I never should have been if I *hadn't* got there. It wasn't what it was cracked up to be though, was it, Hi dear? and now that I know it from my own experience, I shall never want to leave my cosy little home again."

Mrs. Western was right. Very unsubstantial indeed are the delights of fashionable frivolity.

Perhaps there are those among my readers who feel

curious to know how the poet Wimple and his Ida got out of the scrape with his aunt. One fine day in autumn, as this same aristocratic and overbearing aunt was preparing for her morning drive, sickness came along, and, being no respecter of persons, doubled her up, — turban, feathers, jewelry, and all, — and laid her upon a lonely bed. It was ever so much more o'clock than it ought to have been, considering Wimple was an affectionate nephew, before he returned from the city to his aunt's country residence. He didn't look a bit sorry when the servants told him what had happened, especially after assuring himself there was nothing dangerous in the illness.

"Just the thing," he was heard to say to himself, after leaving his aunt's room for the purpose of going to the city to procure a nurse. My readers are not the intelligent persons I take them to be if they have not guessed *who* was "just the thing," and who, in a few hours after said exclamation, was domiciled in the terrific presence of the stately aunt — moving about so quiet and so gentle, anticipating all the wants which querulous sickness invents, laying her little cool hands upon the burning brow of the invalid, and, in fact, making herself so generally useful, that, after a few weeks of trial and endurance, it was found impossible to do without her. So there she remains — the happiest little Ida under the sun.

CHAPTER XXXV.

Effie Lee.

In all these pages has sweet Effie been forgotten? Is there one of my readers that will go back with me, not to old Virginia exactly, but to its next door neighbor, Carolina? Here we are again in the mansion of Colonel Rose, away back to the race week of years agone.

> " When a woman will, she will, you may depend on't,
> And when she won't, she won't, and there's an end on't,"

sung or whistled the old gentleman, with a most lugubrious countenance, as Effie danced off with an "*I won't*" upon her lips, but an "I will" within her eye.

"Hang all girls, say I, with their girl notions, and their highfaluten romances, and their don't-know-their-own-mind-ativeness! Lord save me! if I had more than one to manage, I should book myself for the lunatic asylum at once, and let them slide. She *won't* have Charley Lee — as good a fellow, ay, and as smart and as handsome, as the best lord of the land. Lord! he's a king amongst men, an eagle among barn door fowls — that's what *he* is; and now, after all my trouble to bring the two farms together —

I mean the two children together — she *won't* have Charley Lee! We'll see about that, my lady! Ah, ha! you may laugh as loud as you please; you like Charley, and you shall be made happy in spite of your teeth!"

A loud chorus of voices broke up the old man's soliloquy, and, looking from the windows upon the lawn, he saw the whole party approaching in great glee; all but Charley, who was some length ahead, and quite alone, while Effie hung with most provoking *abandon* upon the arm of his rival, Wells. A bright thought seemed all at once to enter the head of the colonel; for, with a "That's it" on his lips, he hastened to the *porch*, and dragged Charley in out of sight of the company. "Now mind your cue, Charley," he began, griping his hand like a vice, "mind your cue. I've a capital plot in my head — no time to divulge here — only take a joke as if it was earnest. Here they are;" and, bristling up in great ire, he stumped backward and forward upon the balcony, puffing and blowing, and sending out little fragments of angry sentences, till the whole party stood in amaze before him. "To have the impudence!" he went on; "to have the insolence, and unheard-of assurance!"

"*Why, father!*" questioned Effie, in surprise.

"Don't 'father' *me*, miss! Don't speak to me! and yet you were right, after all. You were more discriminating than I was. I thought that fellow there" — pointing sternly at Charley Lee — "was a sensible, honorable man. I thought to be proud of him as a husband to my only child; but now — now — O, I've no words to express my indignation and contempt!"

"*Father!*" Effie had somehow got over to the side of Charley, and stood pale and firm before him.

"Come away from him — I command you! He is disgraced beyond redemption! Thank Heaven, it is not too late! If I had had *my* way, you would have been *his* wife — the wife of a reckless, foolish, miserable gamester!"

"*Sir!*"

"Silence! I was your father's friend; we were boys together; and his last words were, that I should espouse the cause of his son and heir; but now, so much do I despise your unprincipled conduct, that from this time henceforth I demand that you never enter my doors again. Nay, more than that, the marriage to which I had looked forward with such hope I here forbid; and, Effie, the sooner you marry your new lover, Mr. Wells, the better you will please *me!*"

The happy sparkle died out of Mr. Wells's eyes, under the look of imperious scorn with which Effie met her father's sanction.

"What is Charley's fault, father? You are not used to condemn without reason."

"*Reason!* The whole estate squandered; the splendid mansion of his father given over to vile spendthrifts and thieves; the broad lands and wooded hills all gone — lost — staked upon a race of which a child might have known the result. *Reason!* Ask for his betting book, and see the reason!" And the colonel flung up his coat tails, and ranted up and down the balcony fiercer than ever.

"But, father, all gentlemen bet, more or less, on the races. *You* do yourself. Charley is no more to blame than you would be had you lost. It was, at best, a passive fault."

"*Passive!* What do you call a passive fault? I tell you he has lost every cent he is worth on earth; and I dare say, if you were not a girl of too much spirit, he would ask you to share his poverty. Let me tell you an old adage, and a true one—'When poverty comes in at the door, love flies out at the window.' But come, start; we are wasting time. Effie shall be Mrs. Wells before another week comes over her head. And as for *you*, I advise you to leave the country altogether. You'll find no sympathy here, I can tell you."

"Why, father! is it possible you can treat an old friend in this manner? Misfortune is no fault."

"What business had he to be unfortunate? It is time for you to learn to what man's worship clings in this world. When Charley Lee was rich—high in name and worldly goods—he was a desirable husband for any girl of standing; but now, what is there in his future worth any woman's serious consideration?"

"I will tell you, father. A strong will and a stout heart; an arm to battle with the wrongs of life, and a spirit that will not droop under the strongest trials. I will risk Charley Lee, though he has lost fame and fortune; and what's more, I'll stick to him, rain or shine — as the actress said in the play, 'through fortune's might, and fortune's blight, to blazon or to blur.' So you can take yourself off, Mr. Wells, and the sooner the better. Of course I wouldn't be sold to Charley — no, not to the king of the world; but when I find him poor, friendless, and deserted, — when I find my own father turning against him, — it is time I showed my hand."

"Effie, come to me this moment. You don't know what you are talking about."

"I don't care three straws. I'm not a-going to set my face against my old playmate, I can tell you. Why, he has risked his neck a thousand times to humor some caprice of mine; and as for the farm, let it go. If any body, or any *pair* of bodies, can look the future in the face, black or no black, it's Charley and I; so there now. Whenever you are ready, *I* am, Charley," said the excited girl, turning and laying her hand upon her lover's arm.

Colonel Rose could scarcely contain himself for joy at the success of his stratagem. The guests had dispersed in one direction and another, not wishing to become witnesses of family dissensions.

"You'll not even ask the blessing or consent of your father, I suppose?"

"*Ask it!* Of course we shall ask it, like a dutiful pair of cubs as we are; but if we don't get it, I'm afraid we shall manage to do without it. Eh, Charley?"

"No, no, *no,* Effie. If I could have called you *mine* when fortune smiled upon me, nothing on earth could have added to my bliss; but *now,* to take you from a luxurious home, and place you in an abode of poverty and toil — to deprive you of the thousand comforts and luxuries which have become essentials — no, *no;* don't think me so selfish as that, Effie. I don't deserve it. Perhaps the time may come when I shall have redeemed myself — when your father, thinking less harshly of me, may dare to trust your fortune to my keeping; but for the present —— "

Charley made a tragic rush for the door, while the old man turned his back, and converted the laugh in his throat into a cough.

"No, you don't, neither!" exclaimed Effie, seizing him by the arm. "I believe you have all conspired to break my heart — *you* amongst the rest, Charley. If I can't have my way in this, it *is* a pity. I *will* have Charley; I always intended to have Charley; and now that he needs me, I'm more than ever resolved to have Charley." And a passionate fit of crying, such as a child might indulge in, followed her decided avowal.

"Mr. Lee, *will* you leave my house?"

"No, that he shan't, unless he takes me with him."

"Go to your room, miss. Go! I *insist.*" And furiously ringing his bell, he summoned her confidential maid.

"Conduct your mistress to her chamber, and see that you run of no errands for her. Do you hear?"

"Yes, massa."

"*Go!* I've a few words to say in private to my young spark here. I'll settle his claim at once and forever."

"Never doubt *me*, Charley, whatever happens. They can't *make* me marry any body else, if they lock me up ever so tight." And away she flaunted, not deigning a look to her incensed father.

Once in her chamber, she hastily scribbled a few lines on the blank leaf of a book.

"Take this to Charley, as he crosses the park below the lawn, and wait for his answer."

"Yes, missis." And Effie watched the egress of her lover with blazing eyes.

"To control *me* — *me!*" she murmured to herself, stamping her foot impatiently. "I wish they may get it, that's all. There he goes, dear Charley! Mr. Wells is a fool to him. I hope father won't catch Patsey."

Could she have seen the eager grasp of her father's hand upon that of her lover, or have heard that rollicking laugh so hard to suppress, the tone of her indignation would have changed, and Charley Lee's chance of a wife grown beautifully less.

"What did he say?" said she, eagerly springing to the door to meet her maid.

"He'll be here. Never you fear for *him*."

That evening mirth and music reigned supreme at the mansion of Colonel Rose. The beauty and chivalry of the whole state were assembled to celebrate the termination of the races, and among them all none shone more brightly or conspicuously than pretty Effie Rose. She had a word and a smile for all — a compliment or a repartee, a flash of wit or a gleam of mirth, was ever rolling over her beautiful lips. For a wonder, she had chosen a white satin dress, looped with flowers upon the shoulders, while a short skirt of the richest Brussels lace gave an airy lightness to her figure, quite in keeping with the happy expression of her face. Her hair was without ornament, other than the profusion of natural curls which showered over her neck, and lay in quivering rings upon her heaving bosom. No wonder her father gazed upon her in pride, and presented her to his guests with a confident feeling that they too must see her superiority over the mass of women therein congregated. Sometimes a perceptible sadness gathered upon her face while listening to the praises of her father. Short were their duration, however; for from her earliest recollection she had swayed his impulses, as the wind sways the foliage of the mighty oak; and surely, she argued, it would only be a few days' estrangement, to be followed by a life-long forgiveness, even if she *did* go against his will.

The dance was at its height, the supper table groaned with its weight of luxury, when a low sound, something approaching a whistle, caught the listening ear of Effie. Gliding from the room, as she supposed, unperceived, she ran hastily to her chamber, gathered up a few essential articles, which she gave to her maid, enveloped herself in a large shawl and travelling hood, and the next moment was tripping down the back stairs, to elope with the lover that she had a hundred times discarded.

From a window old Colonel Rose peeped out, with a face swollen with suppressed laughter. As the carriage rolled off, a loud ha, ha, ha-ha-ha-r! startled the guests from their mirth, while one or two of the more daring penetrated to the room from whence the sound proceeded. There they found the old man rolling on the lounge in an agony of laughter.

"She's run away; ha, ha, ha-ha-ha-r-r! run away from her old father; ha-ha! outwitted him; out-generalled him; ha, ha! it is *too* good, too good! Ha, ha, ha-r!"

By this time the whole crowd were around him.

"He's crazy," said one.

"She oughtn't to have done it," said another.

"It will all come back again to her," said a third, while the colonel took up the chorus with his stentorian ha, ha.

"Bathe his head!" said an old woman, proceeding to put her advice into practice.

"Bathe *the devil!*" roared out the old man. "I tell you it's all right! It *couldn't* be better! She's gone — eloped — run away with the only man on earth that I would have allowed her to marry!" And between laughing and crying, he told them the whole story; not sparing even the valiant Mr. Wells in the narrative.

The excitement of the scene gave a fresh impetus to the flagging energies of the people, and a new edition of music and dancing commenced, which continued till the last hem of the night's robe lay at the feet of the coming day.

> "When a woman will, she will, you may depend on't,
> And when she won't, she won't, and there's an end on't,"

reiterated Colonel Rose to himself, for the thousandth time, as he laid his head upon his pillow, and composed himself to sleep.

CHAPTER XXXVI.

A Word for all Parties.

Amid the bloom and beauty of a southern home, there dwells a woman who is an angel of mercy to the sick, and a ministering spirit to all who need her sympathy. The poor recognize her and bless her, while many a one of those whom temptation has thrown from their high station of purity, rain blessings on the hand that dared to lead them back again to virtue and religion. She has never forgotten her own errors and misfortunes, nor, while fondly gazing into the face of her bright, handsome husband, does she quite regret the trials which taught her the value of a true love. Martyr no longer, Hagar Meadows does not fail to recognize the hand of Providence in her misfortunes, and thanks her heavenly Father daily for the wider range of sympathy it has given her for the sufferings of the world at large; and when the hour comes that shall close the scenes of her eventful life to those who know her best, no grave will cast a darker shadow than will that of Hagar, the gentle, loving woman and wife.

In the same home that shelters Hagar, wealthy, talented, and beautiful in her full womanhood, lives the widow of Alva Martin, beloved by all who know her. Her lover never recovered from his life-struggle with the villain Laird. He died shortly after, leaving the beautiful Georgianna a sincere mourner for his loss.

Laird became still more a wanderer and an outcast, till, impelled by that restless desire for crime which seemed inherent to his nature, he committed a desperate act of arson and robbery, which consigned him for life to a convict's cell.

Mr. and Mrs. Scammon are still struggling "to keep up appearances," wearing out soul and body in a ceaseless strife with poverty and pride. Mr. and Mrs. Western more wisely adapted themselves to circumstances, and live in perfect happiness and unity, without even a cloud of jealousy to mar their comfort. Ellen Willard sleeps within a vine-wreathed enclosure at Mount Auburn, a victim to consumption, *alias* a broken heart. All through the rich bloom of summer, flowers are heaped upon her bosom with a liberal hand, and many a visitant to that "garden of graves" has paused in her vicinity, awed to silence by the bent and sorrowful old man who haunts its precincts. Uncle Job Thornton and sweet Genevieve patter around the city together — both of them older than when first we met — doing a world of good which never meets the eye of society, but which, nevertheless, finds as much favor in the eye of *Him* who has imbued their hearts with such kindliness and generosity, as if recorded in all the prints in the city. The Welmans suddenly left the city. Some years since, Hagar's husband induced her to patronize a concert in their vicinity. When the curtain rose, and the star of the evening appeared, she was not greatly surprised to recognize in her brilliant dress the once haughty, aristocratic Anna McVernon. What her career has since been I am unable to say, she having since left the country.

I must not close without a passing word of Effie Rose. It was a long time before she became reconciled to the unromantic portion of her romantic wedding; however, she bore up under it bravely. The mansion of old Colonel Rose is still the home of the "brave and the free," although the bravest and the freest of all, his own worthy self, has long since paid the just debt of nature. He lived to see Effie surrounded by blessings in the shape of lovely children, and to know that the match turned out, what he believed it must, a happy one for all parties. He lived to a good old age, in full possession of all his kindly faculties, and died beloved by all the country round.

The unhappy mother of Hagar lived but a few months after establishing the birth of her child.

Minnie is still a resident of the free states, though not without the fear that some time it may become *her* turn to create the excitement and endure the suffering which our laws have so cruelly forced upon those who have had the intellect and the keenness to work out their own escape from slavery.

Lizzie Linder — bright and beautiful Lizzie — goes about in her happy, saucy way, making every body happy as herself. The golden *El Dorado* claims her now, where all good blessings of friends and fortune wait upon her wishes.

The Pinchin boarding house is still among the *elephants* of the city, both sisters, as usual, superintending the affairs of their patrons to the neglect of their own.

Thus ends the catalogue of those who, during the preceding pages, have kept us company. If they have served to amuse or instruct *one* of my readers, or if they have lightened the weary hour of a single sufferer, or awakened sympathy in one heart for the victims of misfortune or of circumstance, my toil has been repaid; and so, reader, we part company, neither, I trust, the worse for the time and interest expended upon *Hagar the Martyr!*

THE END.

A TREATISE

ON THE

CAMP AND MARCH.

WITH WHICH IS CONNECTED

THE CONSTRUCTION OF FIELD WORKS AND MILITARY BRIDGES.

WITH AN

APPENDIX OF ARTILLERY RANGES, &c.

FOR USE OF

VOLUNTEERS AND MILITIA IN THE UNITED STATES.

By HENRY D. GRAFTON,

CAPTAIN FIRST REGIMENT U. S. ARTILLERY

BOSTON:

PUBLISHED BY FETRIDGE AND COMPANY.

1854.

HOME SCENES AND HOME SOUNDS;

OR,

THE WORLD FROM MY WINDOW.

BY

H. MARION STEPHENS.

BOSTON:
FETRIDGE AND COMPANY.
M DCCC LIV.

the subscribers, and at a price so reasonable that it is placed within the means of the humblest citizen.

By persons acquainted with the reputation of the distinguished author of this work, any attempt to urge his claims may be justly deemed a labor of presumption. By those less acquainted with his eminent merits a few words may not be considered as inappropriate.

Most people regard all Histories alike; that is, for purposes of mere information. They are viewed as magazines of FACTS, to be drawn upon as we draw words and definitions from a dictionary. This is a great mistake. The whole of a thing may be so given in parts as hardly to be recognized when in form; and the parts of a History may be so disarranged in detail as to present a confused series of events, which convey no definite idea of system or progress.

History is of but little importance unless it affords rules of conduct, either for individuals or nations; and if an author fails to combine reflection with detail, and to give in philosophical order the events of nations, as causes and effects, as they naturally transpire, he accomplishes but half of his task.

In the UNIVERSAL HISTORY of Mr. Tytler there is a happy combination of the events given, their relations and uses. The attentive reader may be taught not only the history of the past, but the probable destiny of man and nations in all time to come. He is brought in relation to a comprehensive view of the FACTS of the world, and to survey the extent of man's powers and the true logic of knowledge. He is led to see more perfectly that chain which joins effects to causes; to view the gradual progress of manners, the advancement of man from barbarism to civilization, and thence to refinement and corruption; to note the connection of States and Empires; and, above all, to realize the greatest benefit of History — its utility AS A SCHOOL OF MORALS.

The study of History enables a person to have within himself not only a standard of knowledge, but of duty. In view of these considerations, it will be perceived that History is a subject of the utmost magnitude, and that the choice of an author becomes a serious matter of inquiry.

In asking particular attention to this edition of TYTLER, the publishers require no better voucher for the correctness of his views than will be found in the work itself, to which they would confidently and respectfully refer all Students, Teachers, and Professors, in the hope that they will carefully examine it, each for himself. The work is allowed to be well adapted to the use of Schools, Academies, and Colleges, and we need not add that for the general reader its superior cannot be found in our language.

JOHN FOSTER, "the renowned Essayist," in speaking of Tytler and his History, says, "He is an able and practical thinker, possessed of ample stores of learning and general knowledge, well acquainted with History, schools, and questions of philosophy, a discriminative judge of characters, and *writing in a style which we deem a finished example of transparent diction.* It is so singularly lucid, so free from all affected rhetoric and artificial turns of phrase, so perfectly abstracted, with the exception of a law term or two, from every dialect appropriated to a particular subject, *that we have never viewed thoughts through a purer medium.* It is so pure and perfect that we can read on without our attention being arrested by the medium; it is as if there were nothing, if we may so express ourselves, between us and the thought."

FETRIDGE & CO.

RAMBLES IN CHILI,

AND

Life among the Araucanian Indians,

IN 1836.

BY "WILL THE ROVER."

PUBLISHERS' NOTICE.

This book may be regarded as one of the varieties of the day. It is difficult to conceive, while perusing these Rambles, where adventures so

exciting and thrilling are so forcibly told, that it is a true and veritable narrative; but such, we assure the reader, is the fact. The natural scenery of that sunny region is painted in the glowing tints of a faithful picture. The character of that singular people, the Araucanians, the lofty and magnanimous bearing of the warriors, the lovely, confiding, and affectionate dispositions of the maidens, are all beautifully delineated; and so vividly are the various scenes portrayed that we seem to be transported to the field where they are enacted, and feel the varied emotions of the actors. If some of these adventures and incidents were related in a romance, the reader would probably say that they were exaggerated, so much more strange is truth than fiction.

FETRIDGE & CO.

THE FALCON FAMILY;

OR,

YOUNG IRELAND.

BY THE AUTHOR OF "THE BACHELOR OF THE ALBANY."

First American, from the Second English Edition. 1 vol., 8vo., paper. Price 25 cents.

A writer in *Fraser's Magazine* says of the Author and his works, "He seems to have a horror of being one moment dull; such a perpetual volley of smart things was never kept up in that rattling, never-pausing pace, in any other book that has come to us."

"The Falcon Family is superior to its predecessor."—*Concord (N. H.) Freeman.*

"Every passage is sprinkled with wit. Whoever undertakes to read it can hardly lay it down till he has seen the end."—*Boston Courier.*

"It is very witty and amusing." — *Boston Atlas.*

"We do not think the first forty pages surpassed by any thing extant, — *Boston Post.*

"Another glorious novel, by the author of 'The Bachelor of the Albany.'" — *Boston Mail.*

Published by FETRIDGE & Co., Boston. For sale in New York by Stringer & Townsend and H. Long & Brother.

AN INTRODUCTION TO ALGEBRA,

UPON THE

INDUCTIVE METHOD OF INSTRUCTION.

BY WARREN COLBURN, A. M.,

Author of Intellectual Arithmetic and Sequel to Ditto.

Considered by far the best Algebra of the present day, and used extensively in all cities in the United States.

TO THE YOUNG MEN OF THE UNITED STATES.

AN APPEAL.

While you are Young Men, prepare yourselves for future happiness, usefulness, and respectability.

For a small amount of money, saved from some profitless expenditure once a month, you may in a few months be put in possession of a Work from which you may derive interest and profit for a time, which will serve for a study through your life, and which you may hand down to the next generation as a treasure worthy the age in which you lived, and worthy their careful study.

The Subscribers are publishing a popular and elegant edition of

UNIVERSAL HISTORY,

FROM THE

CREATION OF THE WORLD,

BY THE LATE

HON. ALEXANDER FRAZER TYTLER,

LORD WOODHOUSELEE, SENATOR OF THE COLLEGE OF JUSTICE, AND LORD COMMISSIONER OF JUSTICIARY IN SCOTLAND, AND FORMER PROFESSOR OF CIVIL HISTORY AND GREEK AND ROMAN ANTIQUITIES IN THE UNIVERSITY OF EDINBURGH.

It makes two handsome volumes of about 1100 pages.

The study of History is the most entertaining and useful of all studies; therefore the selection of an author is of the first importance. The History by TYTLER has been through more than *one hundred editions* in England, is used in the Universities of that country and this, and takes the first rank among literary works. Be particular, therefore, to inquire for

TYTLER'S UNIVERSAL HISTORY.

Remember that "KNOWLEDGE IS POWER;" and if you have more knowledge than your neighbor, you have a power over him which he cannot successfully resist.

Published by FETRIDGE & CO., 3 and 5 STATE STREET, and 72 and 74 WASHINGTON STREET, BOSTON; and sold by H. Long & Co. and Stringer & Townsend, New York; T. B. Peterson & Co. and Lippincott & Grambo, Philadelphia; Taylor & Co., Baltimore; J. C. Morgan, New Orleans; and by booksellers through the United States.

FETRIDGE AND COMPANY.

THE BALM OF THOUSAND FLOWERS,

FOR BEAUTIFYING THE COMPLEXION, AND REMOVING ALL

TAN, PIMPLES, AND FRECKLES;

FOR SHAVING, AND CLEANSING THE TEETH.

THE FOLLOWING ARE A FEW NOTICES OF THE PRESS.

From the Editor of the London Mail.

BALM OF THOUSAND FLOWERS.

This is the euphonic and very poetical name of a new and valuable cosmetic. Its inventor, Dr. A. De Fontaine, of Paris, has been at great expense and labor in its composition, and has succeeded, to the utmost of his wishes, in preparing an article which will prove conducive, in the highest degree, to the health, comfort, and enjoyment of all who use it. Composed of plants and flowers of the most healthy, innocent, and powerful properties, collected from different parts of the world, being highly perfumed by its own ingredients, and peculiarly pleasant in its operation, it cannot fail to impart satisfaction to all who employ it for the purposes for which it is so happily and wonderfully adapted. It is designed for the toilet, the nursery, and the bath, and as such it is recommended by the faculty of London and Paris, as well as of the principal cities of the United States, and it has been decidedly approved by thousands who use it in preference to all other cosmetics.

Every one who has attended to the philosophy of health knows of what immense importance it is to the true enjoyment of life and a free exercise of the faculties to keep the skin clean and the pores open, by frequent ablutions. A composition tending to facilitate this operation, and at the same time render it more salutary and pleasant, must be received by all classes of the community, and particularly by those of intelligent and enlightened minds. The delicate and soothing sensations which it produces, the delightful softness which it imparts to the skin, the clearness and beauty which it gives to the complexion, and the powerful sanative virtues it possesses in removing cutaneous diseases, will be universally acknowledged. Its application relieves the surface of all impurities, leaving a renovated skin and a pure and healthy bloom. As an emollient for the hair it is unrivalled, promoting its growth, preventing its loss, and giving it a soft and glossy richness. As a wash for cleaning the teeth it is unsurpassed by any dentifrice now in use, promoting their preservation, arresting their decay, and rendering them clean and white as alabaster. As an article for shaving, it is superior to any thing now in use that we have seen tried for that purpose, not only facilitating that operation, but at the same time imparting an agreeable softness and freshness to the face.

Reader, do not class this with the thousand nostrums of the day. No one can be in doubt of its virtues, as its qualities may be tested before purchasing.

From Godey's Lady's Book.

BALM OF THOUSAND FLOWERS,

For removing all tans, pimples, and freckles from the face, for removing grease spots from clothes or carpeting, for beautifying the skin, for shaving, cleansing the teeth, or curling the hair. This is what we are assured this celebrated Balm will do, and we see that the proprietors offer $500 reward to any person who can produce its equal in efficacy. Fetridge & Co., of Boston, are the proprietors of the Balm, and are most enterprising gentlemen. The price is one dollar per bottle, and the money to be returned if the article does not prove satisfactory. We observe by a Boston paper a sign of the prosperity of the firm. It says, —

" City improvements are visible on every hand; among the most conspicuous in our vicinity is one of Fetridge, the enterprising bookseller and publisher. He has recently added two stories to his building on Washington Street, making it six stories in height. One of these is occupied as a library and reading room; so the ladies say Fetridge has a new library idea, and a good one. He puts two hundred copies of every new book that is likely to create an excitement into his library, so that subscribers are never told that the volume they desire is 'out.'"

A Letter from a London Merchant to the Proprietors.

MESSRS. FETRIDGE & Co.

Gentlemen: Seeing an advertisement some time since in the London Times of Dr. Fontaine's Balm of Thousand Flowers, I was induced to buy the article, having been completely covered with freckles ever since I can recollect the appearance of my face. I had tried several cosmetics for the purpose of removing them, but without success. After using one bottle of the Balm, my face appeared much smoother, and I imagined that some of the smaller freckles had vanished, at least by gaslight they could not be seen. I continued to use the article, and am now rejoiced to state to you that they have entirely disappeared. I have likewise used the Balm for shaving and cleansing the teeth, believing it to be the best thing ever discovered for these purposes, as well as for making and keeping the complexion beautiful. I address you this letter, hearing you had purchased the right to manufacture it from Dr. Fontaine; and having seen Mr. Fetridge several times on his visits to London, I thought it might be a service to you to record this testimony.

My kind regards to your Mr. Fetridge, and believe me,

Your ob't serv't,

H. T. JOHNSON,

St. Martin's Lane

The following is from Gaylord Clark, of the Knickerbocker Magazine.

It is not our wont to allude to kindred fabrications, but we can say, from the ocular proof, that the Balm of Thousand Flowers, a preparation for removing tan, pimples, and freckles from the face, shaving, cleansing the teeth, curling the hair, removing grease spots from clothes, carpets, etc., sold by our agents, Fetridge & Co., Boston, is the best article of its kind we have ever encountered. It is, in reality, all that it purports to be.